Library of
Davidson College

The Maypole Warriors

Also by
Fernando Alegría

Changing Centuries
   (Latin American Literary Review Press)
The Chilean Spring
   (Latin American Literary Review Press)

The Maypole Warriors

Fernando Alegría

translated by
Carlos Lozano

Latin American Literary Review Press
Pittsburgh, Pennsylvania
Series: Discoveries
1993

The Latin American Literary Review Press publishes Latin American creative writing under the series title *Discoveries*, and critical works under the series title *Explorations*.

No part of this book may be reproduced by any means, including information storage and retrieval or photocopying, except for short excerpts quoted in critical articles, without the written permission of the publisher.

Copyright © 1993 Latin American Literary Review Press.

Library of Congress Cataloging-in-Publication Data
Alegría, Fernando, 1918-
    [Mañana los guerreros. English]
    The Maypole Warriors / by Fernando Alegría ; translated by Carlos Lozano.
       p. cm. -- (Discoveries)
    ISBN 0-935480-58-7
    I. Title. II. Series.
PQ8097.A734M313   1993
863--dc20   92-21222
                                                                                                                                                                      CIP

*The Maypole Warrior*s may be ordered directly from the publisher:
                Latin American Literary Review Press
                121 Edgewood Avenue
                Pittsburgh, PA 15218
                Tel (412) 371-9023 • Fax (412) 371-9025

Cover photo courtesy of Dr. Mary Hufty
Cover and Book Design by Barbara Alsko

ACKNOWLEDGEMENTS

This project is supported in part by grants from the National Endowment for the Arts in Washington, D.C., a federal agency, and the Commonwealth of Pennsylvania Council on the Arts.

Special thanks to Carmen D. Alegría for her valuable help in editing.

1

"Tap, tap".... The sound on the window pane was followed by a prolonged silence.

"Tap, tap, tap".... The knocking was now more decisive, somewhat hurried, and the silence that followed, deeper, as if the sound of the shutters and the trembling echo of the panes had become a sign of alarm.

"Tap, tap..., tap..., tap".... The lone individual knocking became impatient, peered through the shutters, and began to rattle the window frame.

Inside, the bed creaked. Juan Luis turned over in the dark and, opening his eyes, looked around him in the shadows. The rap of the knuckles against the pane had suddenly sounded to him like a tremendous din. Distressed, he asked,

"Who is it? Who's there?"

Then, he stretched his arm and felt for the switch on the night lamp. From outside, a voice he did not immediately recognize, answered:

"Juan Luis, get up ... it's me, Mario. Get up."

"What do you want?"

"Get up, go over to the house. Elisa is alone . . . I'm on my way to tell Uncle Ramón and Aunt Esther."

"Tell? Tell what?" Juan Luis got up, stumbled over his shoes at the foot of the bed, went to the window and opened a shutter. "What's the matter? What are you doing out at this hour of the night?"

"Father's dead," answered the other and stood looking at him through the opening. Juan Luis looked back at him in silence. Mario was bundled up to his nose in a *vicuña* muffler. There was something absurd in the expression on his young face (in what could be seen of it); something incongruous between his slicked-down black hair, his large, luminous, and cold eyes, and the grief-stricken, fragile voice that steamed out through the muffler.

Juan Luis got even closer to the window and, frowning, tried to smell his breath. Mario continued to look at him unabashedly, apparently not bothered by Juan Luis' silence.

"He died," he said finally, as if suddenly remembering a message someone had sent him to deliver. Having delivered it, he looked at Juan Luis' legs, noticing that he slept in his undershirt and was nude from the waist down. Juan Luis made as if to say something, but aware of the other's gaze, put his right hand to his belly then brought it down slowly and began to scratch his pubic area.

"Mmm . . . too bad!" he said. "And, where are you going now?"

"I'm on my way to tell my aunt and uncle."

"Walking?"

"No taxis; I couldn't find one. In this lousy city they're in by nine o'clock."

"Why don't you try the station? Go up to Mapocho, you'll find a taxi there."

"And what if there isn't? I'll lose time. Maybe there aren't any. No trains come in at this hour: everybody's gone to bed."

"What time is it?"

"I don't know. I left my watch home."

"Wait. I'll look at my watch." He turned and walked towards the night table. Mario watched the bare behind and the thin, hairy legs.

"I'm off: I have to go tell my aunt and uncle. Hurry on over to the house because Elisa is alone with mother."

"Yes, yes; I'm going. I'll dress and hurry over."

"So long."

"Mario! What time did your father die?"

Mario didn't answer; he went off and crossed the street with his short, mincing step. The metallic click of his heels was the only sound in the street. It struck Juan Luis that he wore those heels to look taller. He reached for the shorts and pants lying on the floor and dressed slowly, still half asleep. He put on a sock and shoe and stopped to gaze out the swinging, partially open window. He sensed something in the street that, for no special reason, reminded him of the bottom of a pool. Everything seemed to have become static, as if made of ice: the light from the old street-lamps, the shadows of the gigantic oriental plantains on the gray pavement, the reddish vault of the sky above the black outline of the chapel of San Cristóbal, and a foreshadowing of people who were to walk there and now were motionless, indistinguishable, laying in wait for him. There wasn't a sign of life anywhere and yet, everything along the entire edge of dawn stirred with a certain dull, incomprehensible cruelty.

Unsuccessful in his search for the other sock, he threw himself face down on the floor and groped for it under the bed. It wasn't anywhere. He turned the bed upside down, swore a couple of times, then put on the shoe without it. He poured water from the porcelain pitcher into the washbasin, washed his hands and face, dampened his hair, finished dressing without a sound, and went towards the hall. Seeing an open door, he hesitated for a moment, returned to his room, and went out through the window.

"Someone will have to dress him, that's why Mario has taken off. If Señora and Elisa are alone, they're going to talk me into helping them. The dead man's room will reek of morphine, alcohol, gauze, blood-stained pans. I shall have to touch him. He'll be waiting for me: a long, loose face, gray hairy jowls, beard, a thick mouth all askew, the dark sockets of his eyes still taking in the last bits of life, and the mutilated throat bleeding, a now-twisted and useless tube stuck in it. Will they bury him, tube and all? I wonder what suit they'll put on him? What about shoes?"

The sleeves of the ugly night shirt were too short. Or, perhaps they were made like that in hospitals, and they brought him home to die.

Juan Luis had seen him two or three days before; from the hall, by peering in through the door left open by Elisa. She had gone in to give him an injection of morphine and he had followed her and watched. The sick man was half sitting up in bed, propped up by several yellowish pillows, thin as a rail, not a hair on his head, but heavy-bearded, eyelids drooping, waving a bony, ash-colored hand vaguely, like a shipwrecked survivor. He was choking, but couldn't struggle any more. Blood-stained bandages protruded from his chest; at the foot of the bed, quite near him, were scattered spittoons and receptacles, handkerchiefs, eye-droppers, tweezers. In the dim light of the room, the dying man was like a cardboard statue shaken by invisible worms that were slowly eating away at his entrails. The vision lasted only a few seconds, but he had the impression of having witnessed a self-immolation: silently bursting forth, cutting itself off, choking, flickering like a worn-out wick in an oil lamp.

The streets were still deserted, frozen, transparent. He quickened his step. It was cold. A drop of water ran down the nape of his neck and he wiped it off with the swipe of a hand. A lighted window came into view. Inside, someone was coughing. Someone who could hear his step anxiously, sense him approach, imagine him in the confines of the already ancient night, and become distressed upon realizing that he was going away, just another metallic echo in the deserted street. He cut through the park, crossed the bridge, and walked along the cobbled streets. On a street corner, two men were chatting. He couldn't hear them, but saw them gesticulating as he drew near. Arms upraised, they appeared to be threatening each other. One of them would point at the sky with his index finger, then extend his right hand and strike it with his closed fist until the other seized him by the lapels of his coat and shook him. He passed close to them, but didn't hear what they were saying. Leaving them behind, he once again felt about him the subterranean loneliness of dawn.

The bell tower of the Franciscan Church struck the hour, and behind the sharp stroke that continued to vibrate, the murmur of the river could be heard.

Don Carlos had died, his throat eaten away by cancer. The house outlasted him: it seemed to be supported not by its foundations or the beams that, quite obviously, had been rotting for years, but rather, by the observance of a family obligation, a habit of existing that kept it up, delicate, tottering, stained by the dampness of the winters, shaken by the monstrous roots that seemed to descend from the hill or reach out from the river, peeling like an old piece of furniture, but still proud. There were no sham metal decorations, no wood veneers, in that house: it had an austere facade of old stucco, with balconies suspended in the air, and a dark roof that seemed to flow in the wind like a savage mane. And a staircase, with very high, termite-eaten steps, that rose up and divided it into two wings. The house had about it something of a bird that one day would fly off, like a single, violent flame of protest against the humdrum world that clustered at its feet. The old man had died like that, circumspectly charred in his morning coat, weskit, striped trousers, and gray spats; someday the house would go in the same way, consumed by another cancer, strange and alone in a city in which it could no longer breathe.

The street door and the hall door were ajar. Juan Luis ran up the stairs. There was no one in the hall. A light was on in one of the bedrooms. The old man's. But there were no noises, no weeping, no whispers, as he had imagined. The light and the old man. Nothing more. Where could Señora Raquel be? And the servants? He thought of entering the bedroom. Fear, fear and repugnance dissuaded him. He turned on his heels and went off on tiptoe towards the grandmother's room. The parquet floor creaked underfoot, and, as always, the glass corridor shook. Upon reaching the grandmother's door, he saw that a light was burning there too. He knocked very softly. No one answered his knock. He pushed the door gently and peered in. The grandmother was asleep with her eyes open. She must have read until quite late, for on her breast lay a book whose pages kept rustling under her even breathing. In the other bed, near her, covered up to her eyes, lay Elisa watching him curiously. She saw his bird-like face peer in. He was pale, hollow-eyed, his hair was wet, the knot on his tie askew. She winked at him. Juan Luis tiptoed into the room. When he was beside the grandmother, he bent over her and moved his hand over her eyes. She didn't blink. He then removed his shoes and got under the covers with Elisa. He drew near and tried to embrace her, but drew back with a start. She was fully dressed. She stared at him, then stroked his hair and kissed his eyelids; Juan Luis lay his head on her neck and started to drop off to sleep. But she shook him, took his face in her hands and kissed his mouth. Juan Luis felt her sweep over him, with a fierce longing. Then, they clasped tightly in the depths of the bed. But before completing the embrace, she began to cry and dampened his lips with her tears.

Elisa wept for a long while, almost without moving, uttering confused sounds as if talking under her breath. He caressed her, unconcerned about her weeping, attentive now to certain footsteps coming from the hall and the dead man's room.

"The others must have arrived. They are probably dressing him now. Señora Raquel is not going to help them. Nor will she remain in the room, or if she does, she will look away. She feared him while he was alive. Now, she's probably hard put not to spit upon him. They must be bathing him. His legs are probably quite thin and hairy, and the toenails must have grown out and look hard and twisted like dry garlic. One of the arms will drop and the hand will slip into a receptacle. They'll dry him with a towel, rub his chest, careful not to disturb the slit in the trachea too much; they'll pack the last bandages in his throat and cover it with a silk handkerchief. Afterwards, they will sprinkle him profusely with cologne, pick him up in the sheet like a bundle, and his bones will creak and an odor of perfume and dry blood will hang in the air. Then, they will deposit him carefully in the coffin and he will look greener still, like a lemon, among the white pillows."

Who loved the old man? Who loved him really? Neither his wife nor his children. They were afraid of him, when he returned from Arica; later, when they discovered he had cancer, they felt compassion; more recently, it was disgust. An era was coming to an end with Don Carlos. He had been splendid. He himself said so. The old man spoke in a sarcastic, somewhat infirm voice, grimacing greatly; at times puffed-up with pride, at others crushed by the burden of defeat. The old man was a patriarch from another age, dying in haste so that the new century would not overtake him, hunt him down, and deal him the frightful death of the parasite emeritus. He lived on nostalgia, warming himself with memories, counting his good years while he looked about him, red-eyed, cursing the evil breed that was beginning to besiege him. Who loved him really? Or, actually despised him? When Juan Luis met him, the old man was already an intruder in his own home. Years before, five? maybe ten?, he had abandoned the family, and was now returning without anyone asking, or stopping him from it, either. He was back to die, to throw in the faces of his wife and children the shame of having cheapened himself by having stooped so low as to be forced to do manual labor. Yes, people say he had been a card shark and a pimp in the north. He cut quite a figure, the figure of a son-of-a-bitch crook to the very end. Dressed in his black suit, with amber cigarette holder, heavy gold watch, spats and cane, tall and a bit stooped, he used to walk in front of the old Savoy at the cocktail hour, his chin at a defiant angle, feet flat like a high wire artist on a slack rope: a rope whose days were numbered.

Elisa had stopped crying and was demanding more ardent kisses. He pulled up her sweater and, disappearing under the sheets, began to kiss her belly first, then her breasts. His face flushed with a warmth that seemed to radiate from the rosy roundness of her breasts and sweetly moist, firm nipples. She stirred in the bed and appeared to open up slowly. She slipped off her skirt and let it fall at the foot of the bed. Juan Luis now covered her with kisses and drew the sheets down a bit. He liked to see her like that, sweater rolled up over her breasts, arms spread, shaking her head in a slow, painful negation. He went over her body once again, this time with his tongue. She seized his head and pressed it against her belly. There was a sudden movement in the next bed, and both looked at the grandmother in fear. But the grandmother continued to breathe gently, blowing the pages of the book on her breast, her eyes open but asleep, in a profound sleep. They clasped each other then, kissing now with the urgency of the dawn that was already beginning to tint the window with milky hues. He tried to overwhelm her in a more violent and more desolate embrace, as if with a foreboding of defeat. She denied him gently, pressed her legs firmly together, closed up. Juan Luis besieged her, moaned, pleaded. The light of dawn was filtering in. He had tossed the bedclothes on the floor, and saw her nude, mouth half-parted, and the grandmother as if in a sarcophagus, silent, perhaps smiling in the uncertain light. He then swore at them both under his breath, got up, buttoned, and went out of the room without a backward glance.

The house was still silent. No one stirred in the dead man's room. He crossed the glassed-in corridor on tiptoe and the loose panes rattled. He looked through the blinds. Don Carlos was still in his nightshirt, half seated on the bed, stiff, green, emaciated. In the light of dawn he seemed to rise and float amidst his bottles, tubing, gauze, and pans. Someone would come to cover his face and nail down his coffin finally. Meanwhile, everyone, relatives and friends, had left the house: they wandered about the city cloaked in the uncertainty of the dawn, telling one another about the death of the patriarch in the frock coat, killing time at soda parlors, muffling their steps in the damp sawdust of a forgotten bar, readying the black horses and the trappings for the burial.

Juan Luis descended the stairs and went out rapidly. He had turned up the collar of his jacket; a cigarette dangled from his lips. No one was outside yet. Trees, houses, bridges, and the hills of the coast were already losing their outlines, dissolving into gray and green shadows. A dog came out of a half-open door and trotted beside him. It was a hungry mongrel. The river gangs had painted a red vest on its back, and black and blue circles around its eyes. The dog followed him, looking up at him from time to time. Juan Luis stopped and analyzed one of its glances.

"You are a degenerate dog," he said, "perverted by your masters from the central junkyard. One has only to look at your glassy stare, your slavering mouth, to know that."

He set out again and the dog followed more closely rubbing against his trousers. He stopped a second time, and, without warning, gave him a kick and sent him howling through the air. He then set off more briskly, staring at the streets around the station.

"I've got to find a whore and kick the hell out of her," he told himself. But there was no one to be seen.

It was growing light now, and by the high and blue reflection that rose from the roofs, he saw a cart appear. The horse was a tiny, luminous, smoky shadow, trotting as if lost among the deserted barns and warehouses. In the cab, another shadow puffed on a cigarette and raised his poncho like a black wing to deliver a whiplash. The vehicle passed quite near him, leaving behind the smell of damp vegetables, clay, and leather.

Suddenly, from the other side of the street, he saw a dark silhouette coming towards him. Unable to make out details, he slowly drew his hands from his pockets, clenched his fists. The shape approached but, as the light came from behind it, he failed to see its face. It was but a few steps away when he realized it was a woman. He had no time to look her over; she threw herself at him, seized him by the arm, and, laughing raucously, dragged him off, mouthing obscene remarks at the same time.

"She's not a whore," he told himself, "she doesn't look like a whore, or dress like one." The woman was dark, thick-set, with a pleasant smile, much make-up, a mannish voice, and mocking eyes. He followed her without a word. They reached the door of a flophouse and went up the narrow stairs.

"Pay for the room," she told him, pointing to an old man sitting in a cane-back chair by the brazier.

They entered the room; he locked the door, shot the bolt and, turning his back to her, began to undress. "When she tries to kiss me, I'm going to hit her on the nose, then the mouth, again and again, until she spits out all her teeth, and then I'm going to kick the hell out of her and bash in her belly." He finished undressing, but she didn't approach him. He turned, then, towards the bed and saw her lying on the bedspread, naked, immense, with mounds of hair between her parted legs, looking at him derisively, almost disdainfully. He swallowed hard. Unable to breathe, a sudden panic chilled his stomach and legs.

"Come," she said; "hurry, for it's very cold."

He tried to say something, but couldn't. The woman half sat up, took his hand and pulled him to her.

"What's the matter? Are you afraid?"

He was sweating now and had become quite pale.

"Are you afraid?" she repeated. Seated on the bed, looking at him first with great amusement, then with curiosity, she added, "Don't tell me you're a . . . how old are you? Is it possible?"

He felt he should attack her then, and readied his hands. The woman kissed him on the lips.

"Son, how old are you?" she repeated.

He tried to get up and, with a rapid maneuver, turn her over in the bed and stick her. The woman began to laugh and, throwing her large breasts in his face, crushed him with the weight of her body. She then took his member with her fingertips. He squirmed and began to struggle desperately; the woman guffawed and worked her hand faster. He felt that he could stand it no longer and moaned. The woman hesitated for a moment, grew suddenly serious and lying on her back, helped him. He gave a few rapid and brief thrusts and fell panting on the pillow. The woman let him be for a few moments, then began to stroke his head and neck. There was tenderness in her voice.

"What's the matter?" she said. "Look, just to show you that I'm your friend, I'm going to help you."

And she resumed the attack with her fingers. He vaulted out of bed and lay face down on the floor. The woman began to rant and swear. He no longer saw her, but sensed that she was dressing. Out of the corner of an eye, Juan Luis saw her put on her panties and stockings, and buried his face even more. A strange silence followed, then a rustle of clothes, and the woman turned to say:

"Is this all you have?" She had gone through his pockets and wallet. A bank note quivered in her hand. The door slammed behind her.

Juan Luis got up timidly. He looked all around, as if afraid of being watched, and set about filling the wash basin. Prey to a sudden compulsion to wash, to rid himself of the woman's smell and, with it, the nausea that choked him, he began to wash with deliberation, continuing the operation for a long time. Soaping himself again and again, he doused himself with water, dried off, and began all over again. After drying off, thinking she had probably used the towel also, he washed again. Finally, he used his handkerchief to dry off, dressed, and left.

Something hot in one of the neighborhood cafes would have cheered him up, but he didn't have a cent. Morning was upon him; a light, gray mist clung to the balconies of the hotels and stores, and seemed to rise with the damp vapor that came from the pavement. Buses and streetcars were running already. The corrugated metal roll-down doors of the stores were going up noisily. The streets were slowly filling up with bundled-up, shivering people who walked very rapidly. Columns of smoke rose from the old, gray buildings. Tiny lights turned on and off on the balconies while the sun slowly dissipated the fog. Juan Luis looked into a soda parlor. The coffee pot was steaming and through the steam the white and pink face of a waitress surprised him. He looked at her vacantly; her hair was dripping wet, her arms raised, her hands red from the cold. Juan Luis made as if to enter. A thick, sharp smell -a mixture of hot milk, vanilla, toasted bread, and coffee, enveloped him. Recalling that he hadn't a cent, he withdrew. The girl looked at him in astonishment. He stammered then, and she smiled.

It would soon be time for the university. He went off, hugging the walls, crossed the market square, and penetrated the streets of the park, feeling as if he were gliding down the aisle of a church, through the ochre light of the leafy trees, crunching the damp sand underfoot. A sensation of peace quickened his breath, invading him. He heard the nearby murmur of the river and the deep rustle of leaves in the gentle wind of a winter morning. Through the highest branches of the trees, filtered a white vapor that stirred in him an intense anxiety. He felt that all the sudden movement of life around him came from inside himself, and that the night's struggle had been a victory for him. In some way, that immense woman who opened up to him in a wild copulation, symbolized his own strength, so painfully sought in his nocturnal adolescence. Her face, crowned with black serpents, had been blotted out; there remained of her but a rhythm that, suddenly, was the rhythm of the dawning day, and above her loomed now another body, another movement: the young girl in the rumpled bed, wounded, awaiting him near the grandmother that slept with her eyes open. He glanced at his watch and thought, "I'll see her after the burial."

II

WOULD things really change at Elisa's?
Nothing would change. In recent times the old man lived on his wife's charity. He hadn't a cent. Therefore, if a change took place, it would be for the better: the family would be able to breathe. What a tremendous weight off their backs! Now they could get rid of the bed he occupied, burn the mattress and bedding, dispose of his bottles, fumigate the room, and let the wind sweep away the miasma sticking to the floor and walls. What a relief. A new lease on life for Señora Raquel. And for Mario and Elisa, it would be like being born again. Although, to tell you the truth, the old codger wasn't so bad. It all depends on how one looked at it. He adored Elisa. She was the only one who offered to nurse him. The day he returned from the hospital with the sad news that the "infection" in his throat was, in effect, incurable cancer, he was quite theatrical, hoping to win everybody's sympathy. He had decided to move out and rent a house alone, so as to "die stoically." The family said nothing, nor made any effort to dissuade him. Elisa waited until he was alone to tell him that she would accompany him

and nurse him to the end. The old man was quite a ham, but he appreciated the gesture and it touched him deeply, He had a way with him, and all the tricks of one who has never sacrificed himself for anybody. Also, he was quite good at spinning tales and making people laugh, provided the family wasn't watching. With the family, he was truculent. When he coughed, he spread out his arms, his eyes almost came out of their sockets, beads of perspiration covered his forehead, and he choked, making sure to look at the bystanders one by one while he took mental notes of their reactions, until he passed out, head down, panting. Of course, the old man was actually dying. He had a right to be truculent. But he liked to joke with Juan Luis and tell him about his escapades in the north. Knowing that he was in love with Elisa, he didn't reject him. Nor did he forget that through him he came to recover, if it can be put that way, some of the affection that Juan Luis' parents had denied him. For him it was like maintaining a bond that was precious to him in order to still be accepted by the family. In Juan Luis' case and at his age it was nonsense to speak of bonds. But the old man needed him. Juan Luis never learned exactly how much was true and how much was fabrication in what he told him about the north. He laughed at his jokes, because the old man knew how to tell them, and also because somewhat hypocritically, it was to Juan Luis' advantage to win his favor. The old man winked at his locking himself up with Elisa. And that was very important. Because Juan Luis lived only for those moments: he used to stay up all night, spend the mornings in bed, often without eating, thinking up adventures which made him a hero in her eyes. Sometimes he was a Chilean singer who triumphed in Italy, returned to his neighborhood, and, upon seeing her, abandoned opera and was victorious anonymously in a tango singing contest; at others, he was a boxer of slight build, sporting a right that decided bouts in a matter of seconds, and finally became a contender for a world title in Madison Square Garden and . . . bored with this, he became a famous scientist, while she, married to another man, followed his triumphs in the newspapers until one night in the laboratory . . . . Juan Luis reached the Cordillera suburb where they lived, walked stiffly and deep in thought along the old, dusty streets, enveloped in the fragrance of acacia and jasmine, skirting the canals until, late in the afternoon, Elisa appeared in the small plaza and, taking him by the hand, made him sit next to her on an old bench. There, the hours went by as the colors changed in the sky; looking into her eyes, he saw how the world was slowly becoming filled with all sorts of things: the shadow of a lilac bush, a certain magic light on an oak door studded with copper nails, things that at the time possessed a certain secret, and he now wondered what it could have been. Don Carlos approved in silence. And Juan Luis endured his cough.

Juan Luis crossed the lobby of the School of Education and went out to the patio. He went through the corridors without finding anyone, and entered the student's lounge. A thick cloud of smoke enveloped him and he stopped in bewilderment. The lounge was filled with students in large overcoats; some wore hats. They kept warm by beating their arms and stomping on the floor. The lounge, in spite of everything, was cozy in the August cold. There were a few leather armchairs and some tables. Against the wall a large gas stove roared. Over the chimney, someone had stuck a poster in violent colors. Juan Luis looked around; he could see all his friends. "Who had gone to class? Don Claudio is probably dictating *s's* and *d's* that keep his teeth sharp. Those who count, the ones that matter, are here." Without a word, he pulled off his gloves and began to rub his hands.

"There's a slight danger of chilblains in the little finger of the left hand," he told the group that was at his side. "Gilda is looking at me and is getting ready," he thought. When she went up to speak to him, politely, in her silky voice, he looked at her and unnerved her. It was an insulting look.

"We waited for you yesterday, Juan Luis; I think you are the most obnoxious boy in the school."

Now he looks at her, right eyebrow arched, teeth clenched. It is a grimace that he learned from a photo of Malraux, that produces unexpected effects. Gilda withstands his glance and smiles at him. He lowers his eyes in confusion. "What gives with this woman?" He approaches and stands beside her. There is something about her that repels him. A feature, a grimace, an odor? No. Nothing of the kind. Gilda is soft and her skin has the silky texture of a sun-ripened lemon; very dark eyes, shining, slanted, almost Asian; wide mouth, small, even teeth, and a snake tongue. There is a caress in her voice as she talks to him, as to a child. She sits beside him in class, waits for him at noon to walk with him along the Alameda, invites him to her home, and then to walk through the avenues of Cousiño Park. And . . . something about her fills him with an uncontrollable uneasiness, a feeling of conjugal routine that stinks. He begins to talk nervously with the others.

"The rebels bombarded the university." Undaunted, Gilda comes closer to him.

"Why didn't you come over to study yesterday? There's a written test tomorrow."

"I don't care about the written test. How is it you don't understand that, Gilda?"

She stands there looking at him and he lowers his eyes even more, feeling ridiculous. Everyone must have noticed his retreat. She has come nearer and presses his arm with one of her breasts. She squeezes against him. It has been only a brief, almost invisible contact, but it has left him trembling.

He goes out, flanked by Gilda and Chica, filled with confusion, for he feels that he has a string in each hand that is around the necks of two rare chickens: one is tall, taller than the school of education, the other is midget-like, lost among the bricks of the floor; one sticks out her head over the rectangular patio, over the tiles of the roof, and peeks at the blue sky; the other cackles at his heels. Out in the street the Alameda cloaks them in a fog that the sun is beginning to tint. They change direction, enter the school casino where the light is unreal, filtered as it is by a green glass roof that covers the immense swimming pool. There is no water in the pool. It has never had any. All around it are white cement steps where no one has ever sat. The empty pool is like a cold and dry crystal egg on whose bottom the students have set up a ping-pong table and a few chairs.

In the morning, the bottom of the pool, with its black and white mosaic, is like a chess board. In one corner, dressed in black, wavy hair shining, a young ping-pong player gets ready to beat the air with a turquoise paddle. Opposite him, the top row of tile is interrupted by a green table, and at the far end two girls move their lips in silence. One is very blond, arms outstretched, as if gathering in the light that descends from the roof; the other, more colorless, is made dull by the glare of the glass. Beyond, in a hostile, yet sober and silent attitude, three young men of incongruous appearance stand face to face considering the color of a bottle. Juan Luis goes down the metal ladder followed by the two girls, and makes towards the table at the deep end, under the diving board.

"There's no reason for you to pay," says Gilda, looking at Juan Luis, "it would be unfair."

"It isn't unfair," said Juan Luis. "The trouble is that I'm broke. Flat broke."

Juan Luis is suddenly suffused by a wave of gratitude and tenderness for Gilda and, face alight with a beatific smile, he bends down towards her, while she opens her purse and counts her change, and begin to talk in a confidential tone about the death that had gotten him out of bed and about the ideas that it had occasioned. He repeats certain things recently read in Ortega's "Concerning Love," but combines them adroitly with allusions to a sweetheart, to a loneliness, to a grandmother that sleeps with her eyes open, to his return along the river bank. On the brink of telling about the encounter, he stops because Gilda has been touched more than he had bargained for and gazes at him with eyes filled with humid tenderness.

At the other table the three young men are hatching a plot that touches the most vital part of his life: it is a tiny line, like a limpid and tensile strand of cobweb, that has been surrounding and tempting him, so as to hand him over once again, but now without appeal, to a certain ironic dilemma of violence. He excuses himself from the girls and goes towards them. They watch him approach with hostile indifference, as if to isolate him and force him to leave. But Juan Luis sits down and waits. The eldest, Juan Unanime, has thinning hair, bovine eyes, a fleshy nose, and a spittle-filled mouth. His teeth have many cavities. When he speaks, he stresses his words with thumb and forefinger joined as though holding a flea captive between them, in the manner of a professor of logic. He's obviously the leader of the group, but it is not known why. It could not be due to his rather obvious irony, nor to the weight of his arguments. It had to be something more secret about which Juan Luis had a foreboding, but had been unable to discover until then. Unexpectedly, Juan Unanime says

"Friend, do you have any dough?"

Juan Luis gives a cutting no. The other becomes very serious, looks up, and rambles on. There is something intriguing hidden in his words, something alive. It can be said that while seeking the vital essence behind the name assigned to things, Juan Unanime has discovered the real thing and forgotten the name, as happens to primitives given to magic. And he has been left without a language, but with a mouthful of myths that change and unnerve him at all hours of the day and night. To calm the myths, he drinks, drinks until he collapses with them on his back; in his sleep, they still gnaw at him and sap his strength, fill his dreams and, perhaps, grant him a moment of peace when the light of dawn surprises him stretched out in a ditch, near Blanco Hill, a few blocks from home.

"You're always broke," he tells Juan Luis. "Why don't you borrow from your girlfriends?" The voice wheedles, but its sweetness is that of a hipster. Juan Luis does not reply. "Students," goes on Juan Unanime, "are like Social Security: you deposit your trust in them, their families' trust in them, the entire country deposits something in them, and they never pay real dividends. There you have them, in their wretched neighborhood building, receiving trust and dying of hunger. What does your family give you, friend?"

"The first surprise of the month."

"I say, borrow from your girlfriend and let's have lunch together. Because you must not forget that we are fighting against time."

"I thought there was time to burn."

"A belief wholly yours, friend. And rather typical of your generation. Our country thinks that there is more than enough time, and, in effect, it is living on borrowed time. Its time was up quite some time ago."

"You mean that we must act at once?"

"Have you read today's paper? Have you seen what's happened?"

"I know very well what's happening. But I maintain that we must be patient. The supreme virtue of the terrorist is patience."

"No, friend. Economy."

"Cut the horseshit, friend, please. What I say is that the gentleman here should float a loan with his girlfriends. As for waiting or not waiting, it is a settled issue and there is no use discussing it. There is no waiting possible."

"Yesterday, at three-thirty in the afternoon . . . " began Joel, the second of the bystanders, a young man with a dark, deep look and a black mane that framed his fine face, "something happened that makes any wait impossible: the Nazis who were going to Valparaíso fired at point blank range against the people waiting on the station platform, and do you know whom they killed? Two women selling candy."

Joel spoke in a resonant voice; however, something about it betrayed a certain break, a shameful emotion perhaps; or just timidity or, better still, timidity disguised as presumption. He pressed his fleshy lips together, jutted his virile chin, put an index finger to his nose, demanding attention, but everything in his brief account was wrapped in sentimentality. Juan Luis understood his hate for the Nazis; a hate that one had to accumulate in the mouth and then spit out—a hate difficult to define, in which there was conviction, ideological arrogance, and something else more intimate, more emotional, that was long in rising to the surface. For those born in a time of violence who, like Juan Luis and Joel, were still imbued with Christian spirit, it was easy to accept the voices of redemption unquestioningly, but the sudden intrusion of the wooden soldier produced terror, like the terror we feel at the heedless advance of a monster in a nightmare. In our very city from any corner, from a hovel or a mansion, the sinister Nazi blow could descend, cracking skulls and spitting blood. In Germany, Hitler celebrated his rites of Spring by roasting Jews, and, throughout all Europe went the bluish, thick smoke that intoxicated the menwolves, inciting them to bacchanals of semen and blood in which millions of naked women died and were buried clutching in their arms tiny skeletons of newborn babies.

And in the auditorium at the University of Chile, the hubbub was on the rise. The students hung from the second and third story railings, gesticulating and hurling missiles. Those in the rear climbed onto the shoulders of their comrades and held up placards in red letters. Below, the crowd stomped on the floor, clapped their hands in rhythm, and howled *'Avance, avance, avance!'* From the second floor came an answering cry. The Auditorium, illuminated and resplendent, trembled. Because of its strange funnel shape, extremely high ceiling, iron railings, it appeared to gyrate on an invisible axis ever more rapidly, in its frenzy blurring the grimacing faces, the fists on high, the banners, flags. At the rostrum, Astolfo Tapia from time to time raised a hand for silence. His usually florid face was purple, thick beads of sweat rolled off his mustache, slid down his chin, and collected in his black tie.

Juan Luis looked about him with contempt. Joel was stomping on the floor and biting his lips. The howling increased in volume. In one corner of the hall, hanging almost from the second floor railing, held up by his followers, Parada, the leader of the Nazis, was also trying to speak. His slender body swelled with impotent rage. He waved his hand, breathed hard, and seemed on the verge of flying over the crowd like a bird of prey.

Suddenly Juan Luis noticed that Joel was turning in his seat and that, from a back pocket of his pants, he was drawing a revolver. Silent, pale, perspiring, lips curled in disgust, he raised his hand and emptied the gun. The main light splintered into a thousand pieces. After a moment of dismay, the crowd hurled itself towards the doors crushing, falling, screaming. Juan Luis ran too, jumping over the seats and out into one of the side patios. There, in the darkness, he saw the Nazis, commanded by Parada, descending the stairs wielding their clubs and hurling themselves upon the students. A girl fell at his side, another fell on top of her, and then on top of them a free-for-all broke out. He tried to fight his way through, but couldn't. Little by little, he saw himself hemmed against the wall. Unexpectedly, Joel appeared at his side and began to strike blows and to receive most of the punishment. From the second floor a firecracker fell to the patio. The fuse began to burn with a blue, noisy flame. A Nazi ran out and kicked it among the fallen. Joel kicked it right back. The firecracker burst with a tremendous impact. From the street came the click of the heels of the advancing police. The Nazi troops began to fall back. A few shots rang out in the vestibule. Juan Luis, hugging the wall, got out into the street. Someone fell behind him. He stopped and gave him a hand to get up. The other, moaning, dragging himself along, tried to follow him. Juan Luis then led him by the hand. As they reached the corner of Arturo Pratt Street, a new volley sounded behind them; they hit the ground, bullets whistling around them. Juan Luis looked up and saw the wounded man trying to cross the street. He couldn't warn him in time. A volley caught him in mid-air like a rag doll and cut him in two around the middle. The student bounced on the ground, then rolled all the way to the gutter.

Hate had drawn them together. There was no deep friendship between them. Nevertheless, they sought out one another indirectly, but constantly. Did they need him? No one needed anybody else in the kind of struggle that absorbed them. Affection? With a touch of contempt, perhaps, and even a bit of admiration. Because in their eyes, Juan Luis was a young provincial student seeking to rescue the old bourgeois family whose fortunes had waned. He had come to the university backed by influential names and instead of becoming the epitome of studiousness and good sense—the hero of the old saga who pulls himself up by the bootstraps—he was just wasting time, involved in a senseless adventure. And so it was that in this crowd he was admired not for his knack of loafing, but rather, for his unusual gifts as a terrorist.

In that year of 1938, terrorists all were the students of logic, mathematics, natural sciences, medicine and engineering, law, arts and letters, and applied arts, particularly those in applied arts. Those who didn't study any profession, the humanists who found jobs in business firms or made the pool hall their base of operations, the sons of retired military personnel. In a word, terrorists were the young Chileans who, consumed by the anguish of a hopeless tenement life, put on their patched coats and torn trousers, and sallied forth into downtown Santiago feverishly trying to find their way, bumping against walls, assaulting police barricades, pulling down university statues, shooting and plotting in summer villas, risking their necks in revolutionary cells presided over by lice, pressured by fleeting, implacable time.

Juan Luis qualified under several of these terrorist categories and was to take part in a pending plot.

"How are we going to get the money?" inquired Leonardo,

the third member of the group, a large, thin, slow-moving man with a cavernous voice. "Will they be willing to sell us the ingredients for the bomb?"

Joel didn't deign to look at the questioner.

"There's a way. There's the twenty-five pesos the director donated to rent a moving van."

"What director? What moving van?"

" 'The Great Theater of the World,' friend, for which they need heavy props: the scenery that the Municipal Theater lends the actors in the school of education. Let's go get them on foot."

Juan Luis asked the time. It was nine-thirty. There was time to do it and other things before Don Carlos' funeral. They left.

And even as they marched along the Alameda, other young people went their separate ways with different plans and perhaps more ambiguous ambitions. Their paths, apparently, were not yet destined to cross. That would come later, and time, in reality, could not be an important factor for those who looked upon it like a pool filling up with silt.

Remnants of fog still clung to the tops of the pepper trees. At times, the overhead wires vibrated and a streetcar came to a sudden stop. Old people rested on the park benches, watching with a smile the oratorical air of the statues. A nurse in a starched apron went by pushing a white baby carriage, leaving a halo of light behind her. A student with curly, black hair, his face blue from the cold, walked slowly by; from time to time, as if suddenly inspired, he stopped, looked up at the sky, closed his eyes, mumbled something, and continued on his way. At that moment, nothing disturbed the normal course of the morning. Only three young men attracted attention.

They came along the same Alameda carrying a cross, a harmonium, some candelabra, chasubles, and bells. What penance were they doing? Fugitives from some rural chain gang? People drew aside to let them pass; old retired men frowned; devout old ladies made the sign on the cross; governesses made a face of disdain. Leonardo, even taller and thinner at mid-day, with his many-hued, alcohol-ravaged face, immense dreamy eyes, and long thin mustache—his brown overcoat dragging on the ground—carried the cross on his shoulders. From time to time, he stopped to take a long drag on his cigarette. Behind him, black mane over his face, perspiring, came Joel with the point of the cross under his arm, a copy of the daily *La Opinión* in his hand. At his side, in a faded yellow gabardine, feet dragging, Juan Unanime carried one end of the harmonium; Juan Luis, struggling to maintain the balance that Juan Unanime insisted on upsetting, carried the other end, as well as a bundle of candles and nails.

A block from the school of education, they stopped to rest. Hunger was really getting to them. Leonardo, in his beautiful bass voice, spoke of a certain university order of precedence at meals. They ranked at the bottom of this scale just high enough to burn in the sacred fire of seafood stew and the violet light of wine.

It was seven hours from the caper. Seven difficult hours at the end of which zero hour could come and go unperceived.

Elbows resting on a biblical rock, eyes fixed obstinately on a black decanter, restless feet muffled by the mixture of sawdust and water that covered the floor, they drank the afternoon away. When Juan Luis asked the time so as to go to Don Carlos' funeral, he discovered that the old man had already been buried and prayed over. They drank the afternoon away, while the actors—students—centurions scourged Christ on Calvary, and the Virgin, surrounded by the gentle women of the school of education, gazed through her tears at the radiance of the Jewish sky. The Apostles, the princes, and kings were taking their places; the purple-clad courtesans, the soldiers in gray, and the merchants were already executing the dance of death, and the small stage in the Alameda shook with the rhythm of the drums and the accordion-like lament of the harmonium. The director snapped orders, then became caught up in the final trial of his actors. Dazzled by the winter sun that bled like a fat lamb, they too drank the gall and the sweat, and the water at the feet of Christ. The playlet ran its course and the paper skies lit up and the wax tears were shed. The play over, the twenty-five pesos in their pocket, the terrorists lifted the siege, withdrew from the tomb of the Risen One and walked to Leonardo's house, where they were to pick up the bomb.

Leonardo lived in an enormous tenement with several patios. His father, in better days had been a judge, but now ruined, was a tailor. But, not really. Actually, he got orders from among his old friends and turned them over to a tailor he kept working secretly in a garret in the back. In addition to getting orders, Leonardo's father, most ceremonious and distinguished, took the measurements of the victim with a yellow tape-measure and jotted them down in an old ledger. The house had no electricity.

Entering in silence, they groped their way down a very long flagstone corridor. Someone was singing or moaning in a nearby room. Dogs were barking. A voice asked something, but the unintelligible words vibrated in the darkness as if someone had uttered them in a distant field, in a now dead age. Leonardo finally came out with the chosen weapon: a paraffin bomb in a bottle, wrapped in newspaper. He gingerly put it in his overcoat pocket.

The voice that moaned all at once became distinct. It came over the adobe wall, got tangled in the dark tiles, and left a dry rhythm of hand-clapping and tambourines in the cold air. The friends looked at one another with a wild expression. Upon reaching the door, Leonardo said it would be necessary to pay their respects. In the back of the third patio of the tenement, the neighbors awaited them gathered around a woman that seemed to be suspended by tricolored ribbons: squarely built, she was seated on a stool, feet dangling, her eyes wild. Older hens whirled around beating the earth floor with their heels; a pale, quarrelsome man, three sheets to the wind, flicked at them with his handkerchief. Leonardo took an enormous glass of wine in his right hand, downed it, and passed the glass to his friends so that they could fill it and empty it in the same fashion. When the ceremony was about to be repeated for the third or fourth time, Joel swore and tried to snatch the bomb from his pocket. Leonardo ran through the patio towards the street door. Juan Unanime stumbled after him.

In the tenement, the clapping continued like the crackling of burning wood. Juan Luis could feel it hard and treacherous on his back. At that moment, it was impossible to grasp the reason for the bitterness that emanated from the old patios and settled on the irrigation ditches to reflect the rocks, a few stars, the outline of an alamo above the dark mirror of the clay. The four friends now looked uncertainly towards the sky. Leonardo, swaying like a sleepy mast, mused over the words of the now vanishing song, and urinated.

A few minutes before seven, they climbed into a taxi and gave the address of the Nazi headquarters on Recoleta Avenue. Juan Luis looked about him and felt they were enveloped in a halo of light that, without being a fire yet, would soon become a flame. Joel perceived the intensity of his look and nodded. They were traveling in a vehicle of fire. At sunset, at the moment of slow conflagration, the city of Santiago floated in the air, all ablaze, vibrating like a spark in the crystal loftiness of the winter sky. Something similar to a prophetic exaltation burgeoned on things and peoples' faces, and shuddered across the sky. That sudden charge was going to find an outlet in the hands of the terrorists, but the outcome was going to be as strange as the beauty of that hidden fire that now illuminated the city for an instant before night fell.

There was no need for words. They would go by the two-story building once; the second time, upon reaching the Princess Dollar Movie Theater, Leonardo was to open the door of the taxi; twenty meters further on, he would jump out while Juan Luis and Joel covered him from behind with tiny peashooters; he was to hurl the bomb onto the stairs of the building, return to the taxi at a run, and the deed would be done. There would be no time to see the results. They would have to flee in great haste. Trapped on the upper floor—the stairs and door afire—the Nazis would burn and choke to death like rats.

The taxi turned the corner of the Bridge of Recoleta. Juan Luis turned to look at Leonardo's face: his eyes were half closed, purple splotches covered his cheeks, his lower lip drooped; he held the bottle filled with gasoline as if it were filled with wine and he were about to take a swig. At his side, Juan Unanime dozed.

"You take the bomb," Juan Luis told Joel. "That guy won't be able to take a step with it."

Joel stretched his hand to take it, but Leonardo pulled away brusquely.

"Give it to me," Joel said to him.

Leonardo did not answer. He hugged the bottle against his chest, shook his head and squinted his eyes, trying to identify the buildings they were passing. Juan Unanime woke up and, seeing Joel's maneuver, said:

"Don't take the bottle from him. We all need a drink. Let's see. Driver, stop at the corner, in front of the church, by the Billiards

Academy. We'll each have a swig at least."

"Don't stop," shouted Joel. "Never mind this drunk. Keep going."

"Why spoil things, friend?" said Juan Unanime. "After all, we're on our way to the slaughter by taxi, bottle in hand, like someone going to a military parade at the Park. Paraffined. In the deepest sense of the word. With paraffin in our souls. To set the country on fire with a bottle of rot gut. Funny. Because together with the lard-ass called Von Marees, who sports boots and a brown shirt, hobbles on one foot and strokes his head—with one hand, because he scratches his ass with the other—just like his teacher Hitler, it's possible we may kill a few more. Poor devils, like ourselves. I say funny, because it has to be done."

The taxi went by the Nazi headquarters. In the upper story, through the open windows, they were able to make out, amidst great illumination, swastikas and banners, young men who walked about proudly, raising their hands and howling.

"Stop here, driver," said Juan Unanime, "stop at the Billiards corner."

"Don't stop, shit!" shouted Joel. "Go on, go around the block once."

The driver looked at one, then the other, and decided to mind Joel. Juan Unanime grew furious and made as if to slap at him. Juan Luis pinned his arms.

"Stop, you idiots," Juan Unanime kept shouting.

"Don't stop," repeated Joel.

"Stop, I have to take a piss," said Juan Unanime.

"It's a trick," said Joel. "He wants to back out."

"I won't drop it. I'll go all the way up to the second floor with the bottle and ram it up the Führer's very own butt."

The driver thought they spoke of a bottle of wine or *pisco*, and liked the fun.

"I'll even help you do that," he said.

Juan Unanime stared at him, his eyes suddenly alight with malice.

"Isn't it a fact that he deserves it?" he asked. "Isn't it? And you'd take the bottle and break it over his head?"

"Not quite, no. Because the other bastards up there would

have my ass."

"No, I don't mean that . . . just for kicks, why don't you slip out of the car and hurl the bottle up the stairs. Just to throw a scare into them."

They were already approaching the movie house for the second time. There were some armed policemen in front of the Nazi headquarters; a few curious onlookers stood across the street. Juan Luis analyzed the situation rapidly. What Juan Unanime proposed was a low down trick. At just the right moment, he himself would take the bottle from Leonardo, jump out and hurl it.

As they arrived in front of the building, Joel threw himself across Leonardo at the same time as Juan Luis, and with the same idea in mind. The driver looked at them dumbfounded. Leonardo pushed both of them aside and got out. He reeled for a moment, his huge overcoat dragging on the ground.

"Don't shut off the engine," Juan Luis shouted at the driver. "Be ready to pull away."

Leonardo went on, stumbling on his coat. Howling like a banshee, he raised the bomb to hurl it, but at that instant he tripped and pitched headlong. A single flame of intense brilliance lighted the air, and the explosion reverberated against the ground and walls. Clearly silhouetted against the flame were the policemen with their clubs and submachine-guns, the dumb struck, bug-eyed people, and Leonardo flapping in his burning coat. A stretch of the street was also burning furiously. Juan Luis and Joel leaped from the taxi. But Juan Unanime had anticipated them and, on all fours, was struggling to put out the flames that enveloped Leonardo and drag him towards the taxi. The Nazis had come down on the run and, at the sound of a trumpet blast, began to wield their clubs. The bodies of the four terrorists burned in a single green flame. Juan Unanime kept shaking Leonardo's body and, in the process, looked like a vulture flapping over a dead animal. When they put out the flames, they picked him up and retreated towards the taxi. It was gone. They fled into the darkness of Lastra Street, towards Vega and the river, tripping on the loose paving stones and mud puddles, shouting and cursing, stumbling against the carts and the horses that stopped ruminating for an instant to look at them, guiding on the blue line of the street lamps, with Leonardo's body stiff as a board and still smoking.

III

TELEGRAM in hand, Juan Luis got up from the bench and began to wave his arms; striding from one side to the other like a soldier on guard he would look up, close his eyes, shrug his shoulders, curse, and stride off once more. Elisa watched him without answering his questions. He would tire, seek the warmth of her breast and, aroused, end up by surrendering. It touched her to see him violent, acting before an imaginary audience, believing himself the center of all eyes when, in reality, at that hour in the Forestal Park there were only stray dogs and couples, like themselves, wrapped up in their own madness. But, at the same time, it saddened her to see his wounds and be witness to his poverty, a poverty that did not bother him and, for that very reason, was pathetic. Thin, rather pale-faced, with bright, dark eyes, Juan Luis was dazzling at first glance, then, pitiful in his old, extremely long overcoat over a threadbare sweater —he owned no jacket—and patched, wine-hued trousers. His fine, startling white throat stood out over his black shirt and gray tie. At such times, she felt the urge to caress him, but upon meeting his glance, she had to retreat because Juan Luis repaid tenderness with a sort of furious, cutting mockery that made her eyebrows and temples tremble. He approached her again, and again thrust the telegram at her.

"Their answer is no. That's all. A plain no. Without explanation or hope. Just no. Tell me if it's fair."

As he sat down and crossed his legs, a patch on his trousers became visible and she could not take her eyes off it.

"They could at least have given me some hope, but no. Not a cent."

"Perhaps they can't," she ventured.

"Can't they? A pair of old geese swimming in dough? I'll be damned!"

A couple went by slowly. The woman stared at them brazenly.

"How can you demand it of them?," asked Elisa.

"They could if they wanted. They're just stingy. But, can't you manage something? Even a part of it?"

"No," she said resolutely.

"Yes, I know. It's a matter of my facing up to this, of my being really responsible, and of my getting screwed, royally screwed, so that I'll learn. Isn't that it?"

She kept silent. It was night and the darkness seemed to weigh down and crush the trees. Juan Luis' voice was dull and his words fell like pebbles to the ground.

"Nothing, nothing, nothing, nothing. That's what you and the whole . . ."

He began to insult her with an obstinate fury that drowned in itself only to burst forth anew. He looked at her out of the corner of his eye and, without stopping to reflect, interpreted her silence as an insult. Drunk with words, he went on then, stumbling on his rage, scarcely breathing, face contorted, fists clenched. Until, halting in the middle of a sentence, he watched, panting like a tired animal. Elisa had been weeping a moment before, but now she simply looked off into space, lips lightly pursed into a disdainful smile. Juan Luis let out a vile oath, jumped up and strode off.

She did not stir. Suddenly, she was cold and hungry. Shivering, she pulled up the collar of her green leather jacket, fished gloves out of her handbag, slipped them on, and waited. There was danger of her being taken for a hustler. Steps sounded near her; she maintained an attitude of deep thought, eyes fixed on the background of shadows into which the park was receding at that hour. Another couple went by. Elisa lit a cigarette and smoked avidly, aware of the trembling of her fingers and lips. The night began to brighten and there was a gentle swaying in the shadows: around a bend, the neck and shoulders of a white statue appeared for an instant. Then, nothing. Afterwards, there was something like the beginning of a grimace as a branch swayed, barely rustled by the wind; and, through the coppery density of the leaves, something or someone, and animal, an iron grill, a flickering lamp on a plaster pedestal, and the murmur of voices coming from the Fine Arts Palace, the sound of chisels and hammers, or the crash of pebbles in the nearby river. Now and again, a whistle or stifled laughter.

All at once, she felt the urge, the absurd urge, to feel the beating of her own body. Flicking the cigarette away, she took off her gloves, put her frightened head down, and placed both hands on her belly. A moment later, she looked more intently, scarcely breathing, and pressed in ever so lightly. Nothing. There was nothing. Just as Juan Luis had said: nothing. Not a murmur, not a movement. Nothing yet. Elisa was tempted to scream, let out a howl and start something that would make the world aware of her pregnancy and make it tremble with her, wait and be silent with her. But, at that moment, she felt the touch of a hand on her head and looked up with a start. Juan Luis had returned. He was now looking at her sadly and murmuring unintelligibly. She rose and let him lead her away.

Iris, the soda parlor opposite the daily *La Opinión*, was a combination gathering place, school, pawn shop, isolation cell, and waiting room. The expresso machine hurled explosive columns of steam. A blondish young man was beating on the table, there was a hyena's laughter, somebody was staring obstinately at Elisa. A person would get up and go through the motions of paying, but didn't; someone else would arrive and take his place, pushing away with disgust the coffee-and-ash-stained cup he had inherited. Everybody talked at once—pompously and stridently, without listening.

"And when a family breaks down in Chile? When one feels

that he has crossed the dividing line and the members of the broken-up family start to operate on their own like subversive elements?"

"What about the poor man's home?"

"I'm not talking about homes. I'm talking about families. The poor man has no home. He stakes out his spread at the edge of a river if he is an adventurer, or settles in some government-owned subdivision, if he is a conservative. Or, he'll rent a hovel already set up. The tin, paper, and nails don't really exist. In a tract you can change the house numbers and nobody'll notice. Tables are the same everywhere, and so are broken chairs, toilets, and dogs."

"That stuff about families is utter nonsense," said a tiny, pock-marked youth. "Bourgeois prejudices you still retain, friend, because of your provincial background. You are still talking about families and thinking of the pork ribs they used to cook for you where you come from. Ruined families? Isn't it better to think about who is responsible? The family breaks up for economic reasons. You study. I work. Knight of the plume, that's me."

"You make feather dusters, or something?"

"I live off my pen here in Santiago, and my folks roast to death in the north. Not because you or I want it, but because . . . ."

Joel looked at him with distrust, then turned to Juan Luis once more:

"I can't stand having Political Science brought up when I am talking about my relatives and, as you say, of homes that are like relatives. This kid comes from a shack thrown up at midnight on the *Pampa*. How can he know what is happening to my family? My family can't be worse off than it is, but neither can it be any less attached to the village where we still have some property. Our plot is surrounded by large estates that once were ours and now belong to strangers, to people from another world. Therefore, we can't say that we are subversive elements."

A man, dressed in a blue jacket and gray flannel trousers, got up from a nearby table and approached Joel. Juan Luis heard him whisper his name. Joel thought for a moment, then said:

"Peña wants us to go listen to records at his place. You want to go?"

The other man smiled courteously. His was a serious face of many lines, softened by a sort of childish mockery.

"There's hot wine. With orange and cinnamon," Joel was saying.

Juan Luis took Elisa's arm and accepted in silence. On the way out, he asked Joel:

"Who's this bird? There's something raunchy about him. Difficult to say what about the forehead, eyes, hair, that looks sick. Is he a queer?"

Joel did not answer immediately. He went on, letting Peña and Elisa go ahead.

"I don't know," he said finally, and then, "There's something about this lousy city when winter is almost over, something fascinating: a cold haze that glows from the leafless treetops, the deserted park benches, the ferns and the pebbles on the paths; a sharp, brisk quality about the theaters and, especially, about the ushers like firemen in red and green; a blue-and-whiteness about the pigeons that crap on the Municipal Theater, all in a frenzy, yet weak. Is there anything sadder than those soda parlors where people sit in their overcoats gazing out the window watching the old Lotharios drive by on the way to swanky neighborhoods? . . . it can only be to trysts with firm and elegant women . . . to rub perfumes together until they get down to bare bellies. In winter, Santiago is a city of yellow crimes committed in bed."

Joel had evaded the question and Juan Luis began to feel distrustful.

" . . . I have a tremendous urge to kick the hell outa half the world and come out fighting. This cafe, for instance, look, between the cobblestones and alleys, threatened by the sides of the hill, vine-covered, with the air of a colonial inn. Go on in and you'll see. There are two old sisters there, virgins to their last breath, who make Chilean candy. Sit there—there are only a couple of little tables and some wicker chairs—and they will serve you chocolate, and they'll stick a sprig of basil and, sometimes, some red carnations in a vase decorated with bare-assed little angels. Who do you suppose drops in? The couples that come out of that house with the coat of arms on the door and come in reeking of booze and stinking bed linen."

Peña's house had a sober elegance: a walnut, copper nail-studded front door, a frosted glass entrance hall door, the metal table, a Spanish shawl with red arabesque on a black background, silver picture frames, and the faint presence of a colonial madman, in uniform and with sideburns, hanging on the wall in a gilded frame. And the dumpy mother standing at the door of the studio of her engineer son, a little old lady of extremely white, wavy hair, a string of pearls and a black dress, with her withered, expectant hands, like two pigeons, stretched out to greet them. She took a few uncertain steps and enveloped them in the elegant perfume of her powder, gently warm like the emanation of a priceless parchment. When they entered the studio, the white and wrinkled dowager disappeared.

Juan Luis began to feel uneasy in that room. In the gloom, the thick, blue drapes muted all noises; the leather armchairs seemed to stir as if ready to devour anyone who approached; tiny metallic glints suggested trophies of some sort. Dogs, horses, athletes? And near them, peered out the round, shameless bowls of numerous pipes of varied texture and strange colors. At one end of the bookcase, the outline of a marble sculpture was dimly visible: the suggestion of two upraised arms, or the light of two erect breasts, or the simple gravity of a very young belly, or it could have been something totally different; goblets filled with a green, incandescent liqueur. Higher still, in absolute darkness, appeared to hang yet another picture: its presence was felt in a vague way, perhaps because of the massive filigree of the silver frame, perhaps because of the secret glance of the figure, a smile, or a strange grimace. Nothing there seemed to be defined: not the pictures on the walls, nor the backs of books, nor the faces of the guests that filled the room.

". . . but you study in the same college?"

"No. That is to say, we take a couple of classes together. Psychology, civics."

"Civics? I thought it was no longer taught."

"The professor never comes to class."

"Ah! That's the way. But, you met at the university."

"No. We met long before. A long time before."

"What does he care where we met? Will he go on and ask more personal questions?" wondered Elisa. Moreover, by having him close, very close by, because he sat beside her on the floor, she noticed certain things about him that had escaped her before: a waxy sheen to the wrinkles on his face, an oily patina to his ears, an excessive brilliance in his eyes, and a smell, the strange smell of some herb, or old liqueur.

"In Santiago?"

"Not exactly. An aunt and uncle. Juan Luis' guardians."

"An aunt and uncle?"

"Yes, uncle Ramón and aunt Esther."

The last names bothered him. He fell silent for a spell, then decided to get up and change the records. Stravinsky.

"Don't you think he's delicious?"

Elisa sought Juan Luis with her eyes. He was ensconced in a corner and appeared to be listening to the music with his eyes closed. But, perhaps he was watching her. It was difficult to tell in the darkness. If he was watching her, he was probably jealous. Was it just about over between them? It could not end like that. What if she sprang the great news on him—the toy dancer, the Narcissus with the torn trousers? What if she had the baby? The fact was that life, in reality, was not a poorly drawn sketch that could be erased willy-nilly; life was as it was lived by good bourgeois idiots. A child is begotten, is born, and one has to change its diapers, clean its bottom, and nurse it, work at the lowliest of jobs in order to feed it, get properly married, get hooked, really hooked.

Suddenly, she thought she could make out his face clearly in the dark, so she gazed at it intently. Not merely looking. Intensely rapt, incarnating herself, she put his face into her belly and began to delineate the baby's features, little by little, painfully and joyfully, detail by detail: his forehead, eyes, lashes, mouth, chin, throat; his nervous and fine, yet hairy, hands, his . . . . The transfiguration was also taking place in her face: a beatific, unbelieving smile, loving and sad, played on her lips, until the trance was broken by the hesitant voice of the engineer who kept repeating:

"You love him very much?"

"What's it to you," she was on the point of saying, but kept silent.

"He has the look of a victim. A martyr, perhaps."

"A hero," she offered.

"Maybe it is over between us. It could be. It will end, but for it to end would be senseless. Not real. How can you destroy something not made of anything real? It could be something real. But he doesn't want it."

"That young man doesn't love anyone. He sees himself in you as in a mirror. Watch how he wrings his hands out of sheer jealousy, and tries to hide it by talking to his left and right when, in truth, he has eyes only on you and me. Watch. Let's make him more jealous."

Elisa drew away from the breath that the engineer blew in her ear. At the other end of the room, Juan Luis had worked himself into a lather. He paced back and forth, kicking the pillows.

"Don't explain any more enigmas. I don't know what you understand by violence. Putting yourself in a frame with no canvass and exhibiting yourself in the Museum is in no way different from drying your permanent under a dryer at the beauty parlor. Moreover, Gómez de la Serna is a Spanish sausage."

"You are evading the issue. You hear Huidobro? 'Poets, don't sing to a rose, make it bloom in your poetry . . . .'"

"That's a motto for gardeners. Poets, saltpeter to the rose, birdseed to the birds, and manure to the horses. 'Poets, sell Huidobro apples!'"

"Immaturity, I'd say."

The speaker was a tiny, very blond, one-eyed young man with a slavery mouth and a throaty voice. Studying him, Juan Luis realized that he was in uniform. The creep. His green tunic was too large and, over its stiff collar with the almost indistinct regimental insignia, peered his pale, scrawny, hairy Adam's apple. Legs crossed, rather circumspect, he dangled a lower leg that ended in a monstrous highly polished boot.

"Huidobro said it and that should be enough. Before Huidobro, there was no poetry. Saint John of the Cross, maybe."

"Would you shoot it out over Huidobro?"

"Right here. In the dark."

"With all of us inside?"

"No need. Neruda and de Rokha will do."

In the darkness of the room, stretched out on pillows, hidden behind armchairs and tables, bundled up in the blue velour of the drapes, the abstractionists were baring their fangs; they were the masters of the image, the babies Huidobro was bringing back from Paris, like a stork with an umbrella, through the air; the delicate monsters of Ortega y Gasset's dehumanization—erudite, dangerous, cutting. Juan Luis was provoking them. However, as on former occasions, he only succeeded in becoming furious and, once in a rage, he began to stammer. In order to coexist with them, it was necessary to wield the rapier like a pro, and he preferred to fight with knives.

"Look, the best thing to do is sit here beside me and not let that military creep get your goat. Why do you take him seriously? Are you that immature?"

Juan Luis eyed the man who had spoken to him and was on the verge of mouthing an insult when he noticed a genuine concern in the other's eyes, a sort of gentleness, born of true lineage, smiling, frank, unaffected. He sat down at his side and smiled also.

"The soldier is one of those writers who don't write. All he produces are titles. Miles of titles. Some are way out. Why don't you ask him for one? That is, if you need one. Are you a writer?"

"No."

"Aren't you a writer, really? You talk as if you were. Then, you must be a teacher?"

"Never. I'd die first."

"Why do you attend the school of education, then?"

"Because Elisa does."

"She looks Jewish. Do you ever bite her nose?"

A frightful caterwaul of dissonant chords began to issue from the record player. A trumpet blared forth, like the mating call of a bird among poisonous lianas, and the brilliant disc of the sun answered, lashing asunder the network of savage mahogany trees. Then, the branches moaned and, from the depths of a volcanic cavern, burst fiery forms that opened up like moribund corollas giving off milk and steam. At that instant, a ponderous beating of wings announced the presence of the bird king and, at his feet, a thousand crystalline voices swept down like a cascade over the rocks. The orgasm of wood, metals, rocks, and water upon contact with the fire bird was in the air, but it did not come off: the sun stomped its hoof on the goblet of the lake and the angry bird withdrew, flying off into space, cawing, and the entire forest trembled.

"Do you bite it—or kiss it? Look."

The man had placed an enormous portfolio of drawings on Juan Luis' lap.

"What is it? What do you want?"

"Look at it. Look it over."

Juan Luis began to turn the large pages. In the air he detected a scent, an odor of grass or old wood that emanated not only from the parchment-like, nobly-aged paper, but that was like the breathing of the whole room—rugs, drapes, trophies, books, clothes. He looked up bewildered, sniffing around him. As his eyes searched out the far end of the room, he discovered the half-smiling, half-serious engineer watching him, cigarette on his lips, hands in his coat pockets.

"What is it?"

"Look it over!"

The first page lay spread out on his knees and as he examined it closely, Juan Luis drew back instinctively: from its legs there appeared to sprout a dense tangle of sprouts, shoots, corollas, smoking tree trunks, strange stub-like growths or knotty grafts, twisted like the horns of a stag. That vegetal network clung to a heaven of dense silvery fog that, in its tentacle-like movement towards white abysses, were slowly strangling certain faces. Those faces gazed at him with a cold and obscene submission, hiding their hate behind the sweetness of their crooked mouths. He tried to identify their forms, to lend them some palpable reality, but the faces became lost in the movement of a snake that fled among the roots. Something monstrous was disintegrating there, peering out from a body of changing outline, inhaling in a luminous green bog, discarding its eyes that did not stop looking, mouthless, across the gray scab of the clay and the slow swirl of the ashes.

"It looks like a candelabrum."

"It is a candelabrum. A seven-headed gold candelabrum."

"Did you paint it?"

"The man is in the candelabrum. Look closely. Dressed in clothes that reach the floor, his chest girded by a golden ribbon."

"You paint saints."

"No. Angels. There's quite a difference. Look through the whole portfolio. I am interested in having you look at it."

Juan Luis slowly turned the pages one by one with a heavy

movement of his hand, as if he were moving the wings of big, dead birds. "What are evil angels?" read the caption at the bottom of one of the pages. On the margin, in delicate handwriting, was the answer: "They are waterless clouds, swept here and there by the winds. They are trees, withered as in autumn, or dead, or uprooted. They are the waves, and their nightmares, the foam. They are stars without paths."

"Do you like them? That angel in the short jacket resembles that serviceman a bit. Don't you think so?"

Juan Luis followed his glance and compared the serviceman with the angel that Pepe, the painter, indicated.

"Yes, it's true, they look alike. The serviceman has shorter legs. But the look is the same: that of a one-eyed man with blue eyes."

"They all have titles. This one is called 'I hold this against you.' It is a vision of a soldier angel pressing its uniform before going into battle. There are his spurs and what you see there, beside his prayer book, is his sword. This other one is called 'The Nicholasite.' Condemned for eating sacred things and fornicating."

"It's obscene. Why is he a Nicholasite?"

The angel was descending over a pile of corpses and he was losing his pants as he flew along. A purple light shone in his eyes and his expression was one of rage or hunger.

"This one is called 'The Mansion;' this other one, 'Satan's Chair,' and that one, 'That Woman Jezebel.'"

Juan Luis examined the last page with special care: the woman's image had the resplendent immobility of a mirror. Seated on a marble bench, she looked with a certain hostility at a naked, cherubic, and rascally child who was playing at her feet with a toad. The scene unfolded on a limitless yellowish terrace in some isolated region, perhaps a beach resort or an orphanage. Everything about her was cold and pure. The artist had left a trail of smoke in the sky.

A sudden hush had fallen over the living room. Peña was changing records. Juan Luis felt he was being watched by faces he could not make out and which seemed absorbed by the slow movement of his hands over the thick cardboard pages. He refused to heed that impertinent curiosity, but sought Elisa's eyes in the shadows. She had not stirred from her place; her head was resting on the back of an armchair and her eyes were half closed, one hand drooped indifferently over the glass of wine that Peña had placed on the floor beside her. He had the impression that she awaited with some anxiousness the return of the engineer and that, perhaps, the latter had interrupted something, something important, he was saying when he got up.

"They are the two central characters in this story," the painter was saying. "You understand? Man and anti-man."

He must have noticed a look of surprise, with a touch of irony, on Juan Luis' face because he added quickly:

"It is not the story of the fall that interests me, but rather, the story of what followed the fall. There is nothing heroic about it. Don't you believe it. The important thing for me is to paint angels that are running loose around the streets. With wings or a hat. That's the least important of all. The world is full of such defeated types: they have to have the chance to meet one another and to fight once again. Quite apart from those still flying. The shirtless angels."

All of a sudden, someone got up from a corner and, letting out a blood-chilling howl, spread out his arms, and stopped as if about to take flight.

"I am the one who scrutinizes kidneys and hearts!"

He had placed himself in front of Juan Luis, legs apart, fists clenched. His face was beady with perspiration and his large tortoise-shell glasses reflected the tiny lamps lighting his curly, disheveled hair.

"Who is this jerk?"

"I have given you an open door, because you have a bit of potency! . . ."

"Why does he shout? Is he a drug addict?"

Peña put down the record player's top with fervent care and returned to his place beside Elisa. He sat on the floor and rested his head on her lap. Elisa did not stir. Still standing near Juan Luis, the other man continued to vociferate.

"I know this guy. Why don't you give him something to calm him down?"

"Pay no attention to him."

"Why he doesn't let one hear."

A sustained laughter came out of the corners.

"Pay particular attention to the last two drawings, because the true story is contained therein."

The door opened at that instant and from the threshold Peña's aged mother watched them in silence. She had thrown a mauve shawl over her shoulders and her hands were clasped over her bosom, as if she were praying. Her tiny, clear eyes looked on with a certain hard mistrust, but they softened when they came to rest on Peña. She seemed about to say something, almost stepping forward. Peña looked at her without expression, as if giving an order to a phantom, and the little old lady withdrew silently and disappeared, closing the door gently.

The man had stopped beating the air and screaming. On the other hand, he was improvising a little dance that, due to his obesity, was not easy to make out.

"The worst curse in the Apocalypse is not for the fornicator, nor even for the sacrilegious; it is for the hypocrite, for the one who is neither hot nor cold. For the lukewarm. You understand? The faceless angel. Notice; every time he appears or turns away, either another angel's wing covers his face, or he bows his head, or hides."

A smile accompanied his last remark. Juan Luis turned the last page and, with utter unconcern, lay the voluminous sketchbook on the floor. Then, he looked around the room and, without being greatly surprised, began to recognize the angels. However, the wine—warmer and sweeter each time—had already covered them with a scarlet patina, so that resemblance disappeared in the transition from pure line to shadowy form. Present there were the angel soldier, the one crowned with snakes, and the one in green tights, as well as the one with the golden hat band. All of them stretched out on the rug like vultures in their nest.

"Peña introduces me to old ladies who collect painters. Young painters."

Juan Luis thought that the painter might be able to help him. Something about the engineer's comfort, about his tepid retreat midst records, wines, candy, and drugs, had stuck to everyone's skin. These effete types led an easy life. Obviously. They ate well. Slept well. Comfortably. They wrote and painted well.

"*. . . The soldier's springtime was our springtime. The cherry trees were in bloom in Forestal Park, as were the almond trees in*

Maruri; the nights became broad and deep in Las Hornillas suburb where stick-up men sang tangos, played the guitar and beat their wives and children. We climbed the paths of San Cristóbal with the golden fuzz of the mimosa trees in our hair and hands. We used to attend an interminable matinee at the neighborhood theater and draw together, cheek-to-cheek, legs entwined, and kiss. We used to go to rallies. Neruda, rather dark and serious, dressed in white and recently returned from Spain, read his communiqués and we listened to him fervently, but we didn't know what to do. Later we drank dark wines and listened to Eddie Duchin's piano and the sapo-voice of Fats Waller. We repeated the news of the Spanish Civil War and got a lump in our throats. They shall not pass, but they passed on and on. A city fell, then a bridge, a suburb. César Vallejo was saying but the cadaver kept on dying. I would hide my forehead and she caressed me sweetly and kissed my eyes. Old madman Costa used to appear, shouting in a language he had made up, and he improvised poems, thousands of poems, beautiful poems without words. Anguita used to laugh out his mocking hyena death-rattle, and he was a wax museum dummy, straw-colored at that time, a mythomaniac poet who handled verse as if it were marble in order to create white cathedrals. Volodia used to recite a sort of mathematical poetry; when he wrote, his red mane blazed and he wept upon hearing his own voice. Soto had discovered Picasso at the same time he had discovered his wife, and he painted beautiful guitar faces that at times concealed within them a pieta, and, at others, a white breast, quite white and swift, filled with milk. We listened to Lira, because he seemed a genius, with his tousled, jet-black hair, his thick lenses, moist mouth, tiny eyes, and the chords he played on the piano with his dirty nails. However, Arabela, petite and full like a sweet walnut, grew ecstatic playing Mozart near a grilled window and, as she played, the fringes of all the multicolored shawls she had in her house fluttered, and the immaculate piano keys unexpectedly creaked like a star. It was, as I say, the springtime of the young warrior in the dusks of Santiago. Our indolent city, soft-hued, with the echo of adolescent laughter. We were growing up with an imprecise hope in our breasts and a certain heroic confusion that induced politics, music, poetry, painting, theater, or just plain anger."

* * *

All the angels were weightless bodies ascending in their orbit, beautiful, resplendent, playful bodies. Why could not they help him to scale the heights with them?

Elisa had figured out the answer on her own. The engineer would help Juan Luis.

"How did it start?"

"It didn't start like that."

"They are infantile orgasms that leave a permanent ache in the kidneys."

"A Sunday at the Central Theater. That's the way it was; I recall it distinctly. You know how thick the rugs are there. The house was sold out, so we had to sit in the aisles. Juan Luis sat a step above me, touching my back with his knees. I can even recall the program: 'The Steel Foundry', with Carvajal conducting."

The record player emitted a compact noise of kettle-drums and cymbals. A hesitant, then determined, strident voice affirmed the consecration of the idol in the forest dawn. Fires flared in different parts of the forest and each flame revealed the anguish of some lost wanderer or hunter. A muted sound betrayed the tread of wild beasts on the ground thick with leaves and mud.

"They are good people. Under different circumstances they would engage in hit-and-run raids. Well-dressed Santiago citizens in blue jackets with white handkerchiefs, living in solid middle-class respectability. You know, parlor reeking of mothballs, cracked crystal lamp, gaudy mirror, and a painting of cows grazing, by Benito Rebolledo. They dance tangos, serve punch, chicken salad, and slices of old bread with pate that brings on stomach aches, and finally take pictures that are out of focus and make your girlfriend look like a wind-blown hen."

"I never missed a single concert."

"You always sat in the balcony?"

"Although, at times, I swear that it was torture. Juan Luis taught me to listen. The worst part of it is that the concerts at the Central are in the morning when I am so worn out . . . During the slow movement of a piano concerto, when the soloist barely skims the keys and Ibáñez is a tremendous hush, my stomach starts to growl. At ten in the morning. Imagine."

Juan Luis stared at the wine, cinnamon, and dregs in the bottom of his glass, placed a hand on Pepe's shoulder and said to him:

"I am very grateful really. I'll be there without fail, although I'd rather have you go with me."

"Of course," said the painter. "I'll go with you. Do you want me to go by for you?"

"Where do you live?"

Pepe hesitated. It was an awkward moment. He recovered.

"I'll go by for you."

Juan Luis thought that the painter was concealing his address, because he either lived in a mansion—not so surprising, to judge by his distinguished appearance—, in any case, he was ashamed of his circumstances, which was absurd.

"Jot down your address on this sketch."

"Do you think I'll get what I want?"

"I guarantee it."

Juan Luis became elated; then, the thought of facing up to an uncertain situation made him feel empty inside. He went in search of Elisa. Peña looked at him with a tenderness that offended him, but made no effort to get them to stay. He saw them to the door in silence, bowed slightly and indicated the door with a surprisingly trembling hand. Juan Luis became confused. Was it necessary to promise to see him again? Say thanks? Shake hands? There was no time to decide. Peña opened the door, left them in the street and, still in silence, closed and bolted the door from within.

Once more, rage began to well up in Juan Luis: at first, it was quiet, but keen; then, it mounted, jealous; finally, it grew stormy:

"Don't be an imbecile. Do you think I'm so stupid that I didn't notice? What must that idiot think? And with his head on your lap! I should have kicked him. These dilettante bastards have their whims. They flatter with venom in their hearts, and murder with generosity. And they will try to lay traps for me wherever they can. What a laugh that sneak has. Like a hyena's . . . as if hyenas had anything to laugh about. Consider how well they make out picking corpses . . . ."

The avenue, near the river, was deserted and the trees bowed down with the breeze that was beginning to sweep down from above. In the Franciscan Church, a small shop lit by a shadeless bulb was still open: on the counter were religious objects, scapulars, Saint Andrew medals. Within earshot of the ringing bells slept the down-and-outers in a single pile of tatters and filth. A lone cop went by, swathed in the black, fuzzy mass of his Castilian poncho. Juan Luis' voice was slowly giving out. From one street corner to the next it echoed with intense loneliness and impotent rage. Elisa lit a cigarette and inhaled slowly, deeply.

"It's all very simple. They are going to introduce you to some geographer or archeologist, I don't know exactly, who will give you a job."

"Pepe also wants me to meet him. I wonder what they are up to?"

"They know that you need a job. Why would they set a trap for you?"

"Who needs the money, you or I?"

And the night of the old neighborhood blew on their faces: it was tearing itself away from the small brick houses, thousands of houses, repeated in dark geometric patterns, gloomy reception hall doors with the tiny red shadow of the Sacred Heart; it came off the roof of narrow bakeries that exuded the smell of hot yeast at that hour; from deserted workshops and machine shops covered by a thick layer of oil; from abandoned barber shops; and from a school that watched with one-eyed windows. It was the night of the neighborhood coming to a slow boil, giving off a steam that smelled of dampness and rags, of barren pantries and sleepless people in cold bedrooms.

His rage spent, Juan Luis walked with a quick, firm step. They reached the house and, upon entering through the street door, Elisa looked at him for a moment and stretched out her hand. He held it in his. As he began to withdraw it, Elisa drew him towards her, and they stood face to face, quite close. Juan Luis tried to kiss her and sensed suddenly that in her steady gaze he was seeing himself, and the image reflected was that of a strange ruin: they were two adolescent, two Forestal Park sweethearts with the domestic problems of a respectably married couple. He, in patched clothes, underfed, bitter; she, hurt, bewildered, protecting her belly. But, strangest of all was the handclasp that became an unexpected support: how to fashion one loneliness out of two. And, instead of rage, a tearful tenderness forced Juan Luis to blot out that image from her eyes and he tried to erase it as best he could, with kisses. Beside the old staircase, within hearing of the confused noises of sleeping people, he encircled her waist, pressing her lightly. Elisa drew her body to his and let herself be embraced.

"The archeologist won't refuse what you ask. How much will it be?"

Juan Luis pressed his body against hers, crushing her against the cold wall.

IV

"Let's talk about history a little."

"'Youth,' Rodo used to say, 'is a force.' That is, the youth he used to know through robust Graeco-Roman priests in solid walnut frames by his wine colored desk, in the dusk of a summer in which flies buzzed through the sharp blades of a fan. But, youth, in reality, is not a force, but violence. In that year of 1938, in some arenas where it manifested itself, violence was being readied, distributed, assessed, and then let loose like a dog through the streets of the city. In order not to turn violence into a cardboard myth, one might say that it presided, but didn't rule: it was, at times, the residue in a glass, at others, foam in the morning and, on certain rarer occasions, the image of anguished man rending all his garments, outer and inner, with his nails.

"There was fighting all over the world. In Europe, the old horses galloped, laying bare the graves of pestilence and war. Trains passed one another along the vast slopes following the tight network of cremating ovens. The small Nazi bourgeoisie, attired in the uniform with the black and white stripe of infamy, continued hatching lice-ridden, bald, skeletal children, children that clung to a flaccid breast in order to receive their bath of asphyxiating gases with a howl. All of Europe looked at us through the eyes of those children. And we, in our school benches, continued to memorize *Liederkranz* about black forests and heroic homosexual sergeants. Europe smoldered like a tired cow in its swamp. And the cow mooed sentences by Spengler that we jotted down in notebooks delicately bound with the skin of Jews. Nazi spies shared our seats at the university. They stank of death and oozed oil. However, they could read documents by Menendez Pidal without problem. But when they burned books in a square, or drank beer from a Jewish skull, and when they dropped a bomb on Guernica, then the spies, a knife in their backs and a broken nose, tumbled out of our seats, running wildly through the deserted streets of the Slaughterhouse.

"They were fighting in Spain. For many, civil war was a sinister chronicle in news cables. On the other hand, for us—the red students of the Cervantine prisons—that war was a feast where some strategist dogs chomped away at a defenseless body, the white, lukewarm belly of a lamb; the belly of Garcia Lorca that, despite the American embargo and English parliamentarianism, kept on giving birth to militiamen. The bad thing was that Spain was entirely too far. Poor Spain! Always selling crosses to the natives who, upon hearing her name, fall madly in love with her and immediately want to die for her. Those who could, went. The rest stayed back: lawyers, doctors, engineers, beetle-eyed professors who couldn't make it but who organized gigantic benefits, monstrous rallies, festivals with great to-do; the Jews who clamored in voices choked by sobs, opened their coffers and, bleeding to death, halted the advance of the black boots with their own bodies; a few excited, thin-faced students, shivering with cold, standing at the newsstand with the gruesome headlines. Likewise, the respectable stayed behind and watched as Spain paid the bill. Let them finish off those reds. So the Fascists killed a select group of Basque Catholics. Let them finish off all of Spain, then. They were nearer to the truth, because the Guernica incident could be repeated anywhere.

"Our small, heroic cities showed an odd military air: it was the winter, doubtless, with hunger and typhus; the fog that cement buildings breathed; the cloud formations over the Cordillera; the frost that stretched from the rainy south towards the central valley and went on invading the frozen causeways until it hardened like a steel shroud over the huts near the river, outlining the blue corpses of jobless laborers, pregnant women, and domestic animals.

"And the Popular Front: whoever has heard a proletarian march, played by the chorus of the Red Army, sung by thousands of voices, melancholically epic, hard and sad at one and the same time, will recall the revolutionary funerals of that year. The people of Santiago hoisted red banners and marched in thick columns, singing, shouting countersigns and dragging coaches. From a table in the Iris Soda Parlor, we watched the rosy pages of the newspaper *La Opinión* fly.

"It was of the greatest importance at the time to understand the maneuvering of our great politicians: of the boy-deputy who, the better to identify him by, took on the looks of a flea, pestered like a flea, and spoke with the frenzied voice of a midget (on one occasion, he got stuck to a microphone and was almost electrocuted), opening his eyes wide and betraying one and all; of the mane-headed senator with his soup-strainer mustache, pitted teeth, gray shirt, to be trusted less than the flea-boy; of the egg-headed colonel who made his way from jail to the Senate and who, one day, made the following statement for our edification:

'We will hang all the oligarchs, without exception, from the lamp posts in the Plaza de Armas.' And in a moment of extra inspiration added, 'This does not imply a threat to anyone.'

"It was a martial air. Not far off were the bloody civil struggles. The Socialist Party was splitting. The radicals and the communists proclaimed Aguirre Cerda as their candidate. Baldy Ross, old moneybags himself, bald from his trafficking and cunning, kept telling the country: 'The problems are many, the solution one: old baldy Ross,' with an accent he had picked up no one knew where, either in France or in some British ghetto.

"Cold, cloudy, enveloped in the smoke from chimneys and trains, the city let itself be overrun by groups of alarmists and conspirators, who sought one another out on the downtown street corners and compared weapons—switchblades—and fled pursued by the billy clubs of the police. The impression, in truth, was not one of skirmishes or hasty meetings. Rather, it gave the sensation of large masses, serious, silently choleric, who went about the city in well-drilled columns, marching from neighborhood to neighborhood, from one city square to another, from the local party headquarters to the cemetery, who halted to inspect themselves and speak before the green lancers.

"In any case, the youth of '38—as already stated—was violence itself. But, woe to the violence of the young student awake in the night, arms across his chest, eyes fixed on the ceiling, listening to the betrayal of the times, to an approaching step, to some voice, to a rhythmic thumping in the city that goes by his bed silently, like a giant, muddy, river, massive and hostile.

"Water drips into an empty pan. The dawn wind shakes the trees. From the damp alleys of the Central Swamp comes the rising sound of voices, the rumble of carts moving out, the distant whiplash across the back of a dew-dampened horse. Arms across his chest, still dressed, Juan Luis lay on the unrumpled bed gazing towards the sliver of light that peered like the blade of a knife from under the door of his father's room. He was there: a thoroughly defeated man in the dimly lit room, propped up on his elbows, gray-haired, eyes filled with anguish, smoking. Beside him, the mother slept soundly. Perhaps the father also was watching the line of light on the floor. But his mind was elsewhere."

1930. A September morning at the family ranch: and in a manner that, at that time, seemed diplomatic, Juan Luis sealed his destiny. What a great many things would happen later. But after all was said and done, that day was at the bottom of everything. First a Puerto Montt nocturne; later, to the bedroom he always occupied and the thin, Indian servant with stiff hair pouring fresh water into the porcelain washbasin, opening doors and shutters, moving about warily, never coming too close. That room was his in some strange way; it breathed for him: in the odor of the damp wood, and of clean sheets dried in the air of the orchard, in the sharp aroma that came from the old oak beams, in the subdued gleam of handles, locks, and keys, in the fussy design of the pine wood night stands, he recognized his own childhood and adolescence. And that recognition attenuated the troubles he brought from Santiago. The room received him with the sniff of a faithful dog that approaches silently to lick our hand.

And from the window that faced the garden, he could see them as in an old photograph in an ancient album: his brother-in-law Ramón, in a wicker chair, seemed lost in a dream as he watched with nostalgia the children at play around the pool. Not even in that country atmosphere, alight with homey affection and Spring vacation, did he lose his pride. The white, starched peasant jacket set off his powerful shoulders and athletic torso. He liked to display his firm and slender legs in the tight-fitting black trousers with the white stripes. And, if no one noticed, he would draw attention to them by tapping his heel on the red brick terrace. Ah! you shrewd *huaso*, how well you have succeeded in slowly burying passions, hates, jealousies, like old tools in a forgotten shed! And, standing near him, Eduvigis, the eldest daughter, faded, dried up, in rigorous mourning, bending over her father, as if whispering something secret in his ear. She was good and undaunted, or, better yet, standing like a tree near a dry, whitewashed adobe wall. Further on, his own sister, under a parasol of brilliant colors. Green, yellow, white. Esther, reading a letter. A smile on her face with its fine mouth and proud brow. A bit sad. The high-necked, puff-sleeved dress seemed to make her look taller in the chair, to lend greater majesty to the straight line of her back, and to highlight the white ribbon that crowned her head. There, also, was Ernest, the son-in-law, lighting a cigarette, face twisted, bending down to escape the wind.

His sister spoke to him midst the mooing of cows, the barking of dogs, and sounds coming from the kitchen. Why had he come in the slow night-train? Fanning herself with the newspaper, she gauged the distance that separated him from his brother-in-law. Let him get puffed up and put on airs like a landowner. That was his business. Ramón was respected at the club because of his level-headedness, that is, because of the tight rein he held on his affairs at the ranch, because of the cunning knack he had for handling everyone and standing firm in his fortress. They admired his powerful voice and the sudden gentleness and courtesy he showered upon women, the sliest of glints in his eye, biding his time before tripping them up. Ramón was quite a man. But on his own ranch.

And, for all that, it was necessary to resort to him for help. An old fox who always had a trump card up his sleeve. In everything: business, politics, love-making. And drinking, of course. If after a drink anyone boasted of his drinking prowess in his presence, Ramón would fix a clear eye upon him, pull himself together, and start drinking all over again. Almost as if he had a spare stomach. That's the way he was made: like a tree with several layers of bark. Compared to him, the son-in-law was a mere decoration. Difficult to understand. Because he was not a gentleman farmer. Nothing farther from the truth. But, neither was he a man of the city. Although, on second thought, he could be from the city, but not from Santiago. Not from any Chilean city. A London dandy disguised as a farmer. Or vice versa. He never looked away, and his gray eyes flickered a sort of mockery that was quite circumspect, rather respectful, almost gallant.

The two of them, father-in-law and son-in-law spoke of coups and revolutions. 1930. Exactly. September or October. September, it was. A small red plane that flew over Concepción. How stupid could they get! Only military types and professors could think of such utter nonsense. The plane belonged to Marmaduke Grove, General Bravo, and Vicuña Fuentes. And Grove's too, man. I've already said so. What a strange name for a general. I tell you that he is a colonel, Eduvigis. Carmelita used to mention him in her letters. And Don Gustavo Ross, who footed the bill for the coup. A man with so much money. But not only Ross. There you go again with the Argentinians. What a one-track mind you have, Ernesto. They keep telling you that it was the English. Ernesto would sink down in his chair and take long puffs on his cigarette. And the joker kept his head. Legs crossed, cigarette holder between his fine, bony fingers, blue jacket open, silk handkerchief round his impeccable throat, however silent he might remain in the face of his father-in-law's impertinence, he never lost one iota of his elegance or composure. It was a well-planned coup. Or, so it seemed to him, not knowing much about politics, nor having a great deal to do with the military. And, why did it fail? They got cold feet. You are crazy Ernesto. General Bravo had a lot of guts. The garrison commanders failed him. Those were the days, by god! You could topple a government with a small two-motored plane, some sergeants, and a few bakers who went on strike in Santiago. So, it had three motors. But for the question at hand, it was all the same. Esther used to look at him apprehensively. She could guess his problems. But she did what she could to cover up. The right moment would come. How much would he ask for? How much did he ask for? Consuelito ran into the Lion in Paris... Is it true that they landed at the Hippodrome Race Track? Ernesto was saying that they did not dare land for fear of a catastrophe, since it was Sunday and everyone was at the races. If it had been a Chilean pilot, he would have landed on the straight-away and stopped on the finish line itself. There you go again about the Argentineans. Why, what have the Argentineans done to you? It's all the same in this case. Ibáñez had exiles on every conceivable island. Moreover, General Barceló was waiting with his troops in Concepción.

Someone was talking, talking, talking. But his face had vanished and the voice seemed to know his problem. And to be against it. How could you ever think of landing at the race-track? Were you there? And why didn't you say so before? One has to pull things out of you with a corkscrew. What a way to give information. Speak up, man. The weather was bad, and with the wind blowing from the sea, you did not dare risk it. Moreover, it was growing dark. When the plane appeared in the distance, everyone knew what it was all about and took no further notice of the horse-race. But, no one made any comments, either. You know how people are when in a holiday mood; it's the same here as anywhere else. Who likes to think about revolutions when he is at the races, gossiping about X's dress, Y's sweetheart, and the way so-and-so dopes his horses, and other such things?

Across the years, the voice, the memory of the voice had lost its edge; on the other hand, there still remained the hatred that dominated him, and a disguised disdain. Was his poverty so obvious? Could they take him for a touch artist? Him? Everyone talked, but the words were not what mattered, but what was behind them. In the swimming pool some children were shoving one another around and diving. Juan Luis was there also, to be sure, quite a spoiled cry-baby. And Anita, Elisita, Peruco, the eldest of the Barrientos children, and Georgie, who would die so young. At times, for some strange reason, the children would fall silent and, then, the mid-day light would make them glitter, as they stood dripping, sunburned, enveloped in a green and white halo.

Let them say and think whatever they want! It was still possible to fool oneself and to float upon the water in the dying country afternoon. A fresh, gentle wind lightly rustled the round tops of the willows, and the sky, so high and blue, was like a tent over the dark trunks of the *araucarias*. A young couple walked along the avenues of the park. Who were they? Such a long time ago. Familiar faces. There was something very strange, like the contrast of shadows and reliefs that in dreams transform faces, like the appearance and disappearance of light clothes in the midst of a thick mass of purple, white, and garnet rhododendrons . . . Sarita and . . . who the hell's son? Didn't they get a divorce and she later married the lawyer Darrigrandi? Or, she died young and he married again in a ceremony that created quite a stir. It was Esther's voice. Not Ramón's, nor Ernesto's. His sister's voice. Clear and deprecating. Cutting: a cold refusal, a death sentence, that the rest tried to put off. And the little red plane maneuvered among the dense clouds and approached the stands only to dash off again. The natives of Concepción, the elegant and sober-faced, looked up, observed the maneuvers of the plane and with a serious, accusing eye, wanted to tell it to go away. But the plane insisted and, from its cabin heads peered out and arms waved frantically. A military cap dripping braid and a pair of hairy hands, a tiny revolver, the lawyer's peashooter, and the foreign face of the pilot. A revolution was on, but they said nothing to the pilot, and the most serious problem seemed to be whether to land on the race track or on the grounds of the presidential palace.

His sister went on reading letters, and Eduvigis and the maid were setting glasses on the glass top table. Ramón, hands between belt and trousers, continued to gaze at the children playing, his eyes half-closed, thinking or dreaming. Ernesto was fitting a cigarette into an amber holder. And all that, the silence, the arrested mid-day at the hacienda, shattered. A stiff, thin, old man, mustache and eyebrows covered with dust, a farmer's hat in his hand and the bridle hanging from his wrist, was shouting at no one in particular, waving his arms wildly. He drank *pisco*, one after the other, and he laughed and clawed the air wildly with his hands, wiping his sweaty face and white hair with a many-colored handkerchief. The hell with it. Ramón drank drink for drink with him with the briefest "here's to you," as if gaining time. Then, the clock struck twice. By Heavens. Don Ramón also was going to lose his land. He, the wily peasant, the master of the snare, surrounded by trenches and ambulance chasers. What a shame. Esther retreated into the house and something, suddenly, came unglued on the terrace. Their voices were hoarser, then, and they drank more furiously.

The mortgages were going to ruin him. They were ruining him. And the countryside was shaken by a tremor, that was not exactly the reverberation of the sun in the afternoon. The old man spoke, if memory serves me right, of suicides, of swindles, of skipping the country. And where to? The gringos were jumping out of their skyscraper windows. And here, when he talked about ruin, Ramón was speaking about himself. What he did not know yet was that he had come to keep him company. Unless, by deceiving him, he might get something from him, a little bit, before the boat sank. And then, the old man wiped his forehead and did a somewhat eccentric thing. He took a newspaper clipping from his pocket and read an article by Jenaro Prieto on the wheat crisis. And now a group of young people surrounded him. Who were those young people? They were either returning from the park, or coming out of the house, or were coming out of the grass where they were sunning themselves in silence. Why didn't they speak, why did they look at everyone, especially at him, with such compassion? Perhaps we were already a bit high, or better still, drunk. But, no. Rather, they looked at him with a suspicion and distrust that turned his stomach to ice. It seems that newborn Chinese are on sale at twenty dollars each. If a small Chinese brings 160 pesos why doesn't a big one bring 320? That's what our wheat brings. Not only that, but they save the Chinese baby's life. The young people withdrew with the prudent grace of dancers: the blond, tanned girls and those with dark brown hair, who talked with a graceless air and looked at him with large brown eyes; and the boys in white shirts, all slicked-up, insecure, mocking. But, at the same time, other people were arriving. Drawn by the dry scent of *pisco*. From miles away they came in old, muddy cars, on horseback, on carts. They made their entry vociferously and went to their hierarchical places. The water in the swimming pool took on a dense, dark green hue, and attracted the mosquitoes as if it were a gigantic flower. Spurs clinked, and there were some who embraced, and others who looked one another over threateningly with distrust, disdain. Ramón, circumspect in his rattan chair, observed them all with his little green, malicious eyes, and gesticulated dully, waving his freckled, hairless hands. The sun was sinking rapidly and a sort of halo of fire began to form on the tops of the pines. Green blazes rose up among the oaks and the larches in the park. On the river bank, the dry wood burned noisily. A group of men, whose faces were not visible from the terrace, were busy seasoning the gigantic suckling pigs that turned on the spit over the flames, dripping their golden fat. Other flames rose in other corners of the park and the columns of smoke seemed to become less dense upon reaching the leaves of the alamos, and then to wander off into the blue void of the valley.

He found himself walking far from the group, along the garden paths and among the trees, a man besieged, sunk in a sea of mortgages, letters of credit, I.O.U.'s, discounts and protests. The family breathed easily then, shielded by prestige, friends, props. Who could have guessed at this crack rising treacherously through the foundations? The initial signs came from the stock exchange, from some bank manager's desk, from the college president's office, from certain shops and department stores. Surprise at first, followed by doubt, then horror, and finally, panic. He was being tossed to the sides by a flood of canes, vests, spats, his house at Viña del Mar, his credit, checking account, his club, his tenement houses, his stocks. He was tumbling like a city made of adobe at one fell swoop, with a muffled sound, leaving no other trace than a pile of dry clay and a cloud of dust in the air.

And it was cold in the country; a south wind had sprung up, introduction to a shower. But the sky was quite soft, growing bluer in the glitter of the stars. The fires near the river burned furiously. The farmers ran between shadows and radiance, shouting with all their might, waving whips and knives. Whoever loves you, punishes you. You don't sell your wheat, friend, and I don't sell my wine. They drank like horses by the river, head down, gulping, snorting. They shouted and the fire crackled in unison with their voices. The scorched skin of the suckling pigs on the roasting pit burst, splattering fat and sending sparks through the air. Empty wine glasses were smashed on the ground. Rocks gave off sparks touched off by the scratch of the spurs.

Hands in his pockets, stooped, whistling between his teeth, he groped for the light switch in the living room. But he couldn't see a thing. Some embers glowed pleasantly in the fireplace. He went towards it with a careful step, trying not to bump against the furniture; near the fireplace, he made out the figure of his sister, rocking silently in a chair. "Why aren't you with them? Will you leave Juan Luis on the ranch? Ramón loves him very much, he'll miss him." The two of them read secret signs in the silence and in words: but she confessed to nothing and he lay down his bright tatters like a playing card on the table. The tenement at Vivaceta has been declared unsanitary, and at the one in San Pablo, they threaten to knife me if I try to collect rent. No one is paying. They are years in arrears. You haven't told me if Ramón can help me. No. She said it in that cutting tone of voice that he couldn't identify before. I shall pay every last cent. You'll pay nothing. I owe, owe, owe. A helping hand. They both looked towards the park like spectators in a fashionable box at the theater. The bonfires glowed more brightly. The ranch hands were riding in search of a place for some nocturnal rite. We're in a bad way, Manuel, my brother. It's only a matter of time. Why, at the Club they say that the Bank of London will go under before Ramón. The ranch is as vulnerable as the tenement house. Each one has to hole up and wait out this bad winter in his own anthill. The boarding houses in Santiago and Valparaíso are filled with that type of ant. Sister, I cannot remain here and beg where everybody knows me. What do you mean? And the voice reached him with its edge intact: a note of disdain in the depths of memory. This man has studied a profession, Esther, and his party listens to him. No less. But, what the devil can you do that will earn you a job? It's a government post; no need to know anything. His sister sat rigidly in the chair, no longer rocking. My mind is made up. And, what about Hortensia, and Juan Luis? In the darkness, he couldn't quite make out the features of that face: he perceived only the disdain and an unrevealed and growing euphoria. Neither words, nor gestures, nor even silence were of any use now. He wanted to sign some document and the top of the desk was clear. He started to retreat into the gloom of the living room. He was doubling back along a familiar road that led inescapably to his brother-in-law's study and, there, the heavy door of a safe blocked his way. His sister was smiling now, as if encouraging him to proceed. The flowered drape swirled against the window.

The horsemen attacked one another with whips, and the blood-shot eyes of the horses glittered. They maneuvered among the trees noiselessly, pushing in the night against an unremitting shadow and, as they raised the tips of their Castilian ponchos and lashed their adversaries, they fused with the tongues of fire and the thick columns of smoke. His sister watched him attentively. She would keep on looking at him across the years. Accusing him, pointing out, at times, with her eyes, the current of the irrigation ditch he should follow, watchful of the tiny eddy that would suck him under in the neighborhood sewer that already bore his name.

Nothing remained to be done. The last moments of the silence that both, father and son, shared were fleeing fast like the last grains of an hourglass: a few stars in a cold sky, some shadows swept along by the early morning wind and, from the center of the city, the rumble of streetcars, busses, sellers hawking their wares, sirens. Night had placed its tiny grief on Juan Luis' chest. It was no time to snuff it out. He sat on the edge of the bed, took off his shoes, smoothed down his hair with both hands, and looked once more at the shaft of light in the neighboring room; with a calm resolve, he stood up and went towards it. He opened the door, careful not to make a sound. His mother slept. His father, head on his shoulder, was asleep also. Smoke still rose from the butt of his last cigarette. Sleep was beginning to smooth out the deep furrows on the pained face, the forehead was regaining its nobility, the nose had grown sharper and the fleshy lips were distended into a grimace of childlike surrender. A hand seemed to detach itself from the body and seek an invisible support on the floor. Juan Luis drew near and examined his father's face more closely.

At that hour and in that helplessness, so intimate, so fragile, he could almost touch a life that was ebbing. That man, who in defeat walked the streets of the city selling or pawning the last props of his life, hugging the shadows of mean alleys so as to hide the wretchedness of the shamefaced beggar, head bowed, back bent a little, step growing slower and heavier, dressed in black, smoking endlessly, searching futilely for the narrow exit from this life, that man he had first loved with the illusion of a child and then with the charity of an adult, that man was slowly being reborn in him, surrendering to him, to his own son. Standing beside him at the head of the bed, he saw him recede in time and he could recognize in the sleeping features the root of his own anguish.

Without sound, he snuffed out the cigarette. Bending down, he took the hand and let it rest on the bed. He heard him breathe heavily as, suddenly, he fell into a deep sleep. Taking the bedspread, he covered his father with it, as one covers a child, then put out the light, retreated in silence to his room, got into bed and closed his eyes.

V

ELISA woke up with a start: a sudden thought, a warning signal, her mind not fully awake for a few moments. At ten in the morning she had an appointment at the abortionist's. She got up. After gazing for a moment at her sleeping grandmother, she went out of the room, and waited in the dining room for the others to arise.

Could her grandmother know? The eternal smile that played on her lips, never in her eyes, was unfathomable; as were her silence and her hands that suddenly took hold like desperate claws when they caressed. Her grandmother saw everything. Or pretended she did. But she gave no inkling that she understood anything. Nevertheless, she later looked as if she were up on everything. Never accusingly, but knowingly, almost threateningly.

The last time had been in her bed, the night her father had died. And the grandmother was asleep near her, or pretending to sleep, an open book on her breast. But the act had not been consummated. What a stupid word! As if it were a sacrifice. And, then? She began to figure it out once again. Her last period had been in March. Or, was it April? She thought back to the last concerts. In March. Absolutely certain. She had begun to get sick at K's party, after an exciting session of ping-pong, when they were seated on the floor listening to some jazz records someone had brought from a radio station. She felt a soft, deep, but brief, burning sensation like a tongue touch the inner side of her thigh. At the beginning of March. It was almost two months.

Mario crossed the dining room without glancing at her: bare from the waist up, a towel round his neck, hair standing on end, shuffling in his slippers. The sound of water being turned on came from the bathroom, followed by the din of the old plumbing that threatened to sweep away the whole house down the sewers. Her mother was scolding the maid. It wasn't quite three months. Upon reasoning it out this way, upon feeling that certainty, a spasm doubled her up over the table. She put her hands to her belly, shutting her eyes tight. And, at that instant, her mother came in. She passed close to her, thinking perhaps that she was dozing with her head on the table. The maid brought coffee and toast. Elisa raised her head and, with a decidedly brusque motion, pulled the books and notebooks towards herself and began to read.

Her mother was speaking about a monthly income they were to start receiving the following month. By then, the outcome of her situation would be known.

The springtime of the young warrior: a dark red springtime clinging to the sky like a blood clot. In order to walk along the flowery paths of Forestal Park, by the cherry and almond trees, they would cover themselves with a cloak of blood . . . Hand in hand, along a petal-strewn path, they would bend down to gaze at the reflection of their small anniversary in the waters of the lagoon; and the faces would be rent by innumerable bleeding fissures.

"It won't be much," her mother was saying, "but it will be a help anyway."

"How did you find out, mother?" asked Mario, his nose in the steaming cup of coffee.

"Your father stopped collecting it while he was up north. It accumulated gradually, and in his will he mentioned this money that's in Social Security."

"There will have to be an adjustment, mother; there was one

for retired officers last year. Even the veterans of '79 have been awarded an adjustment."

A feeling of terror was once again slowly climbing from her stomach to her throat, like a cold hand seeking a spot to sink in its nails. Juan Luis' face looked up at her from the sketchbook: a face drawn with a fine, almost invisible, but nervous line. She had made his eyes bigger, his nose more in profile, and she had softened his chin. She had wanted to trace a smile on his lips and a certain tenderness in his eyes, but on paper, Juan Luis' face had imposed its own pride, his impatience, his attitude of flight or attack. She placed her fingers over his forehead, moving them up and down, smoothing out the wrinkles, caressingly.

"Of course, it's absurd, but that's the way things are in this country, that's the way tradition is and you must respect it."

"But father didn't even do his military duty. How can they pay us that pension? Why was it being paid to him?"

"That has nothing to do with it."

"I heard him say once that he was a slacker and that he had been granted an amnesty. I think it was on the occasion of the Centenary."

"You mustn't mention such things. Your father liked to joke. And we have been receiving the pension since the death of his grandfather, the general."

"But, did he serve or not?"

"And, what's the matter with you? Why don't you eat your breakfast?"

"I am pregnant and have morning sickness." How simple it would be to answer like that! And then? What would happen if, instead of sneaking to the abortionist in the outskirts of the city, dirty bank notes in hand, shaking with fear, she were to stand up right then and tell the simple truth to her mother and brother? If, instead of stretching out an iron cot in order to free herself of her sin against family, against classmates, against a good match, she allowed her belly to swell with Juan Luis' seed? What would become of her? Would someone say, "not to abort is a crime"? Her mother? Mario? Juan Luis? They wouldn't have to say it. It was a warning in neon lights at street corners. A part of Social Security benefits, a clause in the regulations for maids and lady clerks, a clause also in the marriage contract, in keeping with a very old tradition. The spoon that scoops up a common grave of national proportions. She smiled at the inner sound of her words, and she thought it would be a good idea to give it to Juan Luis for one of his speeches. It would sound well at the bottom of the empty pool at the school of education, reverberating against the walls, bouncing over the glasses of beer, before the reproach of her gentle classmates. But, would Juan Luis say it? She looked at the sketch once again and the smile became a grimace. What did Juan Luis have to do with all this? Was he pregnant, too? Because a pregnant woman and man were needed to have a child. Did he want to have an abortion? Poor, poor boy. He walked alone, touching her without seeing her, touching himself in her, masturbating with life in one hand and death—the small, miserable death in the unsanitary clinic—at his feet, and he receiving everything like a dented receptacle.

"What's the matter with this girl? What's the matter? What's wrong with her?" her mother asked; her brother turned to look at her in disbelief, while she, doubled up over her notebook, let enormous tears roll down her cheeks. Nothing's the matter. Nothing, yet; a stomach ache. Indigestion. Her mother was scolding the maid. Her brother picked up his overcoat, scarf, and gloves, and went leaping down the stairs trying to catch the bus that was already pulling away. A strip of wallpaper was peeling off the wall, exposing a threatening spot of greenish dampness. The coffee was steaming on the table. A warm breath, redolent of toast, of steam heat, of smoke, rose from the tablecloth, oil cruet, from the cups and knives. The house was breathing. The window panes were fogging up. The brooms and the feather dusters began to emerge, and the furniture was moving from one place to another, creaking. The maid went by with the breakfast tray for her grandmother. In the street, the old motors of the busses roared and, from distant neighborhoods came the sound of the whistles of factories and trains. Elisa picked up her book and went out to kill time.

Señora Ines lived in a small, very circumspect brick stucco house, almost hidden by the trees on the sidewalk; pleated curtains gave it a certain aura of virginal innocence. The metal plate with the Madam's name and the minute plate for the door buzzer gleamed as if they had just been polished. Everything about the exterior of the house inspired friendliness. Nonetheless, the place was a slaughterhouse, and the madam executioner.

Seated on the edge of a chair, clutching her purse nervously, Elisa waited to be ushered into the examination room. There was nothing there to make her uneasy: the light came in, filtered by the curtains, with a bit of the green splendor of the trees that swayed heavily in the street; the parquet floor had been waxed recently and showed little sign of traffic; the few pieces of furniture had the trace of a patina that accentuated the floral pattern of the upholstery and the lace. On a coffee table, a voluminous flower pot cast its purple shadow. There was not a sound in the house, or in the street.

When the door opened, Elisa straightened up with a start. A mature, round looking woman clasping the collar of her coat near her mouth, as if she had a toothache or wanted to hide her face, went by her into the hall and disappeared. She left a strong smell floating in the air, an emanation that she cut off as she closed the door behind her. Elisa squinted her eyes; the gust of ether went over her body unnerving her like something alive that, unexpectedly, was about to possess her, crushing her. She sensed someone behind her; turning around, she saw the madam smiling at her sweetly. She stood up like an automaton and was about to move when the woman stopped her with a wave of the hand and motioned for her to sit down.

"Don't trouble, dearie." she was saying. "Sit down, we'll chat right here."

Maybe she noticed that Elisa was near fainting, so she went to a walnut bar in a corner of the room, opened the little doors, and took out a bottle. Placing two small glasses on the coffee table, she poured the strong drink without a word. Elisa shook as she put the glass to her lips, spilling some of the contents. The woman pretended not to notice.

"Drink it, honey; it will make you feel better. I always get so tired about this time. The brandy is a good one. Napoleon." And she laughed for no reason, as if having brandy tickled her.

Elisa felt a shiver go through her but she closed her eyes and drank it all down with determination. The madam warmed the glass in her hands for an instant, then also downed it without leaving a drop.

"Did you tell him?"

"Yes."

"That's quite right. That's the first thing to do. A woman can't do these things alone. The two of you must put your shoulder to the wheel. It's a big responsibility, my child. What did he say?"

"Nothing."

The woman filled the glasses again and took out a package of cigarettes.

"Nothing? You're kidding. These are American, very mild." Elisa took one and let her light it with a shiny, monogrammed lighter.

"He said nothing?"

"Well . . . he has been saving some money. He has gotten himself a job."

"How old is he?"

"Who, Juan Luis? He's almost twenty."

The woman fell silent. She had lain back on the small, green plush sofa, one leg up, smoking, inhaling deeply. She put the glass to her lips, looking at Elisa through the smoke. In that relaxed attitude, it was difficult to judge her age. The black, loose and wavy hair softened somewhat the corpulence of her back, her bust attracted with its cleanly delineated firmness and, as she bent her leg, her dress was drawn tightly around her hips. Elisa watched her uneasily.

"He is two years away from his degree," she said, as if in answer to a question the other had not asked. Until then, she had not looked at her directly, but the brandy was having its effect now so, after her remark, she tried to gauge the effect of her confidence on that face. A wise smile suffused it, a beautiful smile that revealed a certain awkward tenderness, a bit melancholy, not altogether sensual, though gently domineering.

"We are both two years from graduation . . ." added Elisa, losing her aplomb once more.

"You should have your baby, my child," said the madam, "you should have it, you should tie him up for life, because you love him, don't you?"

Elisa suddenly felt a wave of emotion choke her and, twisting her mouth, she gave in to her sobs, shaking. The madam neither moved, nor said anything: she filled her glass for the third time and took tiny sips. Elisa wept silently, wiping the tears with the back of her hand. She wept a long while.

"I feel so sorry when these things happen!" said the madam, finally, "because I also went through the same thing. And not so long ago. We fall in love like fools, and we fall for the first buck who makes a calf's eyes at us, and follows us everywhere, waits for us after school; we fall for a pair of eyes, for a mouth, for anything, as if he were a femme fatale. And, then, what can one do? Where do kisses lead? How long can we stand being touched? Of course, for you, it's another thing. You, honey, have had a family . . . how shall I put it? A family . . . a respectable family, and certainly never felt alone, nor ever tried to do something foolish in order to escape the dump of an environment in which you have grown up . . . But I . . ." she stopped and watched Elisa's face with distrust. Apparently satisfied, she went on: "There are thousands like me, who have never had the chance we deserve by right. I had to make my own opportunity, and when I did I took it with both hands, but after a few incidents . . ."

Elisa had recovered her composure and was smoking, listening with one ear, maintaining a certain indifference that did not escape the madam.

"Think of me as your older sister," she said, "do not distrust me. I have been around a good deal, and I am sure that I can help you. Have you said anything at home?"

Elisa did not answer immediately. She had mixed feelings about that woman: there was something base in the protection she offered, a sort of complicity that could not originate anywhere save there, in the abortion mill. She tried to evade the confidence.

"No," she answered.

"Well, there is time. But the time will come when you will need someone to confide in. You can't go through this alone. Are you afraid to tell your mother?"

The woman's brusque familiarity enveloped her like an unwanted embrace. The madam leaned forward to refill the glasses, and her hair covered a part of her face. From her neck, breast, and underarms, she exhaled a heady perfume, some expensive, French scent that hung there between them.

"I have no other appointment," she said, apologizing. "This

bit of relaxation will be good for us."

Elisa had not touched her last drink. Before sitting down, the madam wriggled her hips to adjust her girdle.

"Have your baby. That's my advice. First, you'll feel a terrible shame. You'll live in hiding, in exile. And then, that child will slowly fill your life. It will fill you completely, and the morning sickness, the pain, the fear and shame, everything will disappear. And there will be nothing in the world but the three of you. A beautiful, warm thing."

The word "warm" sounded strange to Elisa. She imagined the three of them floating in a bloody liquid, looking for positions, hair loose, eyes swollen, submerged in a white rubber chamber, rising slowly towards some distant, unattainable bubbles.

"... I didn't do it, because my situation was different. Not only the kind of life we led. My friend used to send me gifts with the cook at the boarding school. Perfume, cigarettes, magazines, candy ... Older than me, naturally; lady killer type. I ran off with him and when I became pregnant and he left me, I had to make a decision that, basically, I had made long before. To have a child by him was like giving my virginity for the second time. No, for me, the problem was different. To be sure, I couldn't return home. Nor did I have any reason to. I faced it all alone. But you, you ..."

"Then, you are not going to examine me today?"

The madam turned her head and looked at her as if coming up for air.

"Examine you?"

"You told me two weeks ago to come back for the second exam."

The small living room was full of smoke. A tenuous halo floated around the madam. She looked pale, emaciated, and her hair appeared darker. One of the buttons on her blouse had come undone and through the opening, could be seen part of her white silk brassiere.

"No, my child. There is no need for an examination ... nor do you owe me anything," she added seeing Elisa rifling through her purse. "It would be useless. Let's wait one more month and see. It'll give you time to think it over. Talk it over with your sweetheart. But, don't forget that as the days pass little by little you will be filled with another person, and your way of thinking will gradually change, because you will be another person, a very different person, and then you won't want to . . ."

Elisa had taken the mirror out of her handbag and was trying to erase all traces of her tears.

"Come, come this way. I'll take you to the bathroom."

The madam got up with some difficulty and walked unsteadily along the hall. Elisa looked at her watch: ten-thirty. She could still make her eleven o'clock class. She entered the bathroom and, seeing that the madam was following, shut and locked the door. Alone, she looked the place over. On the walls, papered in pink, the madam had hung little glass fish that ascended towards a fat, red grape. From the white linen window curtains, as from some underpants, hung transparent, black lace. On the toilet's water tank, was a porcelain Louis XV page. In the page's hand was a tiny vase, and, in the vase, a carnation. Below the mirror, set at an angle towards one's middle, gleamed an array of bottles, jars, powder boxes, eyebrow pencils, golden jars, tweezers. It was not the professional bathroom. Professional, perhaps, but not a madam's. There had to be another: white, disinfected, clinical, the one for murders. This one was the experimental lab for another specialty that Elisa failed to ascertain, but that fascinated her. As she came out and made her way along the hall, she saw the madam wiping her lips with a napkin and making as if to fill the glasses once more.

"Thank you, Señora Ines, no more for me, because I have to go."

"No, honey, why do you want to go? Sit down, stay a little longer . . . Look, I am going to tell you something that will interest you. What I told you before is nothing compared to this. Pretend that I haven't said a word. Sit down, then."

The telephone rang at that moment, and the madam got up. Seen from the rear, a hand on her hip, tapping the floor impatiently, she appeared taller, more slender. The skirt of her tailored suit clung to her legs, smoothing out the lines. Until then, Elisa had seen her as fat, hard, old. Now she spoke in a low voice without letting one make out her words: it was a murmur of vague recommendations, underlined, at times, by an intonation of surprise or pique. "Fever. Did she say fever?" She dripped a warm surprise over the telephone, like the astonishment caused by the illness of a loved one; but then, without raising her voice, cuttingly:

"It's your fault," she said, stamping the floor with her heel. And then, "Go threaten your grandmother." And hung up. All smiles she went to the sofa and sat down beside Elisa.

"What was I saying to you? No, don't go yet. Wait Elisa . . . how old are you?" The expression in her eyes was one of sweet irony. "You must be quite young. And, you are very pretty." She uttered the last remark as a final appreciation reached after careful consideration. "And you have class. You understand. Lots of class. You don't say a word. What's the matter? You distrust me, don't you? You'll get over it. You will come to know me and we'll be good friends. You don't realize it, but I can help you very much. Very much."

She stressed the "much" in a sinister way, that Elisa interpreted not as a promise, but as a threat. Did she want something from her? Something shady? She grew afraid, really afraid, but could think of no way to get out of there. Words failed her. The madam was drinking again. Her cheeks appeared sunken and her eyes were feverish: the cheekbone had taken on a hard, provocative beauty. She had put her arm behind Elisa on the back of the sofa, covering her like a bird of prey. Elisa could smell the madam's breath, the perfumed sweat of her breast and underarms.

"At your age, I was a dove. But a dove full of tricks and bad habits. I was so ambitious! I liked men, not only as men, but because of what lay behind them: the luxuries I had never known. I was always mad for luxury: all glitter, gilded, quite new, and rather expensive. But, without money, who can have it? I. I got it. I know practically everyone, and everyone is indebted to me. From the president on down. Don't you like me to tell you these things? Are you afraid? You've got to open your eyes, honey . . . The man I said seduced me . . . It's a lie. All lies. I ran off because I wanted to. Because I was crazy about it. But, do you know what the wretch did to me? Do you? I'll bet you can't guess!"

She was really downing the drinks now, but without losing control.

"Who? Who?," asked Elisa leaning forward to avoid contact.

"Who? Who else! The first one, of course, the first one. I was living with my cousin. Immaculate as a dove. Quite studious. Altogether serious. But I was seeing him. I knew he was married, but I didn't care. And you know what he did to me? No. I can't tell you."

She stretched her mouth, stared at the flowerpot on the table and began to whimper, first in high-pitched grunts, then, with real, deep, enormous sobs. Elisa stood up and approached the window. The relative distance restored her courage. She looked out through the curtains. The street was still deserted, the trees were swaying. It was easy to leave now. The madam had lain back, resting her head on the arm of the sofa. She would drop off to sleep in no time. She was muttering something, waving a hand confusedly.

At that instant, the doorbell rang. Elisa looked at the madam, advanced a few steps as if to open the door, thought better of it, and remained by the window. A key rattled in the lock. Elisa retreated in fear. The door opened, there was the sound of steps, a man appeared: thin, stiff, with his hands in his coat pockets. He stared at her coldly. He observed the madam and seemed to size up the situation. Approaching Elisa, he examined her at close range and smiled. He smiled a child's beautiful smile that lighted his face. Although flustered, Elisa returned his smile and continued gazing at him, unable to look away.

"Is she sick?" he asked.

"Yes," she said.

"Ah!!"

Then, he turned and walked leisurely towards the sofa. He bent down slightly, looked at the bottle, the glasses, drew his right hand from a pocket and gave the madam a big slap across the face. The woman moaned, but did not get up. She beat the air like a drowning person. He laughed and shook his head.

"It's not yet twelve, and she's soused. Can you beat it?"

"You know what he did? You know?" the madam kept repeating.

"What did he do to you?" the man asked her.

"He gave me such a case of the clap . . . He gave me such. . ."

Elisa ran to the door, had trouble opening it, and, without looking back, went out.

VI

THE fortunes of the Acuña's, like those of the Huertas, went rapidly downhill. Don Manuel, ex-hacienda owner, ex-owner of untold real estate, ex-stockholder and stock market speculator, passive member of the Union Club, ex-radical party assemblyman, bore these two letters, *e-x* like a shameful brand on his forehead. That was the weight that forced him to bow his head, that bent his back, that drove him through the slums of Santiago, through the halls of the Social Security, through the waiting rooms of banks, through the offices of real estate brokers, evading and eluding his friends, in a life and death struggle for his daily bread.

The rooms in the house were slowly being emptied; very early in the morning, or in the dead of night, a moving van arrived to load on furniture, then depart as its yellow Percherons pulled it away at a slow trot in the direction of the auctioneer. Señora Hortensia saw her pieces of furniture leave like children off to a distant boarding school; she bade them good-bye from her window, wiping away a tear with her now not-so-fine white linen handkerchief, and followed them with her eyes until they disappeared down the street. Afterwards, she stood there sighing. What irony that our lives are emptied and our dead go off to be auctioned! What are they carrying off in the dresser? And, in the bed? And, that night stand? What about that dark, silent, melancholy sofa? Don Manuel was auctioning off a whole lifetime: his young loves. his dreams, his strokes of luck, Juan Luis' infancy, the victories, anxieties, defeats of a social life lived in the full glare of day.

The grandfather, on the other had, defended himself as long as he lived, huddled in the backyard. Nothing ever left of his lair. There, the old name remained intact. But the old name was an antique shop full of memories. On rainy, cold, desolate winter nights, in that half-way zone that was not exactly a home nor a garret, either—though very close to where the angry cats in heat roamed the city in August—the grandfather kept some coals aglow in a huge copper brazier; a brazier in which he saw the flash of old gunpowder, the gunpowder of the battles of Chorrillos, Miraflores, and Morro of Arica, where he had fought, saber in hand. On the walls hung pictures of military parades, mustached generals, oval-faced ladies with straight hair and velvet bows; trumpets and sabers, and a torn flag or two spattered with blood or mud. In huge trunks in alphabetical or chronological order, he filed the memories of his children, wife, brothers, and sister; and that memory at times took on the semblance of a military tunic, or some silver picture frame, solid watch, or tarnished medals, and newspaper and magazine clippings now gray from the dampness. No one ever bothered him during his lifetime. The history of Chile that he watched over would not have brought a thin dime at the auction block.

Juan Luis was seldom home, merely sleeping there. He got in at daybreak, rounded up a cup of tea somewhere, woke up when his father had left, shared a meager meal with his mother, and fled. She was unaware of his poverty-stricken appearance, continuing to center on his fine features, luminous eyes of a small, depraved angel, proud figure, never once noticing the patches or the darnings. For his father, on the other hand, Juan Luis was a source of remorse, and, as a result, avoided him. He would look away and swallow hard. Everyone, his parents, the maid, and the cats, listened to him. Always. The maid, whoever she happened to be, never failed to see in him a sort of beautiful adolescent preacher, with whom she felt duty-bound to go to bed—after a violent skirmish under the stairs, in the bathroom, or in her own bed, at three or four o'clock in the morning. Consequently, the maid loved and respected him, but as something foreign with whom she could not—it was out of the question—fall in love. His mother listened to him without understanding him, his father, with impatience, sometimes with annoyance.

And it was to such a household that Elisa came timidly. And the house was again resplendent. With her returned the memory of the pieces of furniture gone off to be auctioned. Through her, the old people recaptured the warmth of the summers at the hacienda, a warmth redolent of dry wheat, of cicadas and crickets, as well as the freshness of the park, the laughter of children at the fountain, the playful gallop of Shetland ponies. Her eyes—the deep gold of a faraway sun—still inspired the well-groomed and cultured eloquence of Don Carlos Huerta, the sly melancholy of Don Ramón, lost in his reflections of an old patriarch, the strict elegance of Doña Esther, the ghosts of young people, old people, friends, relatives who had disappeared, fluttering away through a transom and were still flying.

Elisa used to laugh, not saying much, and cling to Juan Luis, or remain alone in her room when he was not there, in bed listening to jazz over the radio, smoking and watching the shadows of San Cristóbal hill through the window.

Juan Luis fell ill that winter. Something from the dampness of the floors, from the cracks in the walls, from the stains on the wallpaper, got in bed with him and began to take its toll of him as it did of the others, filling them with a mangy sadness. Motionless as a mummy, threatened by pneumonia, Juan Luis would spend the day reading by the window that faced the hill, or watching the buses, or waiting for Elisa to come after her classes—sad and melancholy—to sit at his feet and look at him. He had discovered a collection of short novels by Dostoievski in an old Spanish edition with dirt, yellowed covers, and spent hours reading them slowly and taking notes; on houses, the arrival of a horse-drawn coach before a half-open door, the sudden flight of a dove from a cornice, a gust of cold air in a vestibule, the crunch of boots on snowy streets. He also took notes on sunsets, on gestures and exclamations that, later, would appear in his own dreams. He had read the novels several times and, upon rereading "White Nights" for the fourth or fifth time, he acquired a sense of frenzied reality that impelled him to move. Being unable to do so because of the intense pain in his sides and back, he got some relief by screaming whole sentences from the story through the open windows at the buses that passed by in a wake of blue explosions.

It was during this time that their electricity was cut off. The maid wanted to protest, but she sensed the crushing resignation of the rest and said nothing. Candles appeared all over the house. Winter had taken on that hardness so typical of Santiago, a harshness of ice that comes down like a muted breath from the Cordillera. The neighbors used to take their braziers out into the streets, crown them with a tiny, black, tin stove, and squat down to blow on the coals. From his window, Juan Luis watched the men, scarves about their necks, blue-faced and red-nosed, eyes fixed on the tiny blue flame and the sparks that spattered in the dusk. A light, freezing, transparent mist was falling; the rain appeared about to come down, a few big drops beat on the window, but the downpour did not materialize, and the city remained as before: suspended in its ample and luminous niche of frost.

He read Gorki's memoirs, scarcely paying heed to the dramatic episodes, allowing himself to be caught up, rather, in the dazzling sentimentality that surged like a light over a river, and accompanied the young vagabond in his adventures, protecting him in taverns, granaries, prisons. Sprawled out on his bed, scratching as best he could under the bandages that bound his ribs, gazing at the tiny buildings in the neighborhood—watching master craftsmen and apprentices busy at work, Juan Luis glowed from within, gradually overcome by compassion, feeling kinship with them in an aureole of sentimentality that could materialize as easily in a vision of a massacre of imperial guards, or of a strike by tenement dwellers. In rapid succession, he discovered the glorious vagabonds of an anarchical European literature: Istrati, Hamsun. Without transition, he turned to the noble warriors: Roland, Barbusse. He shared with them all a sort of slow-puffing, humanitarian leaven that was rising slowly within him and impelling him to open his arms and join forces in a redemptive march.

His father used to come in and argue politics. Something, a change came over their voices, for in that gloom of flickering candles, the house lost its outline and glided towards an ambiguous zone, between open country and city, and their words would begin to resound and repeat themselves in echoes, as if they were talking by a river bank and what they said gradually became a fairy tale. They both knew that the poverty of their home was but a reflection of the national poverty. Chile had been auctioning off its possessions for a long time. Unlike the grandfather, however, it had also trotted out its military glories and had no trouble finding a bidder: it had pawned off its nitrate-producing province and, before either could round up the money to pay the interest, it had hocked its copper mines. And like them, there were thousands who from their windows watched the moving van carrying off their country's possessions to the Yankee and European pawnshops.

"Chile is a nation of incalculable reserves," Don Manuel used to say, thinking about the loans that rained down on the government palace like bundles. Them he would speak of his country in what seemed liturgical words to Juan Luis and Elisa.

"We must return to our former values," he said, "to the sobriety and order that made the country a model of good citizenship we all admired. In difficult moments, the Chilean has always been able to tighten his belt and face up to misfortune . . ."

"What country is that," Juan Luis would ask. "What Chilean? What belt are you talking about, Dad?"

"The Radical Assembly," answered Don Manuel with venerable pride. And he would reflect on his words: The belt? Tighten his belt? What the devil! He was slowly running out of holes and, soon, he would have to take a tuck in his soul. And then, what?

"Yes. Who kicks out a dictator?"

The revolution that deposed Ibáñez, for instance, in July 1931, was a remembrance of a gray and tumultuous euphoria, somewhat akin to the national holiday, but without the September sun, or better still, with cloudy and drizzly winter skies. The 21 of May. People ran in groups through the downtown streets. Shots rang out a nightfall. A certain brilliance lit the city. "They're fires," the maid would say. "No," his mother would say, "they are the Neon signs at the Mapocho station." A crowd would gather near Santa Lucía Hill. A platoon of mounted police would appear, lances at the ready. An officer brandished a saber. A bugle sounded. From the uneven greenness of the hill, a fusillade of rocks rained down upon the helmets of the police. Young students hid behind the shutters of the two-story houses and fired their tiny revolvers.

"Who boots out a Colonel? A fine thing, son. Why, men of dignity, patriots: a sit-down strike. That's what it was: a strike by doctors, white collar workers, laborers—a general strike."

"Father, I'd like to tell you about a strange thing that happened to me at the time, something that I never told at home, because shyness wouldn't let me: the shyness that a first brush with death inspires, let me explain.

"During the days of the revolution—I am not certain if it was on the 26th of July itself or a day later—I had an escapade of the type one doesn't talk about. I couldn't stand it any longer. I spent my days thinking about the same thing, thumbing through magazines, finding out what I could; I lay awake at nights twisting and turning, touching myself, but determined not to succumb. Until one day I could stand it no longer and left the house at dusk, and went straight to the Eleuterio Ramirez Street. Good Heavens! To the very lowest. I rushed in the first open door, like an avalanche, without looking at anyone, almost breathless, plunged headlong into the bed and buried myself in what opened up to me. It was like diving into a well, black, dizzying, that swept me along from crest to crest, swinging and rocking like a sailor, waving my arms, until I fell into a whirlpool of blows, kicking, rigid, emptying myself in an interminable gush, burying my face in the darkness. I left there empty, shaking. Later, the usual remorse came over me, only that this time with the anguish also came a feeling of loathing and fear. I thought I had gotten myself into a venereal sty. I wandered for a time along the neighboring streets, waiting for night to close in and, when I felt safe, I entered the office of a male nurse. The man looked at me with pity. He led me to a room where his couch, instruments, and syringes were, made me take off my trousers and proceeded to disinfect me with a permanganate solution. I went through the trial without a word. I gave him all the money I had, which was very little, and left filled with gratitude. The man followed me with his eyes, and his look remained indelibly in my mind: a sort of pity, but some disdain also, and even irony.

"I went out dirtier than ever, my insides afire from the permanganate—in torment, repeating the litanies that I always prayed on such occasions. I resolved to go to a church and do penance. But, at that instant, a crowd approached from Matta Avenue. At first, it seemed to be a hundred people or so, but I soon realized in astonishment that from other streets more and more people were coming. The hundreds became thousands, and all ran in silence, with a brutal obstinacy. They ran without trampling one another, filling the sidewalks and the street, faster and faster in my direction, as if in the purpose that spurred them on I had a part to play. Their faces were sweaty, expressionless, pale, their teeth set, their fists clenched threateningly.

"They were poor people, jobless in rags, greasy mufflers round their necks; but there were also workers, and wild-eyed students, ready for anything, some newspaper vendors and shoe blacks, and petty thieves. They swept towards me like a silent avalanche. I flattened myself against the wall, and the swell reached me and passed on by me, running with greater desperation, beating the ground with their heels. They enveloped me; I leaned against someone, got shoved, knocked about, and I ran, ran also, ran with them, without knowing where or why. We ran on for a long time. We gradually approached the Alameda Station. I was sweating and my legs were beginning to give way. But I couldn't stop. They would have crushed me. In front of me, at my sides, behind me, I felt the rush of determined thousands running in silence. At last, the vanguard halted and we all halted. I ended up quite near those in front, facing a modest little house on a street near the Station. Several men were knocking down the door with rocks and iron bars, others pushed and kicked, until the door splintered, and they entered and we entered the room and in the room there was a policeman gasping, his tunic open, cornered against the wall, looking at us, uttering unintelligible croaks, and those who were in front knocked him down with a rock and began to rain down blows with the iron bars, and they split his head open, gouged out one of his eyes and kept on beating him and cracked open his forehead, and the thick blood spurted out a throat wound, and they beat him in the face and beat him on the chest and on the belly, and they began to quarter him, pulling him by the legs, arms, and neck, and his guts spilled out, and the blood was everywhere, and then a man who saw me vomit struck me on the head and dragged me to the street by the hair, saying 'Stupid kid, this is not for you,' and because I was hysterical kept on striking me until I managed to get loose and flee . . . "

"The Radical Assembly, son, with the tenacity and patriotism that have always been its trademarks. And, to be sure, the White Guards, which you don't remember, made up of distinguished young men undergoing military training—get it straight—mi-li-ta-ry, in the parks, soccer fields, and who directed traffic, because the police disappeared from the streets, you know, in fear of the fury of the nation. Young men in blue coveralls . . . What days. An act of civic dignity, of native courage . . ."

". . . I wandered through the streets near the station, hiding behind trees, with a tremendous bitterness in my throat and a cold fear that emptied me completely. I don't know where the people were. I could make out a muffled murmur in the air, but it seemed to come rather from the station, from the trains being switched, or from the roundhouse. Nevertheless, the atmosphere had quieted down and, suspended over the slums, hung a gray fog, heavy as if made of dust and ashes; in it, within it and over it, I thought I saw a red glare that seemed like a blood clot hanging from the sky.

"Later, the same people as before began to pass by. They were not running now, but in as much of a hurry as before and still silent. They went off rapidly, furtively, hugging the walls like rats looking for their particular hole. And I wanted to see their faces, their hands, to ask them something, their names, perhaps. But no one heeded me, just hastened on, away from the tenement room where the cop, the cop's bones, lay stuck with blood to the flowered wallpaper, among family portraits."

"The Party will always be a guarantee that when social balance is threatened, Chile will find its just mean. Our middle class, son, is made of very noble steel. It was forged in the country, not administering haciendas but, rather, working the land. It did not grow by means of loans to industry or commerce, it raised itself by its own bootstraps, from the neighborhood store to the downtown department store. There is your guarantee, young man, in a sober, firm middle class, brought up in the idea of progress, of savings, of order. Don't come around with demagogic slogans of stale revolutionaries. We are in a crisis, but we have been in a crisis before and weathered it. The Radical Assembly."

"Will the Radical Party come to power this year?" asked Juan Luis and, without waiting for an answer, added "What would happen to a junkman's cart if you equipped it with a motor?"

"We don't have roads for motorcars," Don Manuel would say, "our country has only one form of locomotion: the horse."

Then, he laughed, for that was his ironic way of expressing the need for progress.

"Where are you, father, where are you? You used to sit down, one leg in the air, smoke chain fashion, arch an eyebrow, and everything about you, mustache, fingers, eyes, turned golden with the warm stain of the nicotine. You coughed, cleared your throat. In the middle of an old proverb, you would let loose with a plain old nasty cuss. At your heart you were complaining; you did not want to see your own poverty, you wanted to excuse it, to pretend that if it existed, it was not anyone's fault but rather, a fortuitous, remediable accident. I was conscious of the new wrinkles in your face, near the eyes; of the ashen pallor that was invading your forehead; the thin shins with the bones gradually showing through; your sudden fatigue . . ."

"The middle class you speak of no longer exists, Dad, it is buried in the mausoleums of Mutual Aid. The schools run by German teachers were closed, the department stores went broke, progress is a rather ugly word and order exists only in the cemetery. What are you going to do, then? What do you call the social class that pawns its shirt in order to eat, that sends every member of the family to get picked up on the streets, that retires in order to retire once again in order to be a public servant again in order to retire again, that demands a wage for not working, and exists on monthly allowances and travel pay? You believed in your courage, but you believed even more in a dark road that was gradually disappearing. You had grown sentimental, and I knew that secretly, you wept. A fatal resentment gnawed at you. You went along the streets dragging an invisible hurdy-gurdy filled with ingenuous melodies that gave you the sensation of your own death and the memory of us, of me, of my mother, of some friend, some relative who smiled sadly when he recalled you . . ."

"You don't know how to argue," Don Manuel used to say. "You young people lack the civic sense that made my party great."

"Your party is a party of landowners who can't join the Conservative Party because they won't let them."

"Blasphemy. Mine is a lay party of anti-clericals and free-thinkers. But, sometimes we go to Mass."

"You smiled indulgently. The flame of the candle on my desk licked at your beard and mustache tinting them with reddish glints. The cigarette was gradually burning your fingers. I recall your hands very well. They had a quiet strength and a strict nobility in the hard, pink shape of the nails. I used to sit on the floor, near Elisa, and look up at you. In the gloom of my room, I imagined you with a poncho over your shoulders: a heavy, black Castilian poncho, soaked by the rain. And I saw you in the midst of whitewashed adobe walls, and fresh brick corridors, a golden blaze of orange groves and a surging sea of wheat. You spoke of politics and, suddenly, you were speaking of a vineyard that you went to as a child accompanied by your father, and where you used to lie down to gaze at the birds and the clouds—and you used to tell how your father put up a plank for the sparrows, gave them an order, and made them cross over from his vineyard to that of his neighbor. You used to tell other things. You were a zealous provincial man, proud of his assembly. One day I reminded you that the Radical Party had made a statement against private property and in favor of the proletariat in the class struggle. You looked at me as you were wont to do when you sensed that the malice of an astute student was laying a snare for you. You cleared your throat, made a gesture of disdain, arched an eyebrow. 'The times,' you said, 'the times, son.' I, who spat on any mangy assembly, would like to have seen you once, just once more, in the saddle of your corral-colt, sparks flying, cutting figure eights at a rodeo, clicking your silver spurs, downing plenty of chicha, eating plenty of roast pig, electing senators and deputies,

among shady politicians who could dance the cueca and hit the bottle. But they had cut off our electricity, father. And you and your friends had mortgaged your lands, lost them, and here we were in the Capital, hearing the leaks drip into plates, stoking the fire in the brazier, buying this and that by the gram, patching our pants, hitting my godfather for a loan. Somehow, you did not lose your noble bearing, while I, on the other hand, in whom you wanted to see yourself, provoked you and added wrinkles to your brow . . ."

Don Manuel would fall silent, not lighting the cigarette as Juan Luis and Elisa expected. He was hearing something they did not hear. Elisa would go up to him and, absently, caress his head.

At last, Juan Luis' ribs healed and his lung got well, so he went out into the street once more.

VII

A SILVER brilliance enveloped the immense clouds in their slow trip along the Cordillera; light on the gray and golden slopes of the spurs, paling a bit, like old lace, on the pines, acacias, larches, and furze; a suppressed energy, about to burst, on the knots of the cherry trees, taut like dark nipples; and the smell of damp earth, of leaves and roots, breathing under the winter sun.

Juan Luis was making his way through the streets of the slum. It was imperative to get the money his relatives refused, or were unable, to give. There was one door open: the one that the engineer Peña had indicated. The one he would enter accompanied by Pepe, the painter of angels and soldiers. But Peña had to be found in his hideout. The address on the paper napkin might not exist; it was a vague one near San Cristóbal, beyond the river where the tenements began.

Juan Luis thought about Pepe with distrustful curiosity: there was something about his bearing, a distinction associated with foreign nobility; a virtuosity that could only inspire admiration or anxiety. His thick glasses were deceiving; they multiplied the ambiguity of his gaze, by nature disdainful, mocking, cruel. His movements were rapid, and his steps betrayed a lack of coordination, or perhaps a childish uncertainty.

When he found it, the painter's home frightened more than surprised him. Pepe lived near the river, on a rock-strewn street in a low-cost housing area, surrounded by irrigation ditches filled with green water and scum: slum where the bus lines ended and winter began, together with ditches, gruesome night birds, dogs, dust-covered police check-points alongside geranium plants. There the province begins like a ribbon of shiny clay edging along the blackberry fences and crossing endless rivers.

The entry to the house was a small store: just a counter, a showcase, wrapping paper, and the merchandise. The painter lived in the midst of enormous heads of pigs, marinated in red, hot sauce, decorated with sprigs of parsley; they were sad-eyed, attentive heads that gazed at the passersby from huge trays. He lived amidst ears of smooth golden hide, wide and soft noses, amidst pink, thick, long tongues. In the patio were two gigantic kettles in which other heads floated, boiling slowly in a dark, aromatic, dangerous gelatin. The earthen floor had absorbed steam for years and it sweated like a volcanic layer.

Pepe's mother was stirring the juices in the kettles with an immense wooden ladle and, through the clouds of steam, gesticulated to underscore her words. She was a pink, soft-skinned woman with luminous eyes, a clear brow, and white hair tied in a knot at the nape of her neck. She talked and laughed incessantly. Pepe was her whole existence. She shouted it to high heaven in blistering oaths, and was wont to interrupt herself long enough to spit tremendous curses at the oligarchs who wouldn't help her son.

However, Pepe lived farther inside, in a high-ceilinged room lit by a window that faced the Cordillera; it was whitewashed and almost bare of furniture: near the grilled window, a table that doubled as a bureau covered with a white runner, and on it a washbasin and a porcelain pitcher; some chairs, a stool, and the easel. The rest was a riot of objects and colors: tubes, brushes, spatulas, palettes, newspapers, and some hemp rugs that seemed to float on the red brick floor. All these things seemed to lead an independent life: they knew one another, but were not at peace.

On the small bed, a single sofa covered with an Araucanian blanket, lay Pepe, hands behind his head, looking up at Juan Luis without a word, without explaining anything, scrutinizing him. Juan Luis didn't say a word either. He inspected the paintings around the room, looked for a chair, and sat down.

"Who gave you my address?"

"I don't remember. Someone at the Iris Soda Parlor. Perhaps it was the poet Barata."

"Why have you come?"

"You said you'd go with me to the anthropologist's... Peña's friend."

"Ah, yes, that's right. It had slipped my mind. Would you like a drink?"

"At this time of day?"

"At any time. Is there a special hour for drinking?"

He rose very slowly, stretched, and walked towards what looked like a sewing machine. Like that, in his undershirt, denim trousers, and sandals, he looked slimmer, taller, younger. His hair curled up at the nape of the neck, making it look like a girl's. He pulled out a bottle.

"Here," he said, "is some brandy my brother sends me from the south. I'll let you taste it."

"You have brothers in the south?"

"I didn't say I have brothers, I said a brother. The other one is the one you saw as you entered, in the store, eating."

"I didn't see anyone."

"Surely you saw him. You didn't notice. He was eating pork and drinking wine." He punctuated the phrase with what seemed a gesture of disgust.

"I didn't see him."

"Of course you saw him," he added with repressed fury. "He's a postman who was eating there in the entry hall."

Then, he began to dress. He put on a blue shirt over the undershirt, took off his trousers and walked towards the bureau, securing his patched underpants with his hands; he slipped on a pair of gray flannels and, before buttoning up, he secured his underpants with a safety pin.

"These women are good for nothing," he said. "How much trouble would it be to sew on a button?"

Putting on his shoes quickly, he stepped before a mirror and began to comb his hair, careful to give the waves a studied carelessness. He then took out a silk scarf and tied it round his neck Mediterranean style, and finally, put on a blue jacket. With a quick glance at the mirror, he said:

"Let's go."

They went out onto the patio. Pepe's mother was still bent down over the kettles, stirring the heads, without allowing them a moment's peace, pushing them against one another. The steam had dampened her forehead. She saw them approaching and smiled. Pepe went up and kissed her cheek. Then, quite stiffly, his eyes fixed upon the liquid, following the bobbing heads, he stood waiting. She put her damp hand into one of her apron pockets, drew out some rather crumpled and dirty bills, and carefully stretched a few and gave them to Pepe. He took them without a glance and put them in his pants pocket. He kissed her again. Standing there beside the kettles, his arm across her shoulders, the painter relaxed a bit and rested his head on her neck; the woman patted his head and looked at Juan Luis. In her eyes shone a wise tenderness that might have seemed ironic, had it not been for a certain light, firm and almost implacable. Juan Luis blushed and in confusion, passed between the kettles stammering his good-bye. He went out into the street and the painter followed.

"Are you afraid?" asked Pepe.

"Afraid? Of what? Of whom?"

"I was only asking."

"Why should I be afraid?"

"I tell you I was merely asking. I don't know. The truth is that you always look afraid."

Juan Luis turned towards him, teeth clenched, and was about to answer, but the painter anticipated him.

"Don't be offended. I didn't mean to offend. Remember that I'm looking for a face for my seventh angel. Perhaps it's not fear. It could be innocence. Hasn't anyone ever told you that? You look like a lap-dog waiting for a blow or . . . you'll like this better, a caress. You must be lucky with women. I'll bet they kiss and spoil you like a baby. You must be spoiled like hell."

Pepe said those things laughingly. He thinned words down until he transformed them into tiny saliva bulbs that barely peered out between his teeth, and when they did, they left part of their meaning on his lips; the rest rang out in a snooty sing-song voice that sounded hollow.

"You'll fill the bill. The engineer knows how to appreciate your type."

"What should I do?"

"You'll be a hit. There's no doubt about it. Perhaps too much of a hit."

"I don't get it."

Pepe smiled, all curled up in his seat on the streetcar, arms crossed, curly hair floating in the breeze. Juan Luis felt uneasy. The other passengers were watching him.

"Verdoux . . . Verdoux lives like a king. He has a marvelous villa at Apoquindo. You'll see. What does he want you for? To supply commas. So that you'll climb on his manuscripts like a trained fly and leave your specks in the shape of commas and periods, in accord with the Spanish Academy grammar."

The streetcar made its way to the exclusive neighborhood, and the sun was beginning to invest the trees with a spring radiance; governesses and children strolling, gentlemen and ladies waiting at the stops along the avenue, all vibrated like multicolored decals in the gentle breeze.

"Briefly, here's what you'll find: a type with an aristocratic name, French vintage lineage, odd, but not in the sense that bureaucrats use the word, but rather, in a theatrical sense. That is, a mature man that knows what he wants, or better still, who knows that what he wants can only be desired by peculiar types like himself. An over-forty-year-old adolescent who has lived all his life in Europe, and who has returned to establish roots once more in the hope—what am I saying—with the firm conviction of reforming every living thing in this country."

"Reform?"

"Reform. I say reform, without reservation: this little word has something Protestant about it, like raw fish, sarsaparilla. He wants to reform."

"Hmm . . . I'm not the obvious one to help him."

Pepe spoke slyly and, in his hidden meanings, he seemed to hide a grudge against Juan Luis, as if by incorporating him to the anthropologist's regiment he ascribed to him certain values and vices denied him. Upon facing the anthropologist for the first time, Juan Luis understood in part the reason for that resentment: Verdoux was a man of sharp irony, an apt appraiser of every type of aristocracy, for whom Pepe was a beautiful specimen of a flower born midst the irrigation ditches of the Santiago rubble. As someone might put it: he treated him with delicacy, always careful not to hurt or offend him, when what Pepe only wanted was the dignified hardness between equals.

Verdoux lived in a mansion that combined the sobriety of the old Chilean gentleman, with the frivolous indifference of the closet gay who surrounds himself with the young and happy. Entering his study was like stepping into a block of onyx: a clean, pristine freshness, with a green and blue radiance that burst from the depths of exquisite goblets, vases, and climbing plants, from old swords, and resplendent maps and globes. There was a suggestion of the smell of a submarine cavern in whose spacious corners rusted pirate chests and gun mounts from ancient galleons; the scent of papyrus and parchment and, over it, an irreverent playfulness lurking in ukuleles, in marine postcards, in menus from Marseilles inns, in bronzes of a mysterious adolescence, dark as the African jungles, or naked like a frantic Hindu deity. From behind his massive desk, Verdoux presided over an eternal ballet of pearl fishermen.

In the garden, the disciples awaited like a flock of carrion-eating crows. Pepe called them angels. Like vultures, they watched from their perches. It was not easy to distinguish them, at first. Something about the patio closed in by high, gray rock walls, about the luminous emptiness of the paths and corners, reminded one of a cloister. However, the attitude of the guests belied that impression: its bustle was like that of the yard of a sanitorium, or a jail. A general incongruity robbed them of reality. They seemed like people in hiding, playing evil pranks on one another. Their gathering place was a circular pool whose water shone with an intense blue brilliance. They played. Some were nude. In their midst, wrapped in his white toga, Verdoux was like a Roman senator—tall, corpulent, thick-necked like a blond bull. He spoke with affected condescension, but did not fail to poke fun by giving small commands:

"Jump in the water," he would tell one, and the one alluded to would drop his sheet and get in the pool a little at a time, giving shouts and howls that excited the rest, protesting about the cold and inviting others to follow suit. Another and another slipped into the water, arms upraised so as not to get wet, wrinkling their noses and setting their jaws, taking mincing steps, without getting too far from the edge.

"Float," Verdoux shouted at them.

And they floated face down in all directions, their bare behinds peering out, limpid and white, like aquatic flowers. Verdoux laughed, clapping his hands, and the vultures laughed also, flapping their wings. A manservant in white jacket and black trousers wandered among them distributing glasses tinkling with chunks of ice. The sun shown down upon them, distorting their faces. Age disappeared. There were old men and adolescents, men who could be—some actually were—poets and accountants, lawyers, doctors, architects, artists, a policeman, as well as numerous native types that reminded one of produce market porters, slaughterhouse workers, newsboys, or just plain vagrants, and lastly, certain retired types without a specific profession. Instinctively, they were attracted or repelled by one another, moving in short hops like sparrows, or in bold, possessive swoops like majestic buzzards.

Verdoux closeted himself with Juan Luis and Pepe in his study. They sized each other up in silence for a spell. A lap dog ran along the shiny parquet floor and leaped on Juan Luis' lap. He looked at it in disgust, lifted it in the air, and flung it away. The dog hid behind the legs of a chair, moaning and trembling.

Verdoux frowned, but said nothing.

"Juan Luis would like to know what kind of a job you have for him," said Pepe.

"Job?" It's not much," replied Verdoux. "I need someone to put in order my notes on a book I am preparing . . . something not too important. Indexes, files cards, statistics. Type a little from time to time, read to me, edit. Are you interested? I can't pay much, you know. People think I'm a millionaire, and it turns out I'm as poor as a church mouse. How my countrymen insist on seeing millions behind a well-known name! I, my friend, have only the name. And what about this villa? I can read it in your eyes. Don't be deceived, young man. I rent it from a Turk who gouges me for it, but I don't rent for show, but because I need it for my social work. Pepe must have told you."

He looked at them questioningly. Pepe had stood up and was looking through a photo album.

"Will you have the time?"

From the outset, Juan Luis was a snarling cat amidst vultures and songbirds.

"You'll understand," he said, "that I must work to earn money. I don't care what I have to do. I can write a book, arrange your files, or murder one of your guests. I need money."

Verdoux observed him for a moment, without malice, and then looked away, discreetly.

"In this country," said the anthropologist, "that kind of decision is superfluous, but there is need for greater discernment. There is a certain difference, you understand, between putting my files in order and murdering one of my guests."

Verdoux continued to study Juan Luis with unchanging objectivity. He did not seem amused by his aggressiveness, but it did not offend him, either.

"Son, you take things entirely too seriously. It's all right, but there's no use getting indigestion over it. Those friends you see in the garden are very worthy people. Each one of them has his most precious weakness, and some have the seven-year itch. There's no reason to murder them. They harm no one. You see that young man with the short-cropped hair and hooked nose? He's the outstanding economist in Chile right now, and my right arm in the social projects I have undertaken. He's self-abnegation itself. Don't be misled, friend . . ."

Juan Luis saw the economist for an instant as if framed in a poorly focused picture: the sheet covered him from the waist down; his tanned torso had lost the firmness of youth, and revealed a hairy, transparent adiposity; his neck, on the other hand, displayed vigor and pride; the face was lost in innumerable wrinkles that veiled laughter, anxiety, mockery. In semi-profile, he limped around a police sergeant who, perspiring profusely in his green uniform,

Sam Brown belt and straps, pointed his saber at him and laughed uproariously.

"That other man resting in the shade, with the half-closed eyes and profile like a ship's prow, is without a doubt, the most talented literary critic in this country. The most sensitive. He is, as well, a self-effacing, fine philanthropist. A real gentleman. That other one . . ."

"What do they do?" interrupted Juan Luis. "What brings them here?"

Verdoux, toga dragging, began to walk around the room.

"The need to help, to give something of themselves to their fellowmen. They are, if I may be permitted a metaphor, peons to the rebelling angels. Just as an army needs nurses to gather the wounded and restore them to health by dint of affection, tenderness, compassion, and care, my sutlers you see there, in a moment of expansiveness and rest, also gather up the fallen angel, raise him up in their arms, give him support, warmth, faith, confidence in himself, before sending him out to do battle again. In other words, my friend, in this house we receive the young criminal just released, who leaves the Penitentiary like a soul in torment, for whom no one is waiting and to whom all doors are closed, who has no family nor wife, nor friends, nor money, nor anything. He is welcomed here, given a temporary home, seen through his convalescence, taught a trade, or allowed to return to the one he had in his misfortune. And when he has recovered his faith in himself, when his strength has returned and he can look at his fellowmen with clear, confident eyes, he is allowed to leave. You see those halls on the second floor? They are going to be a huge arts and crafts workshop. There, I shall set up my carpenters, my cobblers, my electricians, my mechanics. I shall furnish them all with the tools necessary, all the materials; they will work with a smile on their lips, illuminated by this sun-filled house. And over there, beyond the patio, in that corner of shadows and creepers, is the chapel. Another workshop, for more permanent repairs."

Juan Luis listened in astonishment. On the other hand, Pepe smiled, his face alight with malice.

"The terrible thing," continued Verdoux, seated once more behind his desk, "is that those who have money don't help, and those who help haven't any money. Thus, I can't start my project on a large scale."

"Aren't there any workshops yet?" asked Juan Luis.

"No. In reality, there's nothing. Only a common dormitory where these men have become bored, and, in order not to be bored, think up mischief."

"Tell us, Verdoux, tell us how you have made out up to now with your little angels," said Pepe.

Verdoux was about to say, when the door opened and the great literary critic, who had been resting under the trees before, entered silently, almost surreptitiously, but with calm dignity.

"Will you allow me?" he said. "The sun bothers me. The heat bothers me. The noise bothers me. I am getting old, Verdoux. There is no hope for me."

As he said this, he looked about him with half-open eyes. Then he sat down circumspectly in an armchair and put up a leg, disposed to listen. However, he stopped the conversation when he raised his leg. It was as if he were a strict watchman who surprised his charges in a prank. Verdoux introduced the young men. The writer scarcely looked at them, parted his lips, and then paid no attention, absorbed in the scene of the bathers in the garden.

"The first one he took in," said Pepe, "stayed two days and left with the tools, bedclothes, and some money he found in the house."

Verdoux made a gesture of annoyance, but then his eyes grew gentler, and he commented with melancholy:

"He was a child, just a grown child that's been beaten by his mother, father, teacher, friends. Is it any wonder that he celebrated his freedom by beating an old woman and stealing her purse?"

"Yes, but he stole from you."

"Because he did not understand my affection. He tried to harm me, because it maddened him not to understand. I could see it in his eyes. Such savage eyes, so green, like those of a cornered wildcat, ready to pounce. And he pounced, and he carried off in his claws the telltale signs of prejudice and foul play."

"And the other one? The swindler?" Pepe pressed on.

Verdoux' eyes flashed with fury for a fleeting instant. But he contained himself and the smile of paternal condescension softened his features again.

"But you," said Juan Luis, "you really believe you are going to change this country with a work of charity like this?"

"Change the country? I am not talking about countries, young man, I am speaking of men. A country is an abstraction. I leave it to the economists who play at politics."

"All right. I agree: change men. How many will you change? And why? So the rest will occupy the places of those you reform when the cell becomes available? It's a vicious circle, isn't it?"

Juan Luis' voice had not lost its steely edge, but Verdoux listened to the words, watched the young man's angry face without paying attention to the voice.

"The error made by all politicians," said Verdoux, "is that they think it is enough to shift furniture around in order to fix up a man's life, not realizing that what really matters is to teach that man how to live amidst that furniture. To teach him to live. Man has not learned to live. Neither here, nor anywhere else. Our man, without having to look elsewhere, is distrustful, astute, a liar, and a hypocrite. Why? Because he lives among the distrustful, the astute, the liar, and the hypocrite, and in such a country there is no choice but to be either victim or hangman. When you set out, I am already on the way back. That is the motto of our poor scoundrels, who don't care where they go or come from, so long as they can deceive their fellowmen enroute. Joaquin Edwards Bello, a very intelligent man, once asked himself: 'What is the use of my having been educated like a gentleman, in accordance with the traditions of honesty, truth, and dignity, if I live from minute to minute, day to day, year to year, in a country of scoundrels? If I get up to give my seat to a lady in a streetcar, out of nowhere a rascal slips into it. If I protest, the rascal knifes me. If I remove my hat to greet someone, a petty thief snatches it from my hands and runs off with it. Why, the Santiago petty thieves can steal the tail off a policeman's horse! They sell them to makers of violin bows. Have you ever seen the likes of this!'"

"But you don't realize," said Juan Luis, "that you touch only the surface of things. Symptoms. There are scoundrels in this country, because there are hypocrites, just as you, yourself, said. Those who have governed this country by pretending not to see poverty, abuse, and social inequality; who fill their mouths, pockets, and larders with the wealth that should belong to everybody, feigning indignation when the rabble steps on their corns, when they have grown rich and fat by keeping their foot firmly planted on the rabble's neck."

"Good heavens! What did I say to inspire such a speech? Young man, you have the soul of a politician."

"Man!" the writer suddenly exclaimed. "Man!"

Juan Luis looked at him and began to kick a globe near his chair.

"How you react, man! *L' homme n' est qu' un roseau,* according to Pascal, *le plus faible de la nature.* But he is a reed that thinks," he stretched his mouth and half closed his eyes, seemingly inspired. "The philosopher adds: 'It is not necessary that the whole world arm itself in order to crush him; steam, a drop of water, are enough to kill him.' And you want to dismember him with kindness! One of you will take him by the head, the other by the feet, and, in the struggle, you are going to tear him apart."

"Pascal also said that had Cleopatra's nose been shorter, the face of the world would have changed. Pascal was a clown."

"But son," Verdoux stated again, "you think that only the rabble suffers and therefore, you have fashioned an idea about this country that is a monument-type idea: a gentleman has a rascal on the ground and subdues him by stepping on his neck. Like all monuments, yours is an abstraction in bad taste. In fact, if I were to make that kind of monument, it would be of a gentleman under the heel of a bunch of middle-class hypocrites who insist on living at his expense, who climb up his back, hang from his shoulders, waist, legs, and who have survived like this for centuries. The victim, my dear friend, is not so obvious, and because he isn't, he suffers more. I want those people to get off the gentleman's back, and that everybody, victims and hangmen alike, begin to walk on their own two feet."

"How is that going to be accomplished, Verdoux?" asked the writer. "Our young friend is partly right. Partly. These children you house are the best proof of it. You want to make people walk who have already lived a whole life by dragging themselves. And you want to raise them up with kindness and tenderness. I think you would have better results if you horse-whipped them."

"You are funny, too. Undoubtedly, you think that it should be across their bare behinds, in the Plaza de Armas."

Pepe and the anthropologist burst into laughter.

"I am absolutely serious," the writer assured them, but in his eyes shone a strange gleam. "The bum is a baby and must be treated like one. With affection? Of course, but with the affection reserved for a child. And with a whip. Like a mischievous child. Why, they boastfully call themselves 'bums.' They run like children, hate like children. Our grandfathers who knew them better than we, knew how to deal with them. Our country was one large family—orderly, sober, virile, mighty. It's with the coming of the bum that this country was ruined. Our grandparents could tell a bum a mile away, and kept him in his place, exiled to his lair. There was place in the country only for the gentlemen; note this well, for the gentlemen from any class, even for the gentlemen who came from a tenement, who proved his worth, distinguished himself, became respected and put down roots. What was Martin Rivas but that very type of gentleman?"

"Martin Rivas," retorted Juan Luis, "was not a gentleman, nor a hipster, nor middle class, nor any of that nonsense . . . he was a guerrilla."

"A what?"

"A guerrilla . . ., or a terrorist, if you prefer. He came to the home that fitted his talents, took by storm the woman he deserved, reminded the country that it was alive. That's all. The Carreras and Bilbao were men like that too . . . so was Alessandri, the Lion, before his social-climbing, dude friends clipped his mane . . . that's the way we should all be."

"You must be joking."

Juan Luis gave the essayist a withering look.

"No. Evidently, you are not joking. God help me!"

I have seen that abandoned villa. At the edge of autumn, its tiny white chapel silent, half covered with moss. Somewhere, perhaps among dry poplars, the sun of a distant summer morning still beats down. On the ground, like thick, golden coins, the dry leaves pile up, and along the adobe wall, on the clay roof tiles, time places its signs of ruin. The little fountain is shattered. On its bottom, shiny salamanders crawl. The corridors that never did become an arts and crafts workshop creak and shudder; their glass is gone, but cobwebs have replaced it. The orange trees have died of the plague or of the cold. I have not seen the study with the underwater atmosphere since. I have a feeling that Verdoux' globes still float around bumping against the worm-eaten beams, and that his compasses, rulers, and barometers remain intact, awaiting the opportunity to measure the oblivion that swallowed the presence of the master like a gigantic snout.

Verdoux, hair combed, magnificent, consumed by a love for his country that could not be expressed in metaphors but only in caresses, a lover's love that sought its course in the suburbs of summer, beside the damp shadows of the flower stalls, the length of endless tenements, rotting doors, flooded patios, of foul-smelling movie houses, a passion that could be kind and tender, always committed; Verdoux, misunderstood, maligned, and nonetheless, smiling, a good prospect for a stabbing or for a holdup on some Valparaíso hill, filled with true love for the tender man-child called *roto,* respectful of the hipster, scourge of his own idle, hypocritical class; Verdoux, male nurse, stretching out his arms to the offended, caressing the backs of the olive-skinned people, who rear up like cats at his touch; Verdoux, who began revolutionary plans that could not rule his life, filled as he was with respect for the seriousness and for the frenzied rage of the new adolescent who came to put his files in order.

Verdoux poured tea with an elegant fastidiousness, laughed crying, and burned his ukuleles in the park, in the park already overgrown by weeds. He was both a name and a cause in that year of 1938. There was talk of his charity and his errors. He smiled like a grown baby in his disappointment. One of his lieutenants was shot . . . because of his queerness. But that wasn't the reason. Rather, it was because of his sad clown's face, because of his toothless face, because of his thick tongue, and his genius for gossiping, and because he dared to be gentle among muggers.

Each criminal who came there made off with his clothes, his tools, his money, and his remorse. The floaters in the pool disappeared, the rare aquatic flowers died away, the flock of fall guys departed, the chapel was closed once again and settled back into its smell of pine and wax, the church of the philanthropists came to an end, and a hedge of dry, yellow leaves, heavy with water and mud sprang up and Verdoux took his show somewhere else. But the people's friend remained, wandering through the neighborhoods, wrapped in his golden southern poncho, somewhat withdrawn, writing aphorisms, less corpulent, but also less empty.

Verdoux dismissed the others, closed the door, and began to reveal his secrets to Juan Luis. He worked at a desk, lit by a very bright lamp that created the illusion of a knife shop about him. Verdoux handled his cards with elegance. Juan Luis looked at his pink fingers—the third one sported a soft amethyst—at his thick watch, filled with dials and astronomical signs; his smiling lips and authoritative eyes, and felt something maternal and eccentric about him.

For the most part, the file cards contained isolated phrases, aphorisms in several languages, titles of scholarly works, references to maps and navigational charts, primitive sketches. There appeared also a diary written by the trembling hand of a shipwrecked man: warnings about an inlet in the north of Chile; hasty directions about a buried treasure, names, and a violent tirade about a local official who had betrayed him and to whose death he alluded with ambiguous sarcasm. There were photos also: specimens, Verdoux called them. Men of all ages: beardless miners with straight black hair, damp mustaches, and wild-eyed; fishermen wrapped in ragged vests and heavy sweaters, smiling among baskets of crabs, pants rolled up to their knees; dark-skinned, gleaming, muscular stevedores in their undershirts; brick masons on top of scaffoldings, legs parted in awkward positions; pale, hairy, thin young men in bathing suits, with wry smiles; Indians of a tranquil, coppery indifference, with something devious in their eyes under the upturned brims of their black Andalusian hats; strapping young men jumping on swift tree-trunks down river; natives of Chiloe, wet as if they had just been washed; natives of Tierra del Fuego, round and wide of face, with powerful shoulders and big bellies, standing on thin, mosquito-like legs; easterners from Pascua with strange, dissipated expressions on their ashen faces. Verdoux studied the photos, held them up between his large fingers, pointing out epidermal qualities, details about bone structure, and classified them orally, stressing certain features so that Juan Luis could take notes and be guided, later, in his task.

From the snapshots, they passed on to more particular photos and sketches, to enlargements of details: a single buttock distinguished by a spectacular birth mark; a belly, a shin, a hand, the sole of a foot, ankles, jaws, a lashless eye, an albino's nose, a hirsute underarm, and a gigantic navel, like a mine shaft. From man, they passed on later, to the sea, to underwater mountains, cataclysmic waves, volcanoes, valleys, and then, to the cities. Verdoux was about to start on institutions, when Juan Luis looked at his watch, and asked permission to withdraw. Verdoux looked at him in surprise.

"Aren't you interested?"

"Quite the contrary, I am very interested."

"But, you can't forget time."

"I have a date. I must meet my sweetheart downtown."

"Ah, we'll arrange working hours. You are a slave to the clock. We'll make up a schedule."

"Don't misunderstand me; tomorrow I'll be here on time and we'll start the . . ." Juan Luis stammered. The what? What the devil was Verdoux preparing? Bibliography, history, geography? Any word like that sounded like an insult for a man who seemed to be creating a new science, something like a philosophy of the skin, a herbarium of smiles, a compendium of postures, all of it with the pressing, complex burden of a personal, decisive commitment between the investigator and his subject, a passion between Verdoux and his country.

Verdoux saw him to the street and walked with him to the bus stop. There, on a street corner, half hidden by the shadows of the trees, the wind whipping up a swirl of dry leaves at his feet, haloed by the bluish brilliance of a street lamp, he stood saying good-bye, hands in his pockets, alone and smiling, among furtive shadows that seemed to follow him always, and that he was slow to see.

VIII

WINTER—that Santiago winter that lasts a month or two like a frozen pond near the Mapocho River—not only was giving up the ghost along the leafy avenues of the exclusive neighborhoods, but it was also allowing the sun to show off its radiance in the poorer sections, and boys and girls were the first to enjoy it.

In order to reach Doña Inés', the madam's, one had to walk the length of Maruri Street, immortalized by Neruda in one of his early poems, evoking its sunsets among impoverished families and mimosa trees laden with golden dust that piled up on the rooftops. On the corners of this neighborhood the youthful gangs appeared, sniffing the dampness, flexing their muscles, propositioning the girls, breaking locks, rolling drunks, stealing a little, running a little more, planning a respectable holdup—perhaps a theft downtown—when the spring was more advanced, for a mass rape, one that would fill the newspapers and could be pulled off on the slopes of San Cristóbal or the rocky stretches of the Mapocho River. Those gangs hung out at certain corners, at a particular bar, the Derby, some alleys, the United Breweries, at the Morgue with its spacious football field. And just as the street corner with all its trappings, pool halls, movie houses, was a part of the gang, so too the boy was nurtured by his corner, sprouted there like a dry, stiff tree in hibernation, waiting for the first ray of sun to spring to life anew.

There, at this corner, a curious web had been spun; it was difficult to define it then, though in time its significance would be clear. Juan Luis was considered unreliable, but quite able to surprise with sudden decisions and total commitment. Mario, on the other hand, was a duly decorated and promoted veteran of many campaigns on that corner: in his hands a peashooter always commanded respect.

Mario was an expert in small-time swindles: he forged theater tickets, resold ducats to the stadium, controlled the billiard tables at the Derby with his measured, wise play, pawned his family's flat silver, sold doorbells and plates that he collected in nocturnal operations. He could be quite religious, almost hysterically devout. A certain type of girl lost her head over him: the better-bred type who saw in his spiritual raptures, an upper-class trait. He was faithful to them. To all of them at the same time. And they ended up by hating one another, because of that loyalty. Mothers would then go and denounce him to his mother. And she did not know what to say to them. She recommended prayer: prayer for everything, prayer so that the girls would calm down, so that Mario could be free of the temptations of the devil that weakened him so. And she added that, in Mario's case, Fitina was a good tonic. And Mario, in fact, obeyed her and carried Fitina tablets in his pockets, together with Joinbina pills and passed them out to his friends like mints. Mario, therefore, had sprung roots in that neighborhood. Nonetheless, at that stage of the game, those roots were not altogether innocent, since upon his emergence from adolescence they had become tangled in roots of a different nature: Lucho's.

Lucho had been in love with Elisa since he had reached the age of reason. But, being the bastard he was, raised in a brothel, spoiled by the inmates, Lucho lived in the shadow of the Huertas, like a beautiful, faithful dog, hungry for affection, silent, afraid of Elisa. He could be considered Mario's bodyguard, and, in fact, fought for him. Tall, wide-shouldered, a bit hesitant in his walk, thick and hard of neck, of extremely dark hair and soft, dreamy, blue eyes, Lucho covered the corner with his shadow like a giant tree, and he swept Mario along with him as a graft on his side. His stepmother wanted to make him a distinguished professional man, so she dressed him in costly suits, surrounded him with books, dragged him off to the School of Engineering, supplied him with a regiment of tutors who prepared him for months and years, organized—within her resources—a network of influential friends, recruited from among the most prominent abortionists and night hawks. But she battled alone, and she was destined to lose. No one but she wanted to make Lucho a distinguished professional. The rest insisted on making an elegant, cultured, cruel pimp out of him. An implacable and beautiful pimp. Lucho submitted. Just as he had done as a child, among so many solicitous and interested hands that insisted on dressing and undressing him.

Elisa used to pass that corner: dressed in blue, with a white sailor's collar, her hair more auburn than blonde, pale-faced, circles under her bright and warm eyes, with her natural girl fragrance in spring. Lucho would fall silent and grow smaller and smaller, flattened against the wall. The other boys watched him, examined Elisa's slender, well-formed body, then stared at Mario as if questioning him. He would make a deprecating gesture with his mouth and turn his back on his sister.

"Pompous. He seems pompous to me. He is too concerned with himself. Who is he to put on such airs? It's all because he has a wealthy godfather. But so far as he himself is concerned, he hasn't a pot. His shoes are dirty. That tickles me. They must have holes. But see how he walks. What a stride! You'd think he wanted to scare us. He is very handsome."

"Thanks," said Juan Luis, taking a toasted French bun, and buttering it without further ado.

"It's the head, the wavy hair, or perhaps the forehead; the forehead and the eyes. Damn, but the kid has a noble look. That's why the girl fell so hard. He is well-built. But those airs he puts on must be to hide something. I'll bet he can't handle more than one at a time."

"You are not eating anything, baby. Why don't you take something? You have to eat, particularly in your condi. . ." she interrupted herself seeing Juan Luis' look of annoyance. But she went on: "When a girl is expecting a baby, she should eat and take care of herself, not just for her own sake, but for the baby's. Come, eat something."

Elisa looked at her with an indifferent air and went on smoking and sipping her tea with milk. She had sat in front of the window and, through the panes, a tree seemed to fascinate her with its movements, its pauses, its insistent murmuring. The sky was the winter sky of the slums: gray, damp as a rag.

"I haven't any money, lady," said Juan Luis. "Not a penny to my name."

"Nobody is asking you for any. Besides, you are working, young man." In the madam's voice a family tenderness was almost discernible, but the furious flash in Juan Luis' eyes snuffed it out instantly. "Who is talking about money?"

"You need money for the operation, don't you?"

The man was watching Elisa from a corner, enveloped in the smoke of his cigarette. His look was one of tender, almost paternal, assurance. A certain brilliance revealed an interest, perhaps a suspicion, that she received indirectly, without understanding it or wanting to acknowledge it. She had already seen him once. That morning he had seemed much younger. When he had slapped the abortionist, he had become transfigured. Now she did not notice him; her attention passed through him, towards the window, beyond it, to the tree.

"Change that record, baby, can't you see it's scratched?"

The man got up, crossed the room, and bent down over the record-player. He returned to his chair and lit another cigarette. As though coming out of a tube of smoke, came Gardel's voice:

"Mi Buenos Ayyyyyyyres. . ."

"As I said, I haven't any dough." Juan Luis had eaten all the bread. "I am going to have to get it."

Suddenly, the other man's attitude bothered him. What the hell was he looking at so much? And so mysteriously; like a roll artist.

"I think I have seen you in the newspaper," Juan Luis said to him.

"Juan Luis," exclaimed Elisa softly, "it's getting late."

The man stared at Juan Luis, but did not answer.

"Aren't you a boxer? No . . . . Wait. A jockey. No, too tall for a jockey. You are . . ." Juan Luis was silent, his mouth slightly ajar, unbelief in his eyes. "No, no . . . . You are . . . ."

"Wouldn't you like a bit of vermouth?"

Juan Luis shook his head, smiled, and crossed his arms without taking his eyes off the man.

"Come, sit here, Elisita, here on the sofa. Let's talk."

Suddenly, it was night. The street lamp hung its yellowish light among the branches of the tree. Some people went by hurriedly along the sidewalk. The voices of children died away, became but an echo amidst the sound of car horns.

"Don't screw around," Juan Luis said suddenly. "Elisa, do you know who this gentleman is?" The voice was filled with a wounding mockery.

Elisa turned her back on the two men and sought refuge in the madam's face.

"I'll take some vermouth," continued Juan Luis, and approached the table.

The man got up again and walked with a tired air towards a cabinet, opened its doors, took out a bottle and several glasses. He poured with a trembling hand, gave a glass to Juan Luis, took one himself, then went to the phonograph to change records. He came back humming in a rasping voice:

"Por uuuuuna cabeeeeeeeeeza, metejón de un día. . ."

"You," said the man to Juan Luis, looking at him with infinite pity. "Young man, you are a student?"

Juan Luis laughed.

"Sit down," a threatening edge appeared in the man's voice for the first time.

"By the great mother whore, to think that I'd find him here. Who would have thought so? Because it's him. No doubt about it. Let's see. Let's have a look at him more in the light. How to make him move? I'll muscle him over to the light with my shoulder."

"Here's to you, sir," said Juan Luis as he stretched his arm, and swayed, trying to cover him with his own weight and move him against the wall.

The other man grew taller, raised his glass. Juan Luis was surprised by his height; erect, threatening, the man was growing, perhaps not in inches, but in an inner, raging, resentful way. His mouth was twisted now, and like that, lipless, face yellowish and drawn, eyes blazing, he revealed his identity, the identity that Juan Luis had scarcely suspected up to that moment, and that leaped like a snapshot from a darkened room to the front page of a newspaper.

"Oh, it is; it is, yes! Shall I tell Elisa? Shall I tell her? So this is where he hangs out. Who would have suspected it? With the madam."

"To your health, then, sir; your health."

The Führer approached the window and downed his drink. Then, the anger in his eyes died down, his mouth relaxed. In dejection, he pressed his forehead against the pane and remained there for a long time, staring vacantly, absorbed in the solitude of the street, in the gray darkness that descended like a floating bag over the roofs of the tenements.

"Help yourself," said Juan Luis filling the glasses again. "You seem very sad, my Führer."

The other man did not turn his head, but smiled the faintest of smiles.

"I don't see why you scoff, but that's the way the young are. What do you know about sacrifice? About the sacrifice of life? Of weariness? Of an old secret sorrow? Your young life gushes forth like beer out of a bottle. Mine is pouring out darkly, little by little. Like the last drop of semen, those drops that make one's loins ache, that seem to come from the spine with gray matter and clots of marrow, those drops that leave us trembling and defenseless like an old woman or a young girl before the howling, snapping pack that waits.... What do you know about that, young man? You with your bottle brimming with life. Me with my life's blood gone dry."

The Führer began to whisper and dab at his cheeks with a handkerchief. He approached the phonograph and listened enraptured.

Juan Luis began to cackle, doubling up, grunting, and spitting. He threw out the contents of his glass and clutched his stomach. The madam watched them from the sofa.

"Wine makes my love sad. He must not drink any more."

"You go . . . shit" said the Führer in tears, and Juan Luis laughed all the louder.

"What will they say tomorrow in Congress if they see you like this? You have to rest, sweetie, so that tomorrow you will be at your very best. You don't want to get cold feet. Play something else; every time he plays Gardel he blubbers." It was the madam poking fun now. "Do you know what he is going to do tomorrow?"

"Ines," said the Führer, "shut up, or I'll slap you."

Juan Luis laughed once more.

"Do you know what he is going to do tomorrow?"

"I'll kick the hell out of you!"

"The hell you will. Is this any way to receive guests? What will these young people say? First time they come here together and his highness wants to put on a show . . . Tomorrow, he is going to let Alessandri have it. . ."

The Führer glided from the window like a lizard and, without a word, unleashed a tremendous slap across the madam's face. Juan Luis doubled his fists. Elisa stood up and threw her arms about him, burying her face in his chest.

"Well, did you ever!" This fag beats up on women. And he's so much the Congressman, and he thinks he's so Aryan. . ."

"Let's get out of here, Juan Luis; let's go, let's get out of here, please! . . ."

Juan Luis tried to get to the Führer and, in the process, carried with him a napkin and a cup that fell and smashed to bits. The Führer gave an unbelievable start, whimpered with fright, and cowered behind the drapes. Señora Ines began to laugh and slap her belly.

"Sit down . . ." she said, "sit down . . . your visit is not going to end like this. Elisa, child, don't be afraid; sit down for a bit, we have a lot to talk about. Look, sweetie," she added, and turning to the Führer, "don't drink any more; it's not good for you. Your liver is probably upset, as usual."

She looked at him the way a lion tamer looks at his favorite lion as he arouses him with whip and chair, and then maneuvers him into submission. The Führer was trembling, watching slyly what was happening around him. His light eyes revealed not distrust, but a cold and hard aggressiveness. When he saw that, unmindful of the fray, Juan Luis had sat down, he grew calm and approached the madam with tiny steps.

"My little Ines," he said.

Elisa quailed in fear.

"Inesita, come, get up, let's dance a little tango. Just one more. Don't be mean."

The madam spread her legs and arms, gave him a deep, maternal look, pulled down her girdle, and got up. The Führer grabbed her with feline pleasure, held her tightly, and danced off with her rapidly around the room, sticking a leg between hers, bending her backwards, pushing her away, then to him, shoulders held high, elbows out, head stiff, and a grimace of painful concentration on his lips. Serious, sad, the madam let him have his way. The Führer began to hum in that pell-mell tenor voice he reserved for Congress, then started to mouth Gardel's teary lyrics.

". . . who is going to save the country, who is going to corrupt it . . . , answer me, baby. These kids who think they have all the answers, eh? International Judaism? Bolshevik Judaism, the North American, hiding at the furrier's, at the jeweler's, and at the Stock Exchange of this nation of half-breed monkeys?"

He would take a long step, twisting the madam's back, give a swift half-turn, dip down again, bend her way back, then, facing her, rush as if trying to penetrate her with his knee.

"You'll see. Brown shirt against steel shirt. Steel! Those louse-ridden . . . Have you seen that bald-headed Grove? Back, back, baby; that's it, let me lead; don't stiffen up. Shitty Communists. Bastardly oligarchs. This nation is stewing in a pot of corrupt oligarchs, of middlemen who have sold out to Gringo idiots, sly Jews, rickety rabble. . ."

He raised his voice and began to shout and tap his heels like a Gypsy dancer.

"Let's go, Juan Luis," Elisa kept saying.

The Führer left the madam in the middle of the room, faced Juan Luis, and tense, priestly, pointed a finger at him and shouted:

"You and all the other sissies like you better pay attention to what is going to happen, and don't act like clowns at the university. Stick out your chest, fight, and save this nation from the oligarchs and all your forebearers who have governed this country as if it were a tenement and they had the divine right to raid the treasury and treat the ignorant rabble like slaves, distribute diplomatic patronage, top jobs, and cabinet posts, to croak like frogs, appear important, become pot-bellied, and sport straw hats, and hand the country over to the winos . . . You hear me?"

Juan Luis still seated, looked him in the eye, gave him a look of disgust, and threw his glass of vermouth in his face. The Führer blinked in surprise and retreated to the safety of the drapes once more. Juan Luis watched him, fearful, not of an attack, but of that creature there before him, in that modest home, who was beginning to burn frantically and, who in his holocaust, was going to burn with other creatures quivering with a sort of diabolic tertian fever.

The Führer made faces, clenched and unclenched his fists, kicked the air. But he tired out: his anger, flared once more, then he began to walk around the room, hands behind his back, without a word, frowning, eyes downcast, dripping vermouth. He then returned to his chair by the window, sat down, one leg up, crossed his arms, and did not say another word. In the gloom, his face softened. Señora Ines went over to him, wiped his face with a caress, and bent down to kiss his mouth. After this, she sat at his feet and lay her head on his knees. Out of the shadows emerged the line of her thick hips and, under her skirt, the pressure of her gigantic thighs. The Führer did not stir. She had crumpled at his feet like a living mass, and now was rising little by little, trying to recover some form about his body. She kissed his lap and, with her dark, expert hands, unbuttoned him.

Elisa rose from the sofa, took Juan Luis by the hand, and drew him towards the door. They went out without a sound. The click of the latch cut off the phonograph. Outside, Elisa pressed against Juan Luis' side. It was cold. Juan Luis lit a cigarette. At the corner of Maruri Street the gang—the true soldiers, that is, the corporals of the twilight—was on watch. They spoke in a low voice, watching the lone couple, a glint of hostility in their eyes. Lucho drew aside a bit in order to see them better, then said something greeted by the others with shouts and laughter. Juan Luis turned to look at them. Elisa quickened her step, forcing him to follow her.

"Do you know what those Nazis are going to do tomorrow?" asked Juan Luis.

"What does it matter to me?" she replied.

"What do you mean what does it matter? Don't you know?"

"What difference does it make what they do? It will get them nowhere."

"They are going to make an attempt on Alessandri's life. They are going to shoot him in Congress."

Elisa looked at him in surprise.

"Who is going to do the shooting?"

"The Nazis. The Führer said so."

"He's just talking. Besides, he was so drunk. . ."

Elisa had pulled up her coat collar. Abruptly, she said:

"Juan Luis, know something? I am going to have the baby. . ."

Juan Luis pretended not to hear.

". . . I am going to have the baby, and I think that he is going to be like you, well, not exactly, because a mother fashions him slowly and I don't always love you, you know. At times, you are unbearable, and then I change him a little. But, basically, I think his head will be like yours. His eyes, naturally, will be the same, as will his mouth. He's going to be real quiet and serious, and very intelligent, and will stick very close to me -looking at me with his dark eyes."

"Be serious, Elisa. What did Señora Ines tell you? When does she have to have the money?"

"No need for money now. Wait. It's still six months off. Or is it seven. I'm not sure."

"You're mad." Juan Luis became tense. All at once, he sensed that Elisa could be serious, and thought himself ridiculed. "You're mad. Be serious."

"I am quite serious."

"How can you even think of it? And your mother? And Mario? How can you say such a thing?"

"Why, you are terrified. What are you afraid of, Juan Luis?"

"Afraid? But what's going on? I don't know what's going on."

"It's obvious that you don't understand. I am going to have the baby."

"You have no right. Don't be foolish; be serious."

"I am the one who is going to have the baby. Don't panic."

"And you want me to get married?"

"Get married? Who said so?" Elisa looked at him a bit disdainfully. He had let go of her and was walking with giant strides, ahead of her, in a rage. They fell silent as they approached the house. Mario was at the door, smoking. He had seen them at a distance, but paid no attention. They reached him.

"Ciao," said Elisa and went in without looking back at Juan Luis.

"Where have you been? Have a fight?" asked Mario, pointing with his chin at the glass door through which Elisa had disappeared. "Did you see Lucho on the way?"

"Yes."

"Didn't he say anything? Did he talk with Elisa?"

" No. What are you two mixed up in?"

Juan Luis looked at him with a sudden gravity.

"Us? What do you mean?"

"You know what I mean. What are you going to do tomorrow?"

Mario did not reply. He shrugged his shoulders and took a deep drag on his cigarette.

"What are you going to do tomorrow?"

Mario cast him a furious glance.

"They are going to raise hell in Congress."

"What do you know about it?"

"Just what I told you. Besides, I heard the Führer say it."

"That's a filthy lie. Don't be stupid."

"In a whorehouse. The little Führer. Drunk as a skunk and telling everyone he was going to shoot the Lion . . . He was spilling it all."

"Shut up, you lard-ass!" shouted Mario, shaking with fury. "That's downright slanderous . . . . Only a communist like you can say that." He had clenched his fists, intending to jump Juan Luis.

"Don't get involved; that's the only thing I'm telling you," said Juan Luis. "And I am saying it for your own good."

"Good, my eye! You're butting into something that's none of your business. What's happened. Has the little girl made you jealous? Eh?"

"Mario, shut up."

"With Lucho? Eh? With little Lucho?"

"Don't be an idiot. I'm telling you not to get mixed up in it. The cops are going to knock the shit out of you."

"Juan Luis is afraid... he's afraid of the cops. Poor baby! And he's jealous ... Is my sister sleeping with Luchito?"

Juan Luis grabbed him by the lapels and shook him violently. Mario bounced against the door and made no effort to defend himself. Someone shouted from the balcony: "Mario, come upstairs!" It was Elisa. Juan Luis drew back.

"Don't get mixed up in it."

"We'll meet on the street, you shit."

Juan Luis went off rapidly. At that hour he would still find someone at the Iris Soda Parlor. It was necessary to tell what the Nazis were preparing. The daily *La Opinión* could publish it. He saw a bus and ran. He jumped on. When the vehicle took off, he looked back and had a fleeting look at the second floor of the Huerta house. On the balcony, he thought he saw Elisa. A feeling of anguish overcame him. There was no doubt, Elisa had decided to have his child.

IX

From railroad stations, along the country roads, the length of rivers and mountains, descending from the pampas, like a turbulent but silent human current, the street people had begun to invade the city: thick columns advanced along the periphery of Santiago, people of all ages, covered with rags, carrying their possessions, dragging children and animals. All walked in silence: the men, shoulders drooping, pants held up by rope, toes sticking out of torn shoes, long and dirty hair like a mane over the dandruff-covered collar of their coats, some smoking, others, blowing on their hands to warm them; the women, pregnant, carrying thick bundles of clothes on their shoulders, stepping crookedly in their flat-heeled shoes; the children, barefooted, crushed down in grown-ups' coats, hairy, bleary-eyed, shivering with cold. They all moved with a dark insistence, going with the current, filling the wide roads, protected by the fear they inspired in people.

It was a popular march, voiceless, without flags; a slow multitude that was filling all the streets, avenues, squares, school buildings, barracks, hospitals, stadiums, putting on them the stamp of terror and pestilence. For, those thousands of citizens, were carrying deadly typhus lice.

The entire city was now scratching. Everywhere and under any circumstances. The lice could be seen, but not always. People on a streetcar, eyed one another with distrust, refusing to touch, looking for lice on the collar, shoulders, hands of others. They did not discover any, but they scratched just the same and fled home to inspect themselves, to bathe, to fumigate or burn their clothes. This also happened in offices, in stores, in the street, at the theater. The afternoon newspapers fed the fires of alarm, publishing the number that died daily. In a box, the sinister news: a bank manager, a priest, a respectable matron, notified the police that as they passed a pesthouse, the inmates hurled lice at them. Or, someone hurled lice from the gallery of a theater.

The authorities, the president, the Ministers, the judges and magistrates, the brass of the Armed Forces as well as the troops, doctors, professors, students, artists, workers, all scratched. The government did not try to hide the gravity of the situation, perhaps even exaggerated it, suggesting that in their efforts to put down the epidemic the citizenry should put aside political prejudices and join forces in a patriotic mission. But the opposition press revealed alarming facts: The typhus epidemic, though grave, was not sufficiently so to warrant the measures taken by the authorities. In effect, stated *La Opinión*, it seemed as if the government had decided to put an end to unemployment by letting the lice do their killing job.

In the August cold, families fell one after another, not always victims of typhus, but of influenza. If this happened in the tenements, they carted them off to a hospital or a pesthouse. From the neighborhoods, during the night, ambulances set out filled with typhus suspects, children crying, women cursing, men silent, sirens howling. Along Paz Avenue, at all hours of the day or night, funeral processions went by. The coffins were piled on, four or five to the funeral car. Relatives massed, gravediggers shoved one another, and along the desolate paths of the cemetery, those black lines moving deliberately in the night in all directions, were like new columns of lice and still more lice.

Those not infested retired to their homes to scratch, behind closed windows and bolted doors. They were seen coming out in the early morning, making their way furtively along the streets near the Mapocho River, headed towards Vega or the Central Market. There, they bought, without haggling, filled their shopping bags, and went back to hide once more. They even nailed transoms shut, fearful that the unemployed would throw in rag balls filled with lice. There were no children to be seen on the streets, only the fever-ridden victims, on their shoulder a bundle filled with garbage retrieved from the cans of restaurants.

The lice reached the university and first attacked the School of Medicine. It is not proper to speak of this crisis, without calling attention to the hero who died in the name of everyone. This hero was well-known in the Anti-Fascist student group. He was fat, short, with a sad color about his eyes, an uncertain voice, and a touch of anguish in his throat. He always said just enough and, always, it would have been better for someone else to say it. In the opposition party rose Julio Barrenechea, wide, powerful, like a sleepy-eyed octopus that came out of invisible depths, sounding a horn that set boats lost in the fog back on their course. Barrenechea and Fuentes, our hero, admired each other, but their partisans condemned that admiration and urged them to hate each other. The Sepulveda brothers, beardless, tremulous terrorists—one thin, the other quadrangular—insulted both of them, and turned to attack their neighbors, attacked each other, broke every pact and, at times, laughed with a Troskyite death rattle that filled students with cold hatred. The lice did not attack the Sepulveda brothers. On the other hand, they killed Fuentes.

Gentle soul that he was, not being made of the stuff of victors or martyrs, Fuentes moved heavily through the revolutionary web of 1938 from one group to another, from a student cell to a military one, from the Anatomy Lab to the wretched pesthouse, picking up and caring for typhus victims day and night. During this time, he decided to marry, to marry in haste for reasons that no one understood until it was too late. Infested, the virulence of lice in his bloodstream, eyes burning with fever, he made the arrangements and was married in his garret on Independence Avenue, in black morning coat, striped trousers, gray spats, and bowler. That night, he went to bed, a red carnation in his buttonhole, and died there swarming with lice that, frustrated for an instant, venerated him.

The funeral procession—led by the bride in mourning veils—set out from the university and, along the avenues, the unemployed raised a trembling hand to their hats, allowing the wind to blow the ashes from the cans they carried. At the other end of the Mapocho bridge, men and women hoisting red banners joined the cortege; students unhitched the black percherons and began to pull the funeral coach themselves, advancing slowly, singing the International. At that instant, it started to rain, a drizzle at first, then a heavy, slow rain: the bareheaded students dripped water; flags were drenched; the horses of the police slid on the asphalt; and from the mountain of flowers that covered the coffin rose an intense aroma redolent of dawn in the country. Then, orators spoke forth, standards flashed once more, and dusk fell rapidly. Word had it that the lice were in retreat.

On May 21, Chileans celebrate the glories of their naval war victories. That year, thick clouds covered the sky, a wind presaging rain blew, people looked distrustfully towards the snow-covered Cordillera, the entire city became apprehensive and waited with uneasiness. The hours went by. Along the deserted streets came a car, its little flag fluttering and, after a while, another; children gazed at the flags trying to identify the colors; the dusty, silent houses shook their emblems and waited.

Along downtown streets, between rows of police holding back the multitude, the Army marched by to the strains of The Seventh Infantry, followed by young cadets with their red and white plumes. Behind rigid battalions of marines, Andean troops, and lancers, came the presidential party: pulled at a trot by spirited, red colts, the Daumont coach made its way slowly; in the coachman's gloved hands the long whip undulated elegantly, and the shining, black leather bridles became entwined. Ensconced beside his Minister of the Interior came the Lion, pale, all wrapped up, acknowledging half-heartedly the shouts of his partisans and his enemies. There was fatigue in his eyes, profound melancholy in the top hat that rested on his lap, inflexible will in the leonine head, still quite visible between the now-stooped shoulders.

"Times have changed, Alessandri. It is not easy to recognize these people."

"They want to laugh at me? I'll mess up their magazine *Topaze*."

"Where are the echoes of the '20s, the stentorian voices that resounded against the corridors of Plaza de Armas? Whatever became of Colonel Ibáñez' sabers? If he shows up at a barracks, he'll see what's what."

"Will there be trouble, Salas Romo?"

"Don't worry, Excellency, we have them covered with agents."

"Who is it?"

What is that dark, gesticulating, hysterical mass? Men on tiptoe to give him the finger, a child's hand waving a flag, a bouquet of flowers. Flowers yet! There's some shoving; a man falls on all fours. He can't see clearly enough. These horses have a speedy trot.

"Cruchaga is the man, don't be upset, Excellency. He has them in the palm of his hand. He's such a gentleman."

Alessandri is the same man of the year '20. Don't forget it. But there's the rub. The same man of 1920, in 1938. They'll see, those insolent dogs. They want audiences? Give them the stick. They want revenge? They'll find out how they will make out with Ross.

The coach was already turning and heading towards the gardens of Congress. Some planes passed overhead like slow buzzards. The entourage stopped. The Lion saluted before alighting and then, surrounded by parliamentarians, he advanced slowly. He was entering the Hall of Honor, in the midst of diplomats, ecclesiastics, and congressmen, when there was the sound of a bomb bursting in the distance. The parliamentarians ran; the police ran brandishing their clubs. An officer drew his sword and stood motionless with it on high as if he had descended from a monument. The Lion said:

"It must have been a firecracker." Watch the assembly hall now. The stern judges are there, and the moth-eaten old men. And the enemies. There's that shitty wisecracker who is trying to pull a trick on me. I know you. He doesn't look at him, he senses him down there. What does he want? So slicked-up, with his protruding teeth, and loud suit. Some day he will want to be president. Where are we? Why should he be so nervous . . . Could he be . . . But no, it is not he. It is someone else . . . someone else. Without looking, rather with his eyes fixed on the opposite side, he tries to make sure, he struggles to capture that wave. It is someone else. Somewhere down there, towards the left, no, next to the center aisle, a bit farther back. He'd like to look. But he doesn't do so. He feels a current, something concealed in the air, that turns on and off down there.

The workers wander through the *pampa* starving to death. Someone got the idea to assemble them in a square, or perhaps it was a playing field. There's always some fool who doesn't know how to carry out orders. But, maybe his memories are a bit mixed up. For some of them were gunned down in the nitrate mine, and others . . . where the devil was it? And, wasn't it Cabero who spoke of freight cars that carried the strikers through the *pampa*? And Pedro Aguirre was Minister then. Why don't they say so now?

"In the name of God, this session is declared open."

He opened wide his eyes, raised his head.

"Mr. Chairman, I ask to be recognized in order to . . ."

The secret agents and the police run. Everybody is shouting. One man shouts more than the others. He has the strident voice of a newsboy. The Lion watches and tries to identify the bodies being dragged out. That one is Maira. And that other one. They have him under control now. It's González. They kick him out. Quite right. And screaming. Screaming! Gun muzzles against his ribs. He drops out of their grasp. They pick him up by the armpits and drag him. A few others are taken out. There's time. We'll let a few minutes pass. Give the diplomats time to calm down. That old one looks about ready to drop dead. They eye each other. He calms him with a slight smile. Now.

He is now standing, addressing Congress. His voice sounds fine. Longer pauses. They can be longer still. My heart is O.K. Steady. There's enough strength for three, for four hours. In between pauses, he examines the Congressional seats with a rapid eye. The bastards are leaving.

"I am coming to the end of my mission. At the end of the year I shall hand over the supreme office to the citizen legitimately and freely elected by the people in exercise of their sovereignty . . . I have demonstrated that it is possible to maintain public order . . ." Let's feed them a few statistics. A bit longer. More statistics. He gropes for the glass of water with the right hand. A little shaky. He uses the occasion to look around. And, suddenly, discovers him. There he is. It is he. Can't be anyone else. Wooden-faced. A hand in his breast pocket. "Today, this country is a model of order . . ." And then, before the shot is fired, his eyes look up from the speech and fix on the terrorist. González von Marees, on his feet, fires at him. Fires like a schizophrenic. The shot goes over the Lion and imbeds itself in the wall. The police run over. The Lion looks on sadly. Some of the deputies hit the floor. They have the madman under control now. They drag him out kicking. Well, let's go on. There's time. At least three hours.

X

ALONE in the tiny dressing room, skirt already off, blouse open, Elisa was about to loosen the strap holding up her stockings when she heard her name. She stopped. In the next dressing room, two girls were talking in a low voice. One she knew; the other, who answered in monosyllables and a stifled giggle from time to time, was a mystery. Why had they mentioned her name? Over the open tops of the dressing rooms, the voices sounded indistinct, becoming echo-like as they bounced against the walls of the basement.

Elisa stood there with one leg in the air, a shoe dangling, her thighs motionless. She raised her head and held her breath. But, only snatches of the conversation reached her. The one who had mentioned her was Gilda, and appeared to say that Juan Luis had told her something in confidence; the other one answered clearly: "With the madam?" Gilda was slow to continue: "You'll recall that we left the group after lunch. Imagine, he was gassed up. I didn't notice until he called Valdivia over and asked him for a rubber. Can you imagine? In front of me! Some nerve! I went with him anyway, and

Fina took off with Jorge." "You went with him anyway?" "You know me. I can't resist him. Look, all he has to do is speak to me, stand there with those eyes of his and . . . " "What an idiot." "But, this time . . . listen, I don't know how to say it." "What do you mean?" "That something just comes over me." "Like what?" "I don't know. Just think, he was on top of me when he got sick." "What are you saying?" "That he got sick." "On top of you?" "I hit him a good one. And he fell asleep and when he woke up he was so sentimental and teary and told me what I told you." "Are you a real good friend of Elisa?" "She's nobody's friend." "She still thinks she's somebody" "And, what's it to you?" "Maybe it's on account of him." "You're in love." "Are you crazy? Love is one thing, but sex is something else again. I don't know." "Do you have a pin? This strap is too long. Tie it for me, want to?" "I can't get into this suit anymore. Look. Just look at how my hips stick out." "You're such an idiot! Don't struggle so. Let me help you. Stretch, and don't move. Let me, I'll tie it up in back." "I haven't seen him since." "And wasn't there supposed to be a surprise party this week?" "At the Carvalhos'? He won't go. Maybe I'll see him at the Engineers' Ball. Pass the strap through there. That's it. My, but you have cold fingers! You're tickling!" "And why don't you leave him in peace?" "Then, who's going to keep me in peace." "But, don't be stupid . . . He loves Elisa." "I hang around like a dope waiting for him to call, like a fool I haunt the school of education hoping he'll show up and go off with me. Why, he doesn't even notice me." "He loves Elisa." "And if he loves her so much, why is he running scared and asking for pills? El Pato told me Juan Luis had asked him for money to give the madam. Besides . . . Listen, let's not be gossips. Someone could hear us."

There was a titter. The shoes fell one by one; then there was the sound of bare feet on the tile floor. Someone was smoothing her swim suit over her hips, belly, and breasts. Head bowed, Elisa remained in the darkness of her dressing room, a tuft of hair over her face. She felt grotesque, half nude as she was, one shoe on, a leg in the air, the pink panties girding her belly. She stood up, unafraid now of making noise, fished a cigarette out of her purse, and lit it. The column of smoke rose and spilled over the walls of the dressing room. The other girls must have seen it, but they did not keep still.

"Pass me the lipstick. Give me a towel." "Have you noticed El Pato?" "What about him?" "He's after me. Haven't you noticed?" "So what?" "So, Julio is jealous as a . . . He's caught on. One of these days, he'll knock the hell outa him." "Because he looks at you?" "Well, he doesn't only look at me. Just you watch today. When we do the exercises on the floor, he'll lie down beside me." "Really?" "He rubs against my legs." "No kidding." "All the time. The other day when we were lying on the floor, he grabbed my toes with his and began to squeeze them." "With his foot?" "And he pressed so hard that I almost screamed. I didn't, because Julio would have climbed all over him. He's so jealous." "Did you know there are men who like to caress with their feet?" "On the soles?" "No; between the toes." "Idiot." "I'm going to take this towel with me." "There are towels in the gym." "Juan Luis has another woman." "Another? And, how do you know?" "He told me. He tells me everything." "He just can't get enough." "She's a waitress." "I know. Don't tell me any more." "What do you know?" "Well, you're jealous too. You want me to tell you." "That doesn't bother me one way or the other. If he were my boy friend. . ." "She's one of the kids working at the Carrera Theater soda fountain." "Kid? Are you kidding? She's an old bag." "Well, she's probably thirty, but she doesn't look like it. She has a good figure." "But, she smells like a vanilla shake." "Have you smelled her?" "Juan Luis told me." "And, what does he want with her?" "What do you suppose? To play hop-scotch with her, of course." "What a beast. Where does he find time for all that? With that angel face of his. . ." "Don't you feel like petting him? He's so sexy; you should see him, he talks hour upon hour, looking, touching, placing you . . . Do you know what he did once in the theater?"

Elisa had finished dressing; she picked up her things, put them in her purse, stepped out of the dressing rooms, and slammed the door shut. Outside, it was growing dark. She made her way through Forestal Park slowly.

A gust of cold air had come down from the Cordillera and, having swept the sky, hung over the trees and buildings. A sense of going home was in the air.

Juan Luis' petty treason filled her with pain, with disgust more than anger. Tell someone about it? Shed a tear with someone?

She thought of going to Señora Ines. It seemed cheap. Look for Lucho. Go out with him? She thought of going home, of facing her mother once again. A mean revenge; to unleash her emotions on her mother who would hear without understanding. Seek out Juan Luis? Throw his stupidity in his face? Break up with him? What can be broken off with someone who confuses love with pills. She bit her lips, and realized that she was hurrying, bowed down, perhaps gesturing. How to make him understand things? Juan Luis lived from day to day, deceiving himself with modest dreams. There was a time when he spoke of going away. Let him. He needed to. Even if she lost him. That he might mature and live his real life. She loved him. Oh, how she loved him! But, perhaps it was better to lose him.

Mechanically, she boarded a streetcar and let herself be carried off along Providencia Avenue. Night was falling. Above the hedges blinked the lights of the San Cristóbal funicular and the bulk of the statue of Our Lady lengthened out, its outline lost against the background of stars. Elisa got off and continued on foot along deserted, poorly lit streets flanked by thick trees, and finally stopped at a gate. She rang the bell, waited a few moments. Dogs barked, a shutter opened, someone appeared at the door, and she entered.

She had not come to ask for help, nor did she intend to unburden herself. Yet, once there, seated in the parlor facing Doña Esther, it was obvious that, unconsciously, she wanted just that. The lady listened in silence with that friendly, observant, superior distance so peculiarly hers. She smiled at Elisa, but not too much; she said a few encouraging words; and at one point, she had even put an arm across her shoulders.

"Ramón will be here soon," she said, "we will have a talk with him, and everything will be all right. We will find a way out."

At that point, Elisa rebelled:

"I am not seeking a way out," she said. "I don't want an out."

Seeing her indignation, Señora Esther was at a loss. She appeared to believe that Elisa was looking for an opportunity to confess an indiscretion and nothing more. All of a sudden, she sensed that it was quite a different matter.

"Come, child, come," she said, leading her to the library. There, in that room with the gigantic, dark mahogany desk and bookcases bulging with books, lamps, pictures, metal and marble statuary, they sat down facing each other. Señora Esther began to talk, to question her gently, now slyly, now with solicitude, with insistence and a motherly indignation.

"I realize that you must have had an overpowering reason for leaving home. But, Elisa, such things are thought out calmly, not done helter-skelter. Surely you will change your mind and return to your mother's. Nothing will be changed. I would prefer that you, you," she repeated, pointing a finger at her, "had not done it. You are a sensible girl. You shouldn't. You know what I think of you, what I have always thought of you, Elisa," she added, lowering her voice. "Your father was a weak-willed man. Elegantly fickle. Heaven knows how often we, his good friends, reproached him for it. And your mother," her upper lip contracted a bit, "your mother . . . is an unfortunate woman. You alone inherited the judgment and the strength of the Huertas. Let's not go into the matter of your little brother, however. We have never had reason to complain about you. But, now, what has happened? You are not a spoiled child. You are a strong woman," she stretched in her chair, raised her head, and half-closed her eyes, "strong, dear, very strong and very intelligent. You can't fail now."

Having said this, she considered the battle won. What battle exactly, she did not know.

"Aunt, *you* are a strong woman. I have been . . . a fool. I think I have been a fool."

"And why?"

"Because I have left home, because . . ."

"You have already told me that."

"Not all. Because I am going to have a baby."

Señora Esther closed her eyes, drew back, and was about to speak, but contained herself. She smiled lightly and looked at Elisa, looked at her calmly, then fixedly, plumbing her depths, always smiling.

"A baby?"

"Yes, I am going to have a baby."

After a pause, she asked:

"You told your mother?"

"Yes."

"What did she say?"

"That I would have to see a doctor and have an abortion."

Señora Esther showed no surprise. She crossed her fingers and balanced her bust.

"She said for you to have an abortion?" Her mouth became set once more and her eyes flashed.

"Yes."

"Are you sure? That was your mother's advice?"

"Well, she also said we would have to have it done away from Santiago, that I'd have to drop out of the university, that she would ask you to lend her the money to pay for the abortion."

"She said that? And what did you say?"

"That I would have my baby even if it meant leaving home."

Señora Esther fell silent, gazing at her own hands carefully. Absentmindedly, she played with her wedding band for a few moments.

"And she said nothing about you two getting married?"

"No. She merely said that only a stupid peasant could get a girl like me in trouble; that she was not about to let me marry him."

"Does she know who he is?"

"Yes, she does. My brother knows it too. It's Juan Luis."

Señora Esther blinked again. So, Juan Luis. The timid child with the large brown eyes; the sweet and pious loner who lost himself for hours in the park of the hacienda, while the other children were pulling pranks; later, the silent adolescent, Ramón's favorite, of whom he used to say:

"The rest are peasant idiots, but this nephew of mine, my godchild, is truly noble, and will be a great man . . ."

"What will Ramón say! Although, who knows; men look at these things differently. What did my brother and Hortense say? Do they know?"

"No, I don't think so. Juan Luis never tells them anything."

"Manuel is a failure, like your father. He won't bother about it. Hortense is a good woman, but useless and stupid. Juan Luis never visits this house as he should. He never says a word about what he is doing. But, Ramón has not lost faith in him and is still paying for his education. You know that Ramón . . ."

"Yes, aunt. We all know it."

"And you, Elisa, why have you decided to have the baby?

What does Juan Luis think about it, what has he told you? What do you think of him? To hide, in order to have a baby, frankly . . ."

"That's not my idea. I have no intention of hiding . . . I just don't know, marrying like that is a dirty business . . . I don't know if I can explain it, but I love Juan Luis in a different way. What is happening to me is perhaps my own problem. It seems to me that it has nothing to do with getting married. I just don't want to make a legal case out of it, aunt."

"To have a baby. Well, suppose you do have it. What then?"

"Then? Nothing."

"What do you mean, nothing?"

"I can't go home. Mother doesn't understand me. If I can't continue my studies, I'll work, I'll look for a job."

"Alone. So, you have decided to face it alone."

Little by little, her fingers relaxed, she stopped rocking and looked at Elisa with understanding.

"For the time being, you will stay here. I shall have a talk with Ramón and tell my brother. You will stay with me." She underscored the last word. "In your condition, you cannot go wandering about nor knocking on doors looking for a job. You will be just fine here. Not a word . . . . You will be all right with me."

She recalled her brother at that moment. On a distant summer afternoon, she saw him: round-shouldered, hands in his pockets, whistling a tune; all slicked up, with vest and cane, at the edge of total disaster, begging for more help, for a few more pesos, for a last prop to shore up his defenses and prevent the downfall of his wretched clan, the crash of his tenements, the end of his commissions and manipulations. At one time, that brother had been the very image of success for her: he was young, arrogant, clever, daring. The family's hopes rode on him. Those were the times of ease. He was going to make the patrimony unassailable, take care of his sisters, lend new lustre to the name. Then, his fortunes began to decline. The arrogance turned out to be but a cover-up for his weakness; the cleverness, a sign of sharpness, not of intelligence; the daring, short-lived. He married into the middle class, barely, that is, almost lower class. And, forgetting what he was, he came to ask for help. Always for help. To make a touch, with disdain for his brother-in-law hidden in his eyes. Begging and scorning, but hiding it artfully. This could be his punishment. Juan Luis, his hope, hooked at twenty! But, what about Elisa? There was something about the girl, an attitude that made her glow from within, that was manifest in her will and in her courage. That had to be saved. Class.

"Come with me," she said, and led her to the second floor and showed her the room she was to occupy. "Do you have some things with you? Your clothes?"

"No. I have brought nothing, aunt."

"No matter. We shall send for it tomorrow. You may use a robe of mine. Undress. I will have a hot bath drawn for you. Then, if you feel like it, you can go down for dinner, or eat here, if you prefer. Ramón will not get home till late."

Elisa offered no resistance. The elegant warmth of the house was slowly soothing to her nerves, lulling her into a sense of calm she had not known for a long time. She undressed, followed the maid to the bathroom. In the warm, scented water, she closed her eyes and let the house noises cradle her. Somewhere, someone was playing the piano, and its deep, rich tones reached her vaguely through the thick trees in the garden; there was no shouting or running of children there; no barking as in the tenements, nor the backfire of buses. It was a silence of trees, plants, noble woods, that settled over the house. Her body throbbed under the water. She lay still for a long time. Perspiration began to run down her face. She opened her eyes and saw her ample legs, the erect pubes, her pink belly, and young breasts. She put her hand on her hips, then placed them on her belly, pressing in gently, caressingly. She believed herself falling asleep and thought herself separated from Juan Luis by an invisible barrier, a barrier difficult for him, but necessary for her.

The days passed. Elisa did not return to the university, and Juan Luis made no effort to find her. Little by little, she settled into a routine, as if upon entering that house she had begun to live alone within her own womb with the baby, now beginning to grow. She slept late and was awakened by the ringing of bells somewhere and the rays of the sun that filtered through the eucalyptus trees to rest on her window gently. Then, she read: in the house she had discovered Spanish novels filled with sun, flowers, flies, shawls, canes, legs of lamb, and old people who spoke of markets and churches, beggars and lumbago. She read them because they made time pass. Somewhat tired and pale, stumbling a bit, she would leave her bedroom, and enter a dining room heavy with a smell of butter and olive oil that reminded her of the Spanish novels. Then she would flee to recover in Don Ramón's study with its smell of tobacco, leather, and ink. Later, she used to talk with Señora Esther, and enjoyed submitting to this woman cast in the ancient mold.

"Tell me about Juan Luis," Señora Esther would say to her, and with the command went the desire to know Elisa better, to judge her, to remonstrate with her, but also to provide her solace, for she knew that Elisa was still in love.

"Well," she used to say, "not a bit of what you tell me is true. It seems real, but it is just the foolish dream of a country girl. Do you think that Juan Luis is a special kind of man? Your father was like that. As a boy, Carlos used to live in a town on the San Rosendo spur and spent many summer vacations with us at grandfather Domingo's hacienda. Carlos was a very handsome young man and looked like one of the national heroes found in school readers: slender, wiry, with long legs and slim hips, very wide forehead and big dark eyes. He wore his hair long, almost mane-like. Perhaps too handsome for his own good. And mine. As a child, I used to dream about him. Then one summer he was mine. You understand, it scarcely lasted a few weeks, and not much happened, he held my hands and kissed me a few times. My brother Manuel reacted like a beast. The following summer, after I spent months dreaming up a romance, he did not even recognize me. He seemed to have forgotten me completely... Perhaps Manuel was to blame. I am not sure. A year later, he married Raquel, because of her fortune. He had sold his lands and lost his money in Santiago playing the businessman... But, what about Juan Luis? You will forget him."

"You know that I love him, aunt," Elisa would answer.

Señora Esther watched from her chair:

"He is irresponsible. He will forget you. I'll bet that he has a mistress somewhere, one of those tenement types that students keep."

Juan Luis was not yet looking for her. On the other hand, her brother Mario began to spy on her. He came when he figured that neither Don Ramón or Doña Esther were at home. Maybe he watched from the street corner. He used to ring the bell and slip in with feigned familiarity, refuse to remain in the living room, take her by the hand and drag her practically to her bedroom. There, he walked in front of the window, peering through the curtains, asking his questions without looking at her, boldly making his needs known. At first, Elisa regarded him ironically. Then, she began to feel distrust. What did he want? What did he really want?

"Money? What for?"

"I tell you the old man has a lot of money here at home. I want to get a loan from him. . ."

Elisa burst into laughter.

". . .a loan for a few months. He keeps his money at home, has never deposited a penny in the bank, doesn't know what they're for. His kind wrap up their dough in a pair of shorts and hide it under a bed, or something like that. Where do you suppose he keeps his dough?"

"What's that to me? Or to you?"

"I need money, Elisa."

"What for?"

"I can't tell you. It's not that I don't trust you, but it's very personal. I couldn't tell you."

"Really, whether you tell me or not isn't important. I haven't a cent and I wouldn't ask my aunt or uncle for a nickel for you, nor for me, nor anybody."

Mario would stand looking at her, poker-faced, as if her words could not be final and others, the ones he wanted to hear, would eventually come. Slowly his eyes grew darker, lost beneath his thick, well-outlined eyebrows, welling up with a mocking, cynical smile. His lips stiffened and, unexpectedly, dimples appeared on his cheeks. The slender body tensed up; he beat the floor with his heel, rubbed his chin, and said:

"Elisita, I need it desperately and if you weren't my sister, I'd have already given you a knock on the head and I'd be ransacking the old miser's chests."

Elisa could not take him seriously; she thought him a snob, with his slicked-down black hair, precocious smoker's hoarse voice, and eternally empty pockets. She felt sorry for him.

"Is it for some woman?"

"Don't be stupid."

"Want to buy an expensive gift, play the rich boy? Are you going to Viña del Mar?"

Mario would pace about the room, sniffing, looking with cat-like alertness. The third or fourth time he came, he tried to enter Don Ramón's study. Elisa barred his way. He wanted to search the other bedrooms.

"If you don't stop it, I'll call the maid."

Elisa's voice frightened him. He left and returned again and again. One afternoon, he appeared with Lucho. Elisa received them in the living room. Aunt Esther was to return soon. She felt ill at ease. Mario, more serious and calm than usual, was using different tactics, and that attitude, so foreign to him, made him all the more suspicious.

"Lucho and I have plans for a business venture, something that will make money, Elisa, real money, and we'll repay uncle immediately. We'll even pay him interest, if he wants."

"But, why tell me? What can I do? Why don't you tell him yourself?"

"They listen to you. Mother says they always wanted to adopt you, that's why she doesn't say or do anything now. She says there's nothing they wouldn't do for you. Why don't you do us this one favor?"

So unexpected was this pleading by her brother, so unusual the humility, that Elisa, aware of the duplicity that prompted him, began to play along with him.

"How much do you want?" she asked.

"Well . . . I think that as a start, well . . . How much do you think, Lucho?"

Lucho, hanging on Elisa's every word, did not answer.

"Lucho!"

The big boy slowly came out of his trance. He was watching her in silence, trying to understand the distance that she established between them.

"What was that? How much? You know. You tell her."

"He can't even do that. What did you come for? To look at Elisa?"

Lucho blushed, stood up, and went to a window. Elisa ignored him. Why had Mario brought him? Lucho, in his tailored suits, expensive shirts, American cigarettes, seemed incongruous beside her brother.

"How much? About a hundred thousand pesos. . ."

Mario said it in a calm voice, in an even tone, and let the statement hang in the air, not helping it with gestures or more words. There was something shameless in his attitude as he stood before Elisa. Suddenly, she realized that her brother had come to steal, to beat up uncle Ramón, aunt Esther, or even her. Something in his frayed elegance, in his insolent frown, in the crazy shiftiness of his eyes, something in his hidden hands, revealed danger to her. She looked at Lucho, but he had his back to her. She tried to spar for a time. She would call the maid, offer them something to drink. She might slip out to telephone. But Mario, stiff, silent, did not move from in front of her, barring her way.

"Little sister, where does uncle Ramón keep his dough?"

"I don't know, Mario . . . go away, I beg you, I'll speak to my aunt when she returns . . . a hundred . . . one hundred thousand pesos?"

"Yes, Elisita, one hundred thousand and everything else he may have hidden away. If we take it without a fuss, we won't leave a trace; they'll say thieves broke in during the night and call the police, there'll be an investigation, and nothing will come of it. The old fart will make it up on the Stock Exchange next week. If you fight it . . . there'll be a commotion, things will get nasty."

"Mario, why? What for?"

"We're wasting time. A deal, a good business deal we're involved in."

At that moment, Lucho turned around brusquely, motioned towards the door, and stood waiting. A car had stopped on the street. There were voices, the sound of a gate opening, and someone, a group, advanced along the garden. Mario put his hand to his waist.

"Careful," said Lucho. "It's the old man and some other people."

Mario moved towards the piano, opened it, and began to play with one finger. The maid went by near him to open the street door. Elisa saw them enter and drew near them. Don Ramón had Don Manuel by the arm and, at a distance behind them, Señora Hortensia

followed with a grieved look. Don Ramón said:
"Elisita, tell Esther to have tea served."
"She's not in, uncle, but I will tell the maid."
"And these young men, eh? These young men will stay to tea?"
"Thank you," said Mario in a docile voice. "We were just leaving. This is Lucho, a friend."

Don Ramón watched from behind half-closed eyes, a sly malice shone in them almost imperceptibly.

"You never come to see us, boy . . . time certainly goes by. But, you don't grow a bit, man. You are going to be a midget."

Mario clenched his teeth and for an instant repaid the mocking look of the old man with a hard and disdainful one; then, he relaxed and smiled also, showing his dimples.

"We are on our way, uncle."

The old man, still well put together, placed himself in front of Mario, towering over him like a mountain, and, unexpectedly, pinched him on the cheeks and burst into laughter.

"Go on, then, but come back another day. Good-bye, young man," he said, without turning around, completely ignoring Lucho.

When Elisa returned to the living room, the two young men had disappeared.

XI

MARIO swore as he walked. The way he insulted Lucho and blamed him for everything revealed the sadism of a spoiled child. Lucho strode along smoking, indifferent to the women who could not take their eyes off him. So as not to lag behind, Mario had to trot now and again which irritated him especially. They took a taxi.

"It will be plan number two, then," said Mario.

"That's fine."

"Do you have the bags ready? Both of them?"

"Yes, I left them at headquarters."

"At headquarters? Are you crazy?"

"It seemed safest. At home my mother would see them and start to butt in. They are quite safe at headquarters. Someone's looking after them."

"Who?"

"Chute!"

"Chute Ladislao? You must be crazy."

"Why do you scream so? Nothing will happen to them. I left

them with him because there was training scheduled for the assault troops this afternoon."

Mario bit his nails and thought: "That failed, but not this caper. Besides, we can go back to uncle's another day . . . another night. And knock the shit out of him. How I'd like to get in through the transom. It would be easy. Cross the hall, go up, enter the second door on the left, and straight to the bed and let him have it real good. The old woman wouldn't even hear at the other end of the hall. As for Elisa . . . well, whether she hears or not doesn't change a thing. But this job is better. Cleaner, surer. The important thing is for that lard-ass Lucho not to get rattled. Let him do exactly what he's supposed to and nothing more. Whenever he adds things of his own he screws up. It's better to scare him. Talk to him about party discipline. Scare him with the Führer. He gets panic-stricken about him."

"You can drop me off at the corner of Alameda and Ahumada," Mario told the driver.

"What's the matter with you?" asked Lucho.

Mario looked at him with contempt.

"I'll stop at the hardware store. I need a few more things. I'll wait for you at the vegetarian restaurant. I'll try to get the usual table. Don't come to the restaurant; go straight to the door of the hotel and wait for me there. Don't go up until I arrive."

Lucho began to stir and cough. He imagined himself alone, loaded down with the bags, facing the hotel employee who would greet him with suspicion; then alone in the room, forgetful of the schedule he was supposed to follow. He flung his cigarette down, stepped on it repeatedly, and took out another one which he lit immediately.

"It's no use getting jumpy. Think about tomorrow's meeting, or better yet, about us before the general staff making our report, and when it reaches the ears of the . . . you-know-who, and he seeks you out and finally acknowledges your worth, and everything, everything that will come later . . ."

Lucho saw himself in his gray uniform, blunt cap over one eye, shining straps, black shiny belt, tight trousers. And he saw González von Marees approaching him between two rows of Nazis, hand on high, and then he felt his embrace and heard a deafening roar go up and the drums start a martial roll.

"You are the one who is afraid," he told Mario, without looking around.

The taxi stopped and Mario jumped out. He walked rapidly and became lost in the crowd. He would not enter the restaurant, or approach Lucho while he was carrying the bags, nor would he go up to the lobby with him. Let the jerk do it all himself. If someone is seen, let it be him; if they remember a face, let it be his, so handsome and so macho. He would join him later when he had rented the room. What could he tell him afterwards? That he had decided not to go in with him so that they would not take them for queers. Something like that. In situations like this all the caution in the world is not enough. Get involved, yes. Had to. It is necessary to help the party, to take chances for the cause, give one's life for National Socialism. But if it can be done without showing one's face, all the better. I'll be more useful this way; I'll last longer; I'll accomplish more. And Lucho? The only ones who can't get the better of him are women. He just eats them up. Does as he likes. Could do even better, but the rummy is in love with Elisa, and she won't look at him. Juan Luis. Mmmmm... He's something else. If he tries anything with me, I'll carve him up. Let him come snooping around headquarters. We'll make mincemeat out of him.

Mario did not enter the restaurant, but stood at the corner lost among the old roués ogling the girls. Huddled near the newsstand, he watched the flow of men and women, buses, bicycles, and the gesturing of a very tall policeman who moved his white-gloved hands like a choir director.

No one entered the hotel. Between the street door and the lobby door lay a shadow that he thought unfriendly. The jewelry store next door was empty. A bald-headed, red-faced man dressed in blue, a great handkerchief in his breast pocket, watched the passersby from the confines of his show windows aglitter with diamonds, watches, and rings. Mario looked at his watch; ten to seven. Entirely too early. Had to kill time. If only Lucho were late. He could call Elisa and threaten to go there at daybreak to hold up the old man. Just for kicks. Or Magda. How long had it been since he had called her? Politics! Damn it, once in, you're hooked; it's an obsession, night and day without hope of escape; it's good-bye girls, gang, school, job, everything. Like dope. But he was happy. He had never known the feeling of absolute superiority that the Party and the Führer, especially, now gave him. Cadets, cops, soldiers, firemen couldn't match it. The thrill he got from his uniform, his cap, his shirt, his German boots, the marching, shooting, switchblades . . . Damn. You had to live it to feel it. It was like hold-ups at dawn, a military parade, Sunday strolls with ecstatic-eyed girls, everything, everything rolled into one single thrill. How beautiful was the Nazi Party! Once, when they attacked a mob whistling at them in front of the Maruri Street headquarters, he had hurled himself upon the people, blackjack swinging; seeing the terror in their eyes, he began to strike to his heart's content. In one second, he had experienced what he had always dreamed of: to grow in the face of the mob, powerful as a giant in a fairy tale, his arm and fists become fabulous weapons that punished without mercy, without rest. He could have killed then and could do so in the future, and what he experienced would be nothing but a glorious euphoria, the joy of a saint. For that was the mysticism of his Party and the patriotic courage that emanated from his Führer, and for that, he would steal, kill, or let himself be killed.

It was still early when Lucho got out of the taxi and set his bags on the sidewalk. Mario saw him from the corner, but did not budge. At a loss, Lucho looked in all directions and even examined the hotel sign. He stood on tiptoe and peered over people and cars. He waited a few seconds, then, making a desperate decision, he picked up the bags and entered the hotel. Mario did not stir. The first step had been taken. Lucho would wait in the room; he was too timid to venture out. He would be unable to think of a single thing. Without Mario, he was lost.

Just before ten, Mario went up the hotel steps. Reaching the empty vestibule, he hugged the wall, and slipped along it without the clerk seeing him. He counted the doors. Fifth from the corner, facing Ahumada Street. He knocked gently. Footsteps approached, the door opened slightly. Lucho stood there.

"Open up, jerk. Hurry, so they won't see me."

He slipped in without a sound. Once inside, he breathed deeply, looked out of the window, removed his coat.

"Why weren't you at the door, you fairy?"

"Don't bug me . . . you hurried too much, arrived much too early. I had to buy a flashlight, call the Party . . . Headquarters. . ." he added conscious of Lucho's suspicions. "But, so what? We're here." He went to the bed and lay down.

"Got a cigarette?"

He lit it and threw the match toward the window.

"The important thing is that we're here. Nothing else to do but wait and scratch our balls. Your specialty."

Lucho paced up and down the room.

"Stop it, don't you see you'll make the floor creak?"

"So what?"

"Go ahead now, if you like, but not a sound after eleven. Curfew. Come. Sit here. Let's go over it step by step, for the last time."

Lucho opened the bags and left them on the floor. Mario stood with his back against the wall, then stepped forward counting his steps. When he reached ten, he stopped, estimated the distance from the window and door, fixed a point, and drew a large circle with a piece of chalk he took out of his pocket. Then, he peered out the window and smiled.

"Exactly. Not an inch more or less. This is the spot. I have spent weeks studying it and making my little sketch from the corner," he pointed with his mouth at the newsstand. "Here's the place for the operation; here below, I'll land a million pesos . . . . We don't even want that much; right, Luchito? Place the tools here. No . . . not those. The saw, files, rope. That's it. Keep the sack until I tell you. Give me the gloves. We're set. Now, there's nothing to do but wait. I'll smoke and wait, kid. Lie down, if you want."

"What time do you have?"

"Calm down. There's time. No work till one-thirty."

"Do you think I could go out?"

"Where to?"

"I don't know. It bugs me, waiting with nothing to do. I want to go out."

"Go. Take the key. Try not to let them see you when you return. Come back before one. If you're late, you're screwed."

Lucho went out, closing the door carefully behind him. Mario lay down again, took off his shoes, turned out the light, and slept. He woke with a start. Minutes, hours later? A deep anguish choked him. He tried to get his bearings, but failed. The horror of believing himself in a void seized him. Where was the door? And the window? The light? Where was he? Then in a flash, he recalled his situation clearly, and the details of the task ahead of him. He did not turn on the light; instead, he lit a match and, as he looked toward the center of the room, a scream almost escaped him. Lucho was watching him from the foot of the bed, balancing a hammer in his right hand.

"What? What time is it?"

"After one," said Lucho without batting an eyelash.

"What are you doing?"

Mario got up and stood beside him, feeling unbearably defenseless. Hiding his uneasiness, he knelt down by the bags and said:

"Let's get on with it. From now on, mouths zipped."

Lucho hesitated for an instant, then took off his coat, threw it on the bed, and knelt down too.

"Plug in the saw. Here, right here. Start. Wait." Mario began to tap softly on the floor along an area a few inches in size. "A beam runs along here; move over a little. That's it. Wait." He tapped again until he heard a muffled sound, sketched a rectangle on the floor, and said, "Now, saw away, Clem. Hurry."

The saw made a terrible din that set their hair on end. Lucho wanted to stop.

"Go on, idiot! Go on! Hurry up, there's no time to lose."

Seeing that Lucho was trembling and ran the risk of breaking the saw, Mario snatched it from him and with awesome precision sawed out the rectangle. Then, he removed the flooring, gathered the shavings and, with a fluttering heart, stuck his head through the opening. It was a moment of horror, for he felt he was exposing his head to all the dangers of the world, that an invisible guillotine would chop it off, or that a power from the beyond, some cold claw, would start to throttle him. Accustomed to the dark, his eyes swept the jewelry store to the farthest corner. The certainty of having been right on the nose, of not having been off even half an inch, restored his confidence. He breathed easily, withdrew his head, and looked at Lucho: his trembling lips made him laugh.

"I don't need my flashlight. It's like shooting fish in a barrel.

Perfect. Secure the rope and help me down."

Lucho tied the rope to the foot of the bed and, holding on to it, handed the other end to Mario, who began to descend slowly. As his foot made contact, he stopped.

"It's fine," he said. "I am going to stand up."

He set one foot down resolutely and a shattering of glass shook him all over. It was like an explosion and the pieces of glass continued to sound as they struck the floor. Lucho was on the point of letting go of the rope, but controlled himself. Mario was choking. From his precarious perch, still hanging, one foot inside the showcase, he glanced towards the shop window and the street beyond. The bar opposite was in darkness and closed. He looked up. Lucho was questioning him with his eyes. A few seconds went by.

"Lower me, you shit; lower me."

Lucho played out the rope and Mario stood up on the showcase.

"Now, hand me the sack, the file, the keys. Hurry."

Suddenly, he felt that something—a hand, an arm, a tentacle—had him around his legs. A cold shiver ran through his body, and he stood there frozen, breathless, mouth agape. A few moments passed. The silence became more and more intense. Slivers of glass kept falling to the floor. In some corner, on some wall, a clock struck.

"If you budge, I'll kill you," said a voice very close to his legs.

Mario realized his number was up, but he detected a note of terror in the voice, too, a quiver, a hesitancy, a clear sign of weakness.

"Get down."

Above, Lucho appeared not to have become aware of his fix. He was pulling up the rope, believing that Mario was gathering the booty.

"Get down," repeated the voice and, suddenly, Mario grasped the sense of what could be his salvation: it was the voice of an old man filled with terror.

"Please don't hurt me," he stammered. "I swear we haven't taken anything . . ."

And he started to get down. The man did not draw away, but did let go of his legs and shone a flashlight in his face. At that moment, Mario, lightening fast, gave him a knee in the face and the man fell backwards. The flashlight, and a bunch of keys rolled on the floor; not so the gun that he held tightly in his hand. Mario pounced on him like a cat and kicked the gun out of his hand. Then raising the file, he let him have it in the face, on the neck, and then plunged it again and again into his throat, his chest. The old man lay doubled up in a pool of blood, on the broken glass. Mario wiped his gloved hands on the old man's clothes, and approached the opening. He looked up.

"Hand me the other file," he murmured.

Lucho complied, trembling. He thought he heard footsteps in the corridor.

"I think someone's coming," he said.

"That's all we need."

They remained motionless.

"Go to the door and check . . . carefully, and come back right away . . . while I pick up things."

Lucho tiptoed up to the door, listened without breathing, opened it a crack and looked out. No one. There was no one. He returned to the opening. Mario, probably busy gathering up things, was not to be seen. He knelt down to wait. Time passed. Each noise below, in the jewelry store, was a sound of alarm. The cops would arrive, seize Mario. But, he would have time to escape. Screw him. For a moment, he wished someone would come, catch him, arrest him. Put an end to that madness. But no one came, nothing happened. And Mario was filling his bag. Finally, he felt a tug on the rope and heard Mario calling him:

"Pull me up, stupid! Pull harder; I can't pull myself up . . . harder, harder still . . . . My foot's hurt. Help me, help me . . . ."

Lucho grabbed him by the armpits and pulled him up like a rag doll. Mario was hanging onto the bag for dear life.

"Do we take the tools?"

"We take nothing . . . wait a minute, take the saw . . . it's worth dough. Put the bag in the other suitcase. Leave the rest, to hell with it. Hand me my shoes. Give me your handkerchief. Damn it all. The old man's had it . . . I am cut, nothing but glass . . . ."

Lucho bent down and bound his foot.

"You are bleeding; I'll have to press hard . . . ."

"Press as hard as you like, but hurry . . . . What time is it?"
"Almost three."
"We should be gone already. And the old man?"
"What old man?"
"I wonder what happened to him . . . . Hurry up!"

He slipped his bleeding foot into the shoe, and, limping, took his things, put on his coat, and dusted himself off.

"You take that suitcase, give me the other one."

"No, I'll carry them both," said Lucho. "You'll barely be able to walk. Who goes out first?"

"You go," said Mario, thinking that he would not be able to run in case of danger. "Go on, don't be afraid, go towards the Alameda without a glance back. Make for the taxi stand. Don't wait on me; if you don't see me following you, take off . . . take off without fear. We'll see each other at headquarters. Get going."

Lucho took the bags and went rapidly down the hall. Mario limped after him. There was no one at the hotel desk; the night man was probably asleep on some sofa in the vestibule. They went down and out into the street. Mario looked about him out of the corner of an eye. Not a soul. Lucho was headed for the Alameda. He was about to follow him when the throbbing of his foot made him stop; bending down to loosen his shoe, he saw that it was soaked in blood. Damn it, he was leaving a trail. How idiotic! As he was tying his shoe, there was a slight noise behind him near the wall, that made him turn around slowly and look carefully. On the steps of a bookstore, hidden in the shadow of a half-open door, like a heap of rags, lay a sleeping woman, a baby clinging to her breast; at her feet was a hairy, shivering little boy who looked at him attentively with his large, dark eyes. What age could he be? The ripe age that without giving a hint understood everything and stored it in those eyes. It upset Mario. The child saw the blood that oozed out of the shoe, stained his sock and pants, saw his trembling hands, then looked up at his eyes and held his gaze unflinchingly. Mario felt the urge to approach and strike him with his blackjack, to shut his eyes with a blow. The mother would not even stir. And he could run off. Lucho was almost at Alameda. The boy was asleep with his eyes open; besides, what could he tell? He put his hand to his pocket, pulled out a wrinkled bank note, and threw it at the little boy, who continued to look with the same wise, cynical, absent expression, and did not move.

When Mario turned onto the Alameda, Lucho was already seated waiting for him in a taxi, the rear door open. He got in with difficulty, dragging his right leg, without looking up.

"Ready," said Lucho. "Corner of Recoleta and Davila."

The taxi sped off and Lucho turned to look at his companion. Mario, very pale, was trembling violently.

"What's the matter?" murmured Lucho.

Mario did not answer; he clenched his teeth, and broke out in a sweat.

"What's the matter?" Lucho asked again.

"The old man," said Mario. "What happened to the old man?"

"What old man? Cut it out!"

"The old man . . . below in the jewelry store . . . ."

"Shut up."

Mario doubled up at that instant, striking the window with his forehead; then, he let out an animal-like snort, and began to spit, crying and moaning. The driver looked in his mirror and his face showed anger and disdain.

"He's just had too much to drink," explained Lucho. "It's O.K."

He put his arm around him and steadied his forehead with his hand. Mario was crying convulsively.

"I didn't want to do anything to him . . ." he repeated, "but the old man surprised me from behind. I had to hit him with . . . I had to . . . ."

"Shut up."

XII

A YEAR, in reality, neither begins nor ends anywhere; nor do the months have any reason to follow one after the other, like the pages of a calendar. Months bear the names of cold, heat, of early buds or of tenacious leaves that refuse to fall off trees, and at times, when they end, they start anew—the same months—because they have forgotten some detail and they move back without measure, so that their movement becomes dizzying and people get confused.

When we begin to understand what a year is, that year slips out of our grasp. And we are left empty-handed. If we have other years to remember, perhaps we will understand and we will give a meaning to what happened with the incomplete simultaneity of a lifetime. And, if we have other lives—like those other years—it could be that, by remembering, we might give a semblance of order to what our nostalgia feeds upon. But that order is going to hurt. People and things had a meaning for us when they made us suffer. Now, we are filled with emotion by the image of what no longer exists, of things and people that belong to us, only because in them we die. We recall what touched us so deeply, because it was the opportunity we had to learn to die. And we did not always learn.

In 1938, we were young and believed that we possessed an individual death, a death that concerned no one, a key to open and close the world; a death that we made up and put off at a distance, an unreal death, in truth. And since some of us were marked for an early one, we went in search of it absurdly. On the other hand, among us moved her real soldiers. They were, for the most part, obscure young men, silent, preoccupied with an idea—that of their sacrifice—that appeared to them clear and that, in certain cases, did not even appear to them. But, they died. Like Fuentes, the one with the lice, or Barreto—shortly before—gunned down by the Nazis as he came out of a dive. A violent end. People lived for a violent death, without knowing its strict timetable.

We were young, I say, and in the history of those years, years of civil wars, of persecutions, of anguished waiting, we saw phantoms abroad who, in some way impelled us to act. All of us loved our tiny fatherland. Each one in his own way. I loved it with some adolescent bitterness. I recalled the patriots of old, the hussars with sideburns who galloped from town to town, slashing the flanks of their horses, bearing the news of a newly-won liberty. I thought about night rides along the alamedas, the horses' hooves lighting the rocks of the river, and of the arm that reached out along the way with the brandy for the dawn eye-opener; I liked to cloak my country in hard riding gear. I thought that I could hear the voices of the bearded, frock-coated and dusty, who ran around the country in horse-carriages, haranguing small provincial groups; I imagined the goose quills that wrote on parchments, thick, violent words born in a mining town to be repeated many times on the benches of some school.

And then, I thought about the enemies of the nation who were manipulating the stock exchange, congress, the university, the armed forces, and who shut the doors of the government palace in the face of the people. Then, we young people used to talk of going elsewhere. Thinking it over, however, we spoke of sweeping out that drove of traitors.

Our hero that year was a dark mustachioed little man infected with the plague, a cigarette butt cupped in his hand, a schoolteacher who spoke with the dusty hoarseness of the southern folks. Don Pedro Aguirre was a hussar, too. In his own way. And he loved his country. Not as we did, but with a worthy love also, with a touch of youthful drunken terrorism. No preambles. Right to the point, at once. We wanted to give our lives for our country. Ahead of our time. We didn't know this. We were to find out later. We wanted to knock our brains in, to etch the image of our country upon the world, to impose it like a small clenched fist that from the south, from the most distant corner of the world, struck at the snout of Fascism. We wanted to go forward with a free country forged out of volcanoes, blue seas, ice, Cordilleras. And, since the old people attacked us, our anguish turned to anger. Hence the blows and the blood.

Juan Luis found himself alone, although not entirely. He needed Elisa, suddenly, and he called her at all hours, and at all hours they said that she was not in. At times, Elisa answered and, recognizing her voice, he would ask her:

"May I speak to Elisa?"

Knowing who was calling, she replied:

"She is not in."

And hang up abruptly. Then, he fell prey to an anguish not in the least romantic. And, together with the loneliness, he felt a confused sensation that time was overflowing his life and gushing like water from a broken dam.

"It's absurd, in a pip-squeak like you," Verdoux used to say to him.

But it had nothing to do with age. The time that was fleeing was not a time fashioned out of years, but out of beings, things, and action. He was going through life sidewise, without touching too much, and without letting himself be touched, either. However, if he considered things carefully, he realized that he was cornered: he was harassed by people who expected a worthy life of him, who denied it to him, and at the same time pushed him into all sorts of traps in order to make him submissive.

He went like a sad runner through a field sown with destructive mines. He wanted to find real persons, to beat against them, to lean on them, to sink or swim with them. And the feeling that somewhere they existed began to impel him towards them.

Besieging the house in the Barrio Alto, he knocked, sent messages, tried to get Mario to intervene, continued to call, even asked the madam. A few weeks passed like that. At a loss, he came gradually to depend more and more on certain people who had learned to love him: on Pepe and Verdoux, and on others he discovered little by little.

"Love," Verdoux said, "is an easy word; say it whenever you can. All at once, you will realize that you have infected others and that you have found what you are searching for."

Juan Luis used to sit before the anthropologist in the green darkness of the villa at Apoquindo and, setting aside the file, talk of Elisa; what he said had little novelty, but Verdoux paid no attention to that, but to what Juan Luis was slowly fashioning around himself: the light of a surprising spring.

"Tell me," said Verdoux, "tell me how you love her, explain why you did not speak to her the other day when you saw her."

Juan Luis' voice was beginning to sound like a lovesick oboe calling through the forest, and Verdoux kept time and lit and snuffed out lights with his large, white hands, brought out glasses filled with rose, green, and yellow liqueurs. Juan Luis talked for hours.

Meanwhile, Pepe sketched. Anywhere he happened to be: in a corner, near a heavily barred window, at the desk, surrounded by solid inkwells or in the patio, at the foot of the white chapel. And angels continued to fly from his sketch pad. However, his angels were becoming more human, not hiding their faces so much, no longer empty-handed, they now carried tools and firearms. Juan Luis began to appear in the leading choirs. The truth is that his angels were turning into revolutionaries, and that the violence of other times was acquiring some sense.

The gatherings of buzzards near Verdoux' pool had disappeared, no one floated nor pantomimed with sabers or feather dusters, the recluses had slipped away. Verdoux received another message: he was joining the revolution. And he had done it as he did things: with motherly passion. At his house, then, there arrived other students, other artists, other men in uniform, as well as professional men, to occupy the places of the barmaids, and talk was harsh voices, and there was action, there was fighting, and persecutions.

Verdoux was jailed one day. It was shameful. Eight agents surrounded the villa and, at a signal, broke into the house, opening and shutting doors, checking desks, night tables, trunks, files; pushing the servants around, leaving a stream of papers and clothes over the floor. Verdoux, livid, standing near the library window, let them do as they liked, as if he knew that at a given moment he could fulminate them with a thunderbolt. But the thunderbolt never came. On the other hand, he was shoved out of the house, put in a patrol car, and taken to be interrogated. In order not to attract attention, they brought him through Los Suspiros Street entrance and, without stopping, locked him up in a commissioner's office. They tried to interrogate him. The commissioner had him locked up with cutthroats and petty thieves. They held him in the interrogation room for several days and afterwards, when he was due to appear in court, when the entire city knew about his imprisonment and the incident was assuming national proportions, Verdoux managed to take advantage of the situation. Unshaven, tieless, without belt or shoelaces, he pronounced a lapidary oration against the government, unable to gesture with his hands since he needed them both to hold up his trousers.

They didn't know what to charge him with, exactly. The Lion persisted in ruling with an iron hand during the last months of his administration. Since more than half of the country opposed him, he raided newspapers and magazines, had congressmen beaten up, professors jailed, and students roughed up. He struck right and left. And that is how Verdoux fell. It was not known if it was because he was a follower of Ibáñez, or a communist, or on account of the ambiguity of his private life. It happened that his imprisonment became a political cause, and "For Verdoux' Freedom" became a battle cry.

Juan Luis started to make speeches and receive beatings. Pepe ran with him through the downtown streets, hurling Molotov cocktails. Along with them, went other runners of great endurance and passion, young, old, women, different in aspect, but equal in a certain secret devotion that lit their faces under the saber blows. So it was that Juan Luis was never alone, although he searched for Elisa in the faces of the students that ran with him, and he would continue to look for her.

When Verdoux was freed, neither Juan Luis nor Pepe interrupted their dashes through the downtown. They moved now on account of their own motives. Slowly, they became estranged from Verdoux. Because Verdoux was running in another direction.

During those months, when the country was split into two bands, when fighting was done with all weapons, and all weapons seemed good, and when bombs burst, knives flashed, and horses were spurred, and the balance was always measured in blood, good people and bad sought their way and did not always understand one another. Elsewhere, playing their last hand were: General Ibáñez, laden with sabers; stuttering Colonel Grove; and Alessandri, sad, hands behind his back, head bowed. All these cards were shuffled by the wind.

"Where are you, Verdoux?" Juan Luis asked. "I know, I know that they beat you at the secret police; I know that you don't like military men, that you love the people; but where, exactly, are the people?"

Verdoux replied without losing his enthusiasm, although with a certain melancholy air:

"By choosing the people, a man of principle, is never wrong; he is where there is poverty and injustice, and dignity to bear suffering."

"But that is found in many places, and many claim it belongs to them exclusively."

"And who told you that place is the only one? Whoever says so is already preparing to split your head."

"You are a partisan of Ibáñez . . . everybody says so."

"Ibáñez? Not at all. But if you think it over, you will see that Ibáñez and Aguirre in this case are names, not individuals. People need a big mask from time to time, a totemic mask that will make them feel as their own, virtues they don't possess. An honest man can give it to them in this age of rascals. Ibáñez . . ."

"Committed atrocities."

"In politics, you have to forget. It's the first rule of the game. Aguirre was Alessandri's Minister when massacres were committed in the *pampa*. Who remembers that? They call Ibáñez a Nazi. A few pimply adolescents who don the brown shirt, because they can't be cadets. At heart, they would like to be jitterbugs. They haven't got a penny. Their grandfathers were church-goers, their parents, members of Mutual Assistance Societies; their children will be ballplayers. I couldn't care less."

So, Verdoux passed, then, to the opposition. His name was mentioned in the manifestoes of a Liberating Alliance, whose candidate was Ibáñez; the villa at Apoquindo once again trained juveniles, inside its walls were heard strange voices that, in reality, were voices of command, and instead of the water fountain, was heard the military heel that climbed and descended stone stairs, walked the empty corridors, looking for the moment to march to the government palace.

Juan Luis did not interrupt his task as archivist at the villa, but another place became his hangout, and with different people: the vestibule of the market run by Pepe's mother on Independence Avenue became the first Secretariat of the Popular Front Party. At the entrance, where formerly hung garlands of tricolored paper, now flashed a cloth sign in red letters; and in the window, where the pig heads garnished with parsley and stained red with chili used to wait their turn, now was displayed a picture in a silver frame of Don Pedro Aguirre haranguing a group of peasants. A platform for speakers had been built and a large table had been set up with a motley display of pamphlets and proclamations. The sale of pork heads continued, although on a lower scale, and its consumption, for the most part, was communal.

Juan Luis began to attend daily, first the assemblies, then the more intimate gatherings, and finally, the council that planned and ran the campaign.

One night, the candidate attended. He came accompanied by a caravan of cars. The whole precinct came to receive him: Maruri bakers, male nurses from Saint Vincent's Hospital, racing fans from the Hipodromo Chile, field workers from Renca and Quilicura, students from the School of Medicine, workers from United Breweries, jobless from Cerro Blanco. There was shouting and singing. However, it was not what was said that was leaving its mark on the precinct. Seated on a narrow bench, lost in the crowd of workers, scarcely able to breathe from the smoke and the acrid smell of sweat, Juan Luis watched with astonishment the strange mutation taking place there, which, perhaps, was also taking place throughout the country, and hopefully would come to be the image everyone sought. The orators were beginning to bury a world, and the shovel, as it began to cut into Chile, also pierced other distant, unknown peoples. Walls came down, windows, doors and roofs flew off.

Someone spoke of the southern miner in his wooden cage descending into the abyss of coal and ocean, and described his dazzled look when he returned in the morning to meet his squalid children and pregnant wife; someone spoke of the life and death of the miners in their salt tombs; and someone else wrote poetry about the cave hollowed out in the hill, the shanty town of boards and tin where Chilean families were gradually handing over their souls like dirty rags.

Faces of men were movable shadows and lights that would reach other nations with the mysterious passing of tiny stars across time.

Juan Luis was smoking, leaning against the wall, a few steps from some children peering from between some grown-ups' legs, when he heard a voice at his side:

"The speeches bored you . . ."

Juan Luis looked up in surprise. It was a thin woman with a delicate face and large, brown eyes. He did not reply. From the hall came the sound of applause and yells, in the street they became confused with the singing of crickets, the creaking of frogs, and the barking of dogs.

"What do you think of the little old man?" asked the woman.

"I like him," replied Juan Luis, withstanding her gaze, and smiling, too. "I am not exactly wild about him, but I like him."

"Of course, the politician shows in him . . . The old guard. I see it also. I think everybody realizes it—the young people, at least. But he's got something. Something of the common people that is pleasing. In Chile a clean-shaven face, a starched collar, an enormous handkerchief in the pocket and a voice on the preachy side, are enough to lose an election. Add to that some connections at the Stock Exchange. An election is lost. On the other hand, take an olive-skinned old man with a whiny voice, fingers and mustache stained with nicotine, sly peasant eyes, some smallpox marks, a wrinkled collar; make him out a Mason-Catholic tending towards socialism, and he'll win hands down. Moreover, this old man is sincere," she added, snuffing out her cigarette and crossing her arms. "Sincere because he doesn't deny what he is. An assemblyman of the old school who suddenly found something resembling his own ideas in the new wave. I think he knows that he is getting in over his head. But, who does not agree about educating the people? And the old man is a teacher. The rest, they could have made up. He is playing the school teacher. Not the university professor, but the public school teacher, followed by his starving, barefoot kids. He suits me. I know his tricks, but he suits me."

From the hall came *vivas* and *down withs,* whistling, and the stomping of feet.

Juan Luis now looked at her more closely. Where had that woman with her mocking, somewhat cynical words, come from? He had never seen her before, not at the university, or at Verdoux', nor at Pepe's. She dazzled him a bit. He waited for her to stop speaking.

"He suits me just fine, too," he observed, "although I take him more seriously. Are you a communist?"

"They are coming out," she said. "We better move out of the way."

Men and women came out stumbling over one another, shouting, pushing to get near Aguirre Cerda who, hat pulled down, cigarette butt in his mouth, was trying to get into his car.

"*Viva!*" "*Abajo!*"

Children and dogs ran, women slipped on the mud in the street and fell laughing and swearing. The light from the small street lamp was insufficient to light up that stretch of the slum agitated by revolutionary oratory. Those were tenement voices being raised there, they would cling to the candidate like cans tied to the car of newlyweds.

Pushed back by the crowd, Juan Luis seized the woman by the waist seeking to protect her with his body. He struggled his way from the crowd and managed to enter the place once more with her.

A short, thick, gray-haired man with a smiling face watched them and asked Juan Luis:

"You are coming with us tonight?"

Juan Luis did not recognize him, thought he had never seen him before.

"Where?" he asked.

"Come," said Pepe, "let's go write on the walls."

"Mural propaganda," explained the other, without taking his eyes off Juan Luis. Behind the metal-rimmed glasses, the eyes had the edge of a knife.

"Let's go," added the woman. "I need exercise."

"And who'll fix the coffee for us later?" asked the gray-haired man.

"You make it, if you like," she answered. "I am going to paint walls."

They went out into the street. The woman walked beside Juan Luis, the gray-haired man behind them accompanied by a tall guy in a long, green overcoat, who limped along carrying a can and a brush.

At that early dawn hour, the street lamps cast an imprecise circle on the street and, from corner to corner, the circles became endless resplendent tracks. Lights and shadows in a fine frost. The limping man would set down his paint can on the ground and the woman painted enormous black letters that gripped the walls of the neighborhood. The paint dripped in thick drops: *Long Live the Popular Front! Down With Reaction! Long Live Aguirre Cerda!*

Suddenly, another group advancing in the opposite direction appeared. They also carried cans and brushes, posters and glue. They were in uniform. In the vague light of the dawn, Juan Luis made out the brown shirts of the Nazis. They were probably armed. How to defend themselves, if attacked? Instinctively, he sought the woman. She had lit a cigarette and stood waiting beside the gray-haired man.

The Nazis advanced at a run and tried to cross out the words on the wall. Behind the brushes appeared the clubs. Juan Luis barely managed to see their faces and, on their caps, the swastika—an undernourished spider—presiding over their swift billy clubs and switchblades. The gray-haired man drew a tremendous chain from under his overcoat, wrapped it around his hand and began to unleash it over the attackers. With each blow, he swept three or four of the enemy who fell bleeding. Clubs flew off, knives tinkled to the shining pavement. The limping man picked those knocked down by his companion on the bounce, and nailed them. Nailed them with precision. Not to kill. Merely to mark them.

A car traveling at great speed arrived at that moment, and from its interior, police jumped, submachine guns at the ready. The two groups, then, broke up and fled in silence. Some Nazis lay on the ground. And, on the walls, the still dripping paint had finally become fused with real blood.

Juan Luis saw his friends again in the house of the gray-haired man. There, Juan Luis learned his name: Elías. The woman, his wife, was called Ximena. He appeared gentler, now, more open and mild; she seemed older, but no less beautiful, in a quiet, dark way.

Elías was a photographer. Naturally, he did nothing else and just managed to exist. The walls, furniture, window frames, even the flower pots on the balcony, took a hallucinatory movement with his compositions: open fields—transparent poplars and distant skies —sea—rocks, clouds, seagulls—or men who walked beside dusty carts, or who raised enormous hammers over endless tracks, fishermen who hurled nets at dawn and pulled them in spattered with swift silvery fish. Here and there, callused hands, bronzed faces, rocks, eyes, peered from a corner.

In this manner, Elías conspired and his sentences emerged like photographic arrangements with a secret, undisturbable balance. However, the woman placed hostile elements in that movement. But, the balance, instead of being lost, became firmer, not on a normal level, but in eccentric dimensions.

"Doesn't it sicken you to have to hit some poor devil you have known all your life?" asked Ximena as she applied disinfectant to his wounds.

"What are you referring to, comrade? The object is to win. Let others choose some poor devil they don't know. Leave the known to me . . ."

"And another thing," she added, "there is a level at which I separate politics from swindle, and that level for me is the commitment we have to humanity, to pure and simple humanity. At that point I understand why some poor wretch like ourselves risks having his head bashed in, we are above that level. We equate death with what motivates us. But, if Ibáñez and the Führer decide to give us their vote, is it necessary to crush them?"

"After the elections," answered Elías.

"Ximena is not thinking of the elections," Juan Luis dared to venture. "Old ones compromise, we fight, and the result is that we are going to be saddled with whatever is elected. Not the old people. We inherit the commitments, or the open road to fashion a new world. Such things are exasperating, it is true. And there are others that are depressing . . ."

Pepe looked into his eyes with that derisive air that made his glasses glitter.

". . . faces that anger, and faces that depress," he said. "I showed them to you some time ago and you have already forgotten them. I shall finish my work after victory."

"That's fine," added the photographer, "because what is at stake is a final act of sacrifice. It has to be like that. Do you think that everything is against us? All right. The enemy is experienced, united, it carries secret weapons, helped by liturgical formulas. They say 'communism' and shipments of shiny guns will appear on Chilean beaches. But, if you examine the matter, you will see that everything can just as easily be in our favor. Because we, like the diver, are coming up for air. We are a large body that stretches the length of Chile. What is it to us to go out into the streets to fight and to die? It is all the same to us. We are always in the street. What about them? Just imagine what it must mean for some bigwig or his well-heeled kids to stick their feet in the stinking cesspools of a tenement. Are you going to tell me that they are in their own element? They should like to go out of a sense of charity, but they go in order to get the votes. People cannot fail to see that they say one thing, but mean another . . . ."

Seated on pillows on the floor, they heard the juicy voice of the photographer and, above the steam of the coffee, they saw coming towards them a light that seemed to rise from the swamps of Centenary Park, from the very heart of the mud, clay, and rock of the Mapocho quarry, lick the adobe walls, climb and wait at the window until the sun rose to swallow it.

". . . Day and night we shall have to go out into the street to move with our people, to fight in a square, in the fields, wherever it may be, keeping the body alive so that it will rise in October and walk with such a determined step that no one can stop it."

"Your speeches are O.K., photographer," thought Juan Luis, "even though they are slightly cracked and corny."

Salvatierra, the lame, pug-nosed plumber, strolled about the room, trying to inject a well-thought out phrase, but as he started to speak, stopped, because his thought came out sad and phony. He was as loyal as a dog, but he inspired no sympathy; he seemed to be made out of leftovers, like a turned, lengthened, and patched coat.

Others arrived: bakers, stonemasons, painters, elementary school teachers, students—men and women. They came at any hour of the day or night. Came in, heated coffee, drank wine, or cooked; read the newspapers, left or took pamphlets. And they talked, talked, talked.

Ximena watched and listened to their opinions, gave them what they asked for, heard confidences, acted as mediator in altercations. In the morning, there were unexpected bodies sleeping on sofas, chairs, the stairs, or simply on the floor. And in his dark room, Elías manipulated developers and film, without worrying about the neighborhood that was slowly growing in the middle of his living room like a stinking mushroom.

Juan Luis spent the first night there and returned, afterwards, at all hours. He sensed that this was the place to organize his revolutionary activism, with men and women enacting a sort of red parable among ghostly bakers and pitch dark nighthawks.

Ximena stirred, but did not tempt him. He had discovered her secret after the night run: Ximena was an unpublished poet. She wrote poetry about civil heroes, somber deaths and resurrections. Listening to her he thought he could detect something oddly sensual in her voice, precisely when she tried to be hard and proletarian. While she recited, the photographer sized her up with his sharp macho expression, crossing his arms as if calling attention to a strength to which, however much she might read and read, Ximena would ultimately surrender.

Juan Luis soon unburdened himself and she listened in surprise.

"If you have left her and don't go in search of her and tell her what you are telling me, how the devil can you think that she'll come back to you? Because you spend your time talking about her? What good is that to her? If you love her so much, why haven't you gone looking for her?"

It had been weeks since Juan Luis had seen Elisa. He thought of her constantly, spoke of her unceasingly, but he had simply not tried to look for her. He felt that Elisa belonged to him, that it had always been so and would continue to be so. And, now, Ximena shook him.

"If she slams the door in your face, you deserve it. More likely than not, she is already running around with someone else."

"It can't be."

"And why can't it be?"

Juan Luis told his story, the rest of it. Ximena listened with a sad air, smiling faintly, playing with the cigarette smoke that enveloped her face. As he talked, Ximena took his hand and caressed it. The child was a new way of loving Elisa, of belonging with her as he never had before. Juan Luis now wanted the child.

Suddenly, Ximena kissed him and, taking his face in her hands, told him:

"At your age it is probably a sin to love like that, but don't change. Go look for that girl tomorrow and tell her what you are telling me now; say it a hundred times. You are going to grow with your child; perhaps it's what you need."

Juan Luis knew one thing for certain: he would go on pasting posters, painting slogans, beating up on the Nazis, fleeing from the cops, and looking for other people in the tenements, factories, schools, workers' communities, for people who were beginning to recognize him, because he came with good news.

But it was Elisa who went in search of Juan Luis. She found him in the empty pool of the School of Education. From the edge, she saw him seated at a table, a cup of coffee in front of him, lost in the headlines of a newspaper. Juan Luis looked up and went to her. Standing below her, in the bottom of the waterless pool, on the black and white mosaic, looking at her, hands stretched out to her, there was something of the dancer or mime about him, as if he expected her to jump in the air and into his arms. Elisa descended the metal ladder and went with him to the table. There was no one in the pool at that hour of the morning. Just they, lost in the thousand facets of the mosaic, lit by a strong green light that spilled down from the glass roof.

Elisa pulled off her gloves, lay her bag on the table and, gazing at him intently, said:

"Juan Luis, something terrible has happened."

He made as if to take her hand and she withdrew it.

"Don't be foolish. I am telling you that something terrible has happened."

"Has something happened to you?" he said in a teary voice.

"To Mario. I think something frightful has happened to him. But I am not sure. Juan Luis," she added. "Listen to what I am going to tell you. Don't say anything. For God's sake."

"Elisa. . ."

"Listen to me. I want you to promise that you will not repeat what I am going to tell you . . . I think that Mario has killed someone."

Elisa lowered her voice; she was whispering now, quite close to him. Juan Luis caressed her hand and put his cheek to hers.

"Some days ago, over a week, he came to my aunt and uncle's and acted very strangely; I had never seen him like that. He was with Lucho. They returned several times. One day, I realized what they wanted. . ." she hesitated for a moment, but then blurted it out, "they wanted to rob Uncle Ramón. Open the safe of his desk, what do I know. The fact is that they didn't dare or couldn't. I realized that they not only wanted to rob, I had the foreboding that nothing was going to stop them, that they could even . . . kill."

"Mario? You are mad. He may be wild, but not to that extent."

"Have you seen the papers the last few days? Have you read about the robbery in a downtown jewelry store?"

"No, I didn't notice . . . well, I did read something. Wasn't the watchman killed?"

"Exactly."

"But they have already caught the criminals. They were two Argentine Mafia types."

"No. They were not caught and they were not Argentine

gangsters."

"How do you know?"

Elisa wrung her hands and in her eyes there was anguish that alarmed Juan Luis. She seemed to have forgotten all about him.

"Mario . . . Mario has some stolen jewels . . ."

"And what does that mean? It does not mean that he committed the crime. He could have bought them. He is such a dope."

"He has not bought them. What could he buy them with? He and Lucho are trying to sell them. Mother found out, because they tried to sell a friend of hers some earrings and, when she didn't want them, they offered rings. Besides. . ."

"Besides what. . ."

"The police are after Mario. They went looking for him at home. They have already talked with Uncle Ramón. It seems that there was a witness. Someone denounced him."

"Idiot," thought Juan Luis, "he had to get mixed up in something like this, trying to act the rich kid and the young Nazi hood."

"The paper has a different account. Look," he told Elisa.

According to *El Mercurio*, the crime had been committed right downtown; the robber had checked into a room in the hotel right over the jewelry store, cut a hole in the floor, and lowered himself to the store below. Details surrounding later events were equally clear. The room clerk insisted he remembered the criminal perfectly. He had checked in around ten o'clock: a corpulent man with a foreign accent, thick horn-rimmed glasses, sixty to sixty-five years old, whose baggage consisted of a single satchel, and who had left the hotel shortly afterwards limping noticeably. The police, going on this description, were searching for an Argentine gunman, accused of similar other crimes, an old-appearing man, but of Herculean strength. The watchman, concluded the article, had been unable to make a statement; when found, thanks to a call by an unidentified citizen, he had already bled profusely and died before reaching the emergency ward.

Newspaper in hand, Juan Luis smiled at Elisa.

"You see? It has nothing to do with Mario. It was an Argentine gunman, a sixty-year-old man! The clerk at the hotel, who saw him, says so himself."

"Nevertheless, they are after Mario."

"It must be for something else, for his Nazi nonsense."

"Mario and Lucho have the jewels . . . Juan Luis, please, help me to find Mario. I have to see him and ask him myself . . . . It would be horrible . . . You don't realize it, but for days I have been nearly out of my mind, thinking about him, imagining him pursued by the police, beaten . . . Juan Luis, help me find him . . . please . . . ."

Elisa was in tears now. From afar, it seemed as if the young girl disappeared beside Juan Luis' dark figure as he followed her towards the metal ladder.

"Don't cry. I know where to find him."

"Can you find him? Really, Juan Luis?"

"Don't worry. You'll see him."

They went to Verdoux's. The anthropologist received them in his bathrobe, seated behind his massive desk. When he saw Elisa, he rose, took her by the hand, and led her gently to a leather sofa near the window facing the patio with the orange trees. Elisa looked at him in surprise. It was not the first time she saw him, but standing there, wrapped in the huge, white Mandarin robe, enveloped by monsters, dragons, and salamanders, bending towards her, he made her uneasy. Juan Luis had come for something specific and was not long in telling him.

"I don't know him," Verdoux answered politely, but rather curtly. "Although so many young men from the Alliance come here, very likely I have seen him and spoken to him. I don't know him by name." He seemed to suspect something unpleasant, for he added: "He hasn't been here during the last few days. You know. Young men forget me, forget my advice, they are only interested in some money they insist I have, and which I don't have. Not a penny, my dear girl."

"Mario is very active in the National Socialist Movement."

"Oh, he is? How the devil should I know him then! There you go trying to link me with that damn Führer. What is the matter with you? Where did you get the idea that I have anything to do with the Nazis?

"I did not say that, Verdoux. But they follow you, pursue you . . . . It is quite possible that you have met Mario."

"Miss, pay no attention to what they say about me. I am a

scientist. The young men are something else again. Not always, not all of them. However, some believe they see a rather brutal truth in what I say and write, and they seek me out. They are not yet tainted by the mangy hypocrisy of their elders and they have broken away from the clutches of their prudish, pious mothers who crush them, believing they can add another blind knot to the umbilical cord. There is good stuff in our young men. They are overflowing with energy, are serious demolishers who beat on one another out of sheer good health, and there isn't a man or woman or anything in this unfortunate country to inspire them. What do grave fools have to offer them? A soccer ball! To a youth burdened with the anguish of all humankind, and who would like to kick the world apart in order to put it back together again with his own hands . . . . A soccer ball! Don't laugh. As if I didn't know them!" He smiled now as he looked out the window, evoking perhaps his pool filled with floaters in the summer. "You give these young men anything and they will tear the country apart . . . . Today with switchblades, tomorrow with machine guns and bombs . . . . Do I know them! We have to save them in order to save ourselves."

"But Mario?"

Verdoux looked at them as if they were Martians, made a gesture of impatience.

"Ah, you come to the point! You are people in a hurry. You are not interested in my ideas. Well," he said, thinking it over, "You know the street where Peña lives?" looking seriously at Juan Luis.

"Yes, certainly. He lives on Bellavista, near the Park."

"Very well. Look for him, ask him, if you like. Or, follow him. That's it," he added laughing. "Follow him like they do in mystery movies. Follow him tonight. There's a meeting. It is possible that your brother will also attend, Miss. You know what these devils are about, don't you?" Possibly he thought Elisa was a Nazi, because he looked at her with open hostility. "That's it, plotting, is what those demolition men of Von Marees are about. Mounting little revolutions with little tin soldiers! Imbeciles. . ."

Juan Luis rose and took Elisa by the arm. Verdoux resumed his initial graciousness and led them to the door, floating in his voluminous kimono.

"Come back, my child, come back to see me and we will talk

of other things, not about insipid politics. Bring her, Juan Luis."

"We'll return, Verdoux."

"Good-bye, children."

Elisa, dumb with astonishment, saw him disappear into his study like a balloon into space.

Mario was seated near the head of the table. The place at the head itself was unoccupied. Unmistakable sign that the Führer had had the intention of attending, but that something of greater moment had kept him from it. Above Mario, shone a sad single-bulb lamp whose shade simulated a bunch of grapes, but in reality resembled a cow's udder multiplied in yellowish teats, ulcerated by time and flies.

Opposite Mario, next to the head of the table, presided retired General Termopilas Cienfuegos. Then, on both sides, came captains, majors, lieutenants, and orderlies of the Nazi battalion Relámpago, Purisima Ward.

"There will be no shouting here, shit!" General Cienfuegos was saying at that moment, directing his good eye, the one that was not crossed, at Lieutenant Armando Bragueta, who had unexpectedly interrupted Mario with excessive violence. "You understand?"

"Yes, my General."

"Continue, then, Mario."

Mario stuck a finger in the collar of his brown shirt, stretching his neck as far as he could.

"The events that preceded our job," said Mario, "were as follows..."

"You have not understood yet, or you have wax in your ears..."

Mario pursed his lips and waited for the explanation of that new interruption.

"We care nothing for the events that preceded your job."

The general blew through his eyetooth, as if trying to rid himself of a piece of meat, and looked indecisively with his crossed eye. His face was like an image reflected in yellowish, putrid water, with skin that was sallow, yet not entirely green; out of a gaunt, not quite gelatinous, forehead—unreal and deformed—protruded his devious, lashless eyes.

"Nothing. You understand? Absolutely nothing. You act as if

you were new here. And you are not new. There's the rub. Our party was not formed so that no-account lard asses can brag by exaggerating their achievements and putting on airs as heroic militants. You just did your duty. Very well. Damn it!" he added pounding the table with his fist and making the furniture and glasses vibrate, "Very well! You anticipated the strategy of the party and on your own initiative, *on your own initiative*," he underscored, "you carried through on something that redounds concretely to the benefit of the movement. Very well! That is the way to do things. Don't spoil things now by dwelling upon the lousy minutiae. What you did, you did alone. You understand me?"

"Yes, my general."

"Completely alone. Don't try to involve us in your filthy maneuverings. The results are what counts! That is the ethics of our movement and that is the mystique, understand me right, the *mystique* of our new soldiers. Continue."

Mario began to feel dizzy. He had not eaten that night and, on the way, Lucho had gotten it into his head to stop in at The Derby for a drink—on an empty stomach. His intestines began to growl. First a long, sibilant sound, then a whirling one like that of an emptying drain, and some dry blows. The general looked at him attentively, shaking his head. It was not the head, really, but the damned crossed eye that wiggled. Besides, from some sideboard in the shadows, perhaps behind him, came the smell of rancid butter. Or perhaps it was the general who had opened his vest.

"Shitty old bastard," thought Mario, "he keeps suet in the sideboard, to feed his wife and son."

At the other end of the table was his son, good Iginio, quite dark, smiling, bespectacled, a little retarded, but in an inoffensive way.

"He has one helluva time with his studies, that's why the old man wants to militarize him. Will he make a fine Nazi!"

And as he thought, Mario slowly gave an accounting of the money he had for the coffers of the party.

"Is that all?" roared the general.

"That is all, sir."

"Sir, my eye! Cut the nonsense. You will have the rest of the money by Friday. You understand? Friday without fail, dammit!"

he struck the table again. "And don't come to me with delays. You work it out. And don't you get caught!" he said, suddenly becoming friendly. "Because if they don't liquidate you, we will. Did you take that down, treasurer?"

"Yes, me general."

"Very well. Now, the following militants may withdraw. . ." He called off the names of the staff and they saluted as they left, tails between their legs. The general scratched his chin and looked all around carefully.

"Now, we are going to discuss something very important, something of *national transcendence*. National! Stand up! Let's take the oath."

They stood up and, at attention, one hand on high, swore the allegiance to the Führer, flag, country, and National Socialism.

"Very well. At . . . ease!"

They sat down once more.

"Iginio!" the boy jumped up as if launched from a pad. "Check to see if all the doors are closed."

The boy moved quickly from one door to another.

"They are all locked, my general."

"Fine. Sit down. Next Sunday," he began in a low, deliberate voice, "our party will celebrate a historic convention. All of Chile will have its eyes on what we do. Young Nazis will come from the entire country, from Arica to Magallanes, young men like yourselves who have sworn to save this country from the pack of international Jews who are raping our treasury, and from the drove of communist bums helping them. It will be the first time that our Führer addresses the whole world to announce that in this corner there has sprung up a new generation of men dedicated to the salvation of humanity by the strength of their faith in discipline, abstinence, patriotism, and desperation! The cowardly fears of the Judeo-Christian myths for others! We accept the role of desperate men and, although we don't have Aryan eagles to impel us through the paths of the Black Forest, on the other hand we have a mythological Araucanian torrent coursing through our veins to inspire us in our sacrifice. *Blut und Boden!* By reason or by force! Our watchword is that of the victors. Never forget, young Nazis! Our forebearers bathed their newborn in the waters of the Bio-Bio.

We will bathe ours in the blood of the speculators and the Bolsheviks."

Mario's intestines gave a twisted growl and, then, a watery rattling signaled a near avalanche. The general observed him with his crossed eye. His outline had grown darker; his dark suit had lost its outline. The general was a shadow and his face a shapeless, flickering light. Only his eyes trembled with a definite purpose. The length of the table, other shadows rested, undecided, and gazed also with lashless eyes, as if searching among the dining room chairs, or near the fly-specked painting of fruit and mints, or perhaps in the half-eaten fish that a cat was dragging on the floor, for an earthly support, for something to hold them up and prevent their being lost in the ceremonial emptiness. The general mouthed on implacably:

". . . the future is ours because the nation understands that its salvation lies in our strength. Our love for our country is a heritage from Portales! He taught us to love it with a hard, pure passion, without the stinking sensuality of the Judeo-Christians. A firm hand! Discipline! Abstinence! We are Portalinos and will recover the time that the hypocrites and the Masons have squandered. To nationalization! More planes, more tanks, for the conquest of Antarctica! Punish Bolivia! New uniforms! National Machitun! Attention! The oath . . ."

The shadows jumped up and with upraised arm, swore allegiance.

"Now," he said, "let's forget theoretical nonsense. Down to brass tacks . . . . Sunday night, the provincial delegations will return, but they will not return, that is, not all will leave. The cream of the Nazi crop will remain in Santiago. It will remain for its baptism of fire. What will that trial by fire be? I cannot say. My lips are sealed by a solemn oath. But I can say what your duty will be. Nazis! Atten . . . shun, stea . . . dy!" the shadows jumped up and raised their arms. Let's take the oath."

After the oath, the general went on:

"Our Führer asks of you the final sacrifice. Are we ready to give our lives for our Führer, for National Socialism, for the freedom of our country?"

"Yes, we are!"

"Our Führer has issued the following order of the day for our battalion: 'The Relámpago Battalion will remain in barracks on war footing, from Sunday, September 4, until further orders.' On war footing! Get it straight! On war footing from Sunday on. That means that no one is going to wiggle out of it for any reason whatever. No nonsense about the Colo Colo team playing on Sunday afternoon, or having tickets for the theater, or having a sick mother, or similar bullshit. No one gets out of it! Each one at his post to carry out his assignment to the death! Understand? To the death!" The general looked at them one by one, focusing on them with his good eye, while the other one danced like a compass needle. "To the death!" he kept repeating, looking first at one, then another, and another. When he came to his son, his mouth twisted into a grimace of disgust, but fixed his gaze upon him for a long while. "To the death," he concluded. Then, he checked the hour on his pocket carillon, and stated solemnly: "Boys, the fray is unequal! Our Führer will lead us to victory . . . ." He fixed his gaze on Iginio then, and with an imperceptible raise of the eyebrows signaled to him. The boy rose without a sound, approached a cabinet, opened it, took out a manual phonograph, adjusted the speaker, and released it as one sets a dog to walking. He had not quite reached his place, when the first trains of "Die Walkurie" rang out.

The march of trombones vibrated, the irate horns howled, and the cymbals crashed in a metallic cascade, while the base, hoarse and digestive, puffed like a tired belly. The general had risen and was singing. He was singing to some blond tresses that had tied him in Austral forests, and to a pair of blue eyes that appeared and disappeared in the Magellian archipelago and, then, swore fealty to his charming commercial gods, swore to chop wood and sharpen the axes to uproot the trunks of the motherland and lay them as an offering on the lap of the Teutonic goddess, who would dance issuing children from between her legs like an erupting volcano. It was a loud and alcoholic ballad, whose refrain always ended with a grunt of virile resonance. The tears ran down the cheeks of the general; huge droplets as from a broken roof that washed his beard and went on to leave a greasy spot below his tie.

At another of his signals, Iginio advanced with a copper dish and placed it at the head of the table. On the dish lay a somewhat dented knife. The general took it in his hands, traced a swastika in the air in front of the Führer's empty place and, immediately, passed it to Mario. He lifted the sleeve of his left arm and, without hesitating, made a small cut in it. Blood appeared. He passed the knife to his neighbor, who repeated the sacrifice. And so it went around the table until it came to the general, who had also bared his arm and was pricking it carefully. But the blood would not flow. He tried again with more violence. The blood did not appear. He bit his lips and made a gesture as if to degut a fish and, from the scratch, a yellowish liquid oozed out.

The Wagnerian beats were at a frenzy of exultation: cymbals, bells, and tambourines, flutes howled, and drums broke; in the tumult, one could almost see the flight of the conductor, tails flapping, tie in a whirlwind, mane lost in the currents of snowy air. Then, the general turned off the lights and each militant took out a candle, and they intoned their Araucanian incantations, repeated Goethe's oration to turtle soup and Nietzche's litany to rebellious mange and, the music over, they rose, linked hands, and went out into the corridor singing martially the "Song of Yungay."

At the river's edge, exposed to the freezing wind that came down from the Cordillera, Juan Luis and Elisa waited for the Nazis to come out. They smoked in silence. There was no one to be seen at that hour, not pedestrians, nor cars; nothing but night, the black, star-studded sky, and the tortured, dry branches of the trees. In the distance, below the Archbishop's Bridge, a bonfire.

"They can't be much longer," said Juan Luis.

And so it was. They came out single file, as if the general's vestibule door were too narrow, or they were seeking the darkness of the alley walls.

"There goes Mario."

Elisa hurried forward and, before crossing the street, she shouted to him. The group of Nazis stopped, appeared to come together. It was all over in a moment and, then, someone howled:

"Squealer! Spy!"

And they jumped Juan Luis like a mad pack of dogs. They swarmed over him before he could defend himself, clubbed him, kicked him in the back, chest, and head; rolled him on the clay ground, and left him spread-eagle and senseless. Then, they fled. Elisa knelt down beside Juan Luis. She tried to call, looked in all directions, and managed to scream,

"Mario."

But there was no one in the street any longer. Not even the echo of her brother's heels. On her knees, Juan Luis' head pressed against her breast, she wanted to call but no sound came out. He was moaning with a muffled rasping sound, drowning in blood. She tried to pick him up and cross the street with him. Juan Luis fell once more and lay legs apart without making a sound.

A shutter opened in one of the windows in the general's house. Someone was watching the scene from there. Some shadow or shadows with sad idiot eyes, smiling perhaps, lashless. Elisa waved with her hand. No answer came from that window. Nobody answered from there, nor from the other side of the river, nor from the neighboring houses. She then sat down on the ground, cradled Juan Luis' head on her lap, and waited. Waited for a long time. From time to time, a gust of wind swept down to shake them, a light mist was slowly dampening her hair and Juan Luis' face; he would open his eyes, gaze at her for a moment, and fall back into a stupor. Dawn was coming. Along the hills of Apoquindo rose a greenish light. The morning air went from hill to hill, stirring birds and trees.

With the dawn came the first carts: men in dark ponchos walking abreast, who looked away, lashed out at their animals, and went on. From the bank of the river below, some children were shouting something unintelligible and dogs were barking. Elisa no longer tried to call. She caressed Juan Luis' forehead and wept in silence. Suddenly, a car stopped. The driver got out and stood watching them open-mouthed. He bent down the better to see and immediately straightened up, looked at Elisa, then at Juan Luis in disbelief.

"This young man is badly wounded," he said. "How is it you have him here? What happened to you?"

Elisa did not answer.

"Miss, let me help you."

A cart driver had also approached and between the two of them picked up Juan Luis and placed him in the car. Elisa gave her home address.

"No," said the driver. "He must be taken to Asistencia Publica or, if you prefer, to Santa María Clinic which is nearby."

Juan Luis opened his eyes, raised his head, and said:
"Tell him to take us to Elias' house."
"What Elías?"
In a firmer voice, Juan Luis gave Elias' address, and closed his eyes once more.
"As you like," said the driver, "but in the state he's in, he's better off going to the emergency than visiting friends."
As always, Elias' door was open. Juan Luis went up leaning on Elisa.
"Don't worry," he said, "they are good friends."
"Who?" asked Elisa, discovering that a man was sleeping on the stairs, and a couple in the living room.
"All of them," answered Juan Luis. "Knock on that door."
She left him in a chair and knocked. Several times she knocked and, finally, the door opened and Ximena appeared in a nightgown, trying to open her eyes.
"Yes?"
"Well . . . there he is," said Elisa pointing at Juan Luis.
Ximena frowned, stepped forward and examined him closely.
"Dear heart," she exclaimed, "And what a job they did! You are Elisa? All Juan Luis does is talk about you. About the two of you." Taking Juan Luis by the chin, she turned his head, and assessed the damage. "Look, my child, we better get Elías out of the bedroom and put Juan Luis in there. He has to be put to bed."
"How can you think of such a thing," said Juan Luis.
"Come this way. Can you walk? Help him. I'll go fix the bed."
Elías appeared, hair disheveled, without his glasses, in an undershirt and pants, barefooted.
"Go to bed."

Funny that there was no foreshadowing of the approaching disaster: I mean, things that generally are subject to man, and adapt to him, do challenge us at times, stubbornly, in order to point out the danger. In some ancient civilization pots and spoons rebelled once in order to strike men in the face, expressing thus the ire of the gods at men's astuteness, hypocrisy, and cruelty. We should have been similarly warned by rifles and pistols, knives and clubs.

The retired general, who trained his monkeys in suicidal practices, must have been warned by his own misery, or by his wife's anguish. His young commanders knew what was coming: Pérez, the pink giant, commercial entomologist, curly-haired, large of foot and strong of arm, already bore crossed carbines on the nape of his neck; Parada, gloved gallant of the black hat and punishing smile, carried the image of his fatherland, like a bleeding Sacred Heart of Jesus, over his own bleeding heart; Huerta, the veteran panty-raider, savage seminarian, was already between two bayonets, tongueless and eyeless, a bayonet in the belly at twenty.

Everything remained the same: the Cordillera was snowcapped, the poplars dry, the chimneys smoking, the tenements freezing, the bells pealing, the city breathing an invisible gas. All the same: the country sober and democratic, the middle class patching its pants. Nothing seemed to announce that death was besieging the government palace and sniffing around the Social Security Building.

Death was on its way to take out an insurance policy. And we screamed, launched a proclamation, not knowing that death was astutely signing policies in our own names.

It was strange that trains should reach Santiago laden with young men from the provinces and that some of these young men should remain to dig their own graves.

It was strange, because it was already September and in the flowering trees, as in ourselves, a familiar breath was blowing, and they and we burgeoned with buds. The tiny homeland was stirring, and it was a temptation to move along with it.

The day passed. People came and went. Somebody read the paper, somebody else left behind a stack of fliers, another mentioned the assembly, and still another counted the casualties. Juan Luis, in shorts, on his back, took up all of the bed of comrade Elías. At his side, Elisa rubbed his back, his ribs. It had been her first night out. The things Aunt Esther must be saying! It made no difference; nothing that she said could explain anything.

"Only the nighthawk knows what he does with his night," said Ximena upon hearing her misgivings; "the rest will always say that he spent it in carousing."

The whole day went by in the same way. Then, Juan Luis, aching and bruised, but not sick, without mentioning Mario any longer, began to talk of the coming days, trying to make Elisa understand this new thing that he saw coming. It encompassed them all: the unborn child, them, the photographer and his wife, Pepe, Verdoux, the young terrorists, the anonymous people of the neighborhood in whose faces were mirrored thousands of other faces, all of them necessary.

"Ximena, this country is waking up," he said as she entered carrying a glass of *pisco* that she put to Juan Luis' lips, "like a monster and begins to rid itself of the debris that has always covered it, shakes its tail; the parasites are beginning to drop to the swamp, the monster is about to open its jaws . . ."

Ximena observed how Elisa's sweater had gathered above her waist, how her legs touched Juan Luis' bare legs.

". . . no vermin will survive."

"A few hours, just a few hours. How little it costs! And how difficult to begin. You will never convince people with words, no matter how long you talk or what you say. Perhaps in time you will convince them. I mean, with some heroic acts."

"A few hours . . . a few hours are enough," repeated Elías from the door. "You are not aware of the great truth you have uttered. A few hours! Stop the damned bribery that is going on, the money that we cannot lock up. . . . Stop it for a few hours. You have stated a great truth, boy. A few hours are enough for us."

Ximena approached the door and took the photographer by the arm.

"You talk too much," she said, "action is what we need. Rest, don't worry about a thing, we'll shut the door."

And they left. Through the little bedroom window, the afternoon brilliance scarcely reached them. Elisa undressed calmly, lay her clothes on a wicker chair, made her way to the bed and, careful not to hurt him, lay at his side and allowed herself to be embraced.

The limpid, blue sky looked down like a distant eye upon the sleeping city. Moist air pressed against the buildings and clung to the men and women who came out of the offices and let their bodies fall like bales into the chairs of the neighborhood restaurants. The bells of La Merced struck twelve. Suddenly, the spring midday burst like a crystal goblet.

A caravan of automobiles descended at great speed from the Alameda and came to a skidding stop in front of the Social Security Building. The occupants got out in groups, approached the grilled door which was already closed, and began to force it open. The traffic policeman came to investigate. One of the boys drew his gun and emptied it point blank into the man's chest. The man bent in two like a puppet and dropped to the sidewalk. He lay there bleeding, dying. They entered the building, stopped for a moment in the lobby, and waited for a group of men and women to come down the stairs.

"Against the wall!" ordered a tall, blond boy with thick-lensed glasses.

The employees, smiles slowly fading, complied open-mouthed.

"Turn around, and up the stairs, you shits," came the order again.

They had to retrace their steps and climb the stairs with the guns at their backs. Others were herded along with them; all walked in silence, still without panic.

"It's a mistake. . ." someone started to say.

"Shut up!"

"Why, I don't even work here."

"Shut up or I'll blast you! All of you, up!"

They reached the seventh floor and were crowded into an office that faced the interior of the building.

"If you stay here quietly and don't try any funny business, nothing will happen to you. If one of you tries to skip. . ." The blond boy waved the barrel of his gun. "You understand. Not a peep."

He closed the door and led the rest of his men along the corridor at a run.

"From there," he pointed, "from that office and that other one. Quick! The barricade. Bring out all that furniture. Throw up the barricade."

They began to drag out chairs, tables, desks, bookcases, and pile them up on the landing until a solid barrier was formed. They then deployed along the corridor. One group stationed itself on one side at an angle, commanding the barricade and taking advantage of the curve of the stairs; another group took up positions the length of the walls, and another remained by the office windows facing the street; the rest climbed to the upper floors.

"Hello, hello . . . hello, hello . . . Relámpago to Huascar . . . Hello, hello," static thundered from the radio, "Relámpago to Huascar . . . Hello . . . *Blut und Boden* . . . Come in, I read you loud and clear, come in, Huascar . . . yes, first objective taken . . . little resistance . . . some clown dead . . . come in, Huascar."

"Huascar to Relámpago . . . second objective complete success . . . There's fighting at the university . . . hold your ground, reinforcements on the way . . . one regiment has joined us . . . Possible action at the school . . . third objective has not fallen yet . . . hello, hello . . . Huascar calling . . . come in, Relámpago . . . *Blut und Boden* . . . come in . . . ."

And the wait began.

Mario pressed his cheek against the butt of his carbine and kept its sights on the door of the presidential palace. He didn't know who his target was. The president? He laughed. Lucho watched him from his position near the other window of the office and frowned questioningly.

"Nothing," said Mario in a very calm voice. "I was wondering what if the president came out the door of the palace."

Lucho appeared not to understand or hear him; he bent over the sill of his window and tried to look down. He was unable to see anything. But he did think he could make out something like a blanket of fog, something like a meadow filled with wild flowers, or a stream of running water.

"What are those bums waiting for? Why don't they come to try to get us out?"

"Listen," said Mario.

"What's up?"

"What's that?"

Lucho, pale, squinting his eyes, drew back. "It's the sun," he told himself. "It's the sun that makes the street move. Because there's no one down there. There's no one yet."

And he looked again. And he had the same sensation: the fog, not so thick now, the grass, the flowers, the water, and he recalled a summer afternoon on the slopes of San Cristóbal hill. A hike with Mario, Elisa, and other girls and boys. And he, seated on a rock looking towards the city of Santiago, chewing on a twig, made drowsy by the sound of the water, and the hum of the dragonflies and the bees and the crickets. And suddenly, Elisa passed near him wearing a very light dress, scarcely more than a halter, her back bare, her armpits moist, and that smell of her, and the nape of her neck wet under the brown bow, and she went by quite near and he was touched deep, deep down, and he followed her with his eyes telling her how much he loved her and how he would have taken her in his arms, and . . . .

"Hello, hello . . . Relámpago to Huascar . . . come in . . . ."

" . . . young patriots, by defending the national flag, when the armies of liberty make ready their weapons, and the people . . . ."

"Hello, hello . . . they're fading . . . we have lost them . . . ."

" . . . not a single traitor will be spared, not a single . . . ."

"We have lost them."

Just then, a shot rang out in the street and then another, and a bullet splintered the window where Lucho was sighting. Glass flew in all directions. Everybody hit the floor. Mario peered out.

"Listen, Lucho . . . Lucho"

Glass continued to rain down and, above the tinkling, could be heard something like air escaping, something like a fan that has been turned off and is slowing down.

"Lucho . . . Lucho"

Mario raised his head a bit more, then stretched himself out full length, and managed to see him. Lucho was on the floor, his face resting on the window sill. The left cheekbone had a hole the size of a fist, and in that hole could be seen the splinters of the face bones, and in between the splinters thick, almost black blood that had spilled out and was oozing down over his mouth towards his chest.

Mario let out a hoarse cry and retreated until his back hit the wall. From there, eyes closed, trembling, he began to moan, pointing at Lucho with a finger. The others turned towards him, but they didn't understand at first.

"Hello, hello . . . ."

"Forget it."

Pérez, solid, ruddy-faced, adjusted his glasses and crawled in the direction of Lucho. He reached the window and tried to take one of his arms. Lucho's body pitched headlong and lay there, bent double, face on the floor, rear end on high, his feet twisted grotesquely.

Not a sound below.

Nothing but a jungle-like silence, the silence of shadows setting in, of leaves, of wind, of the soft sniffing of animals.

Pérez was sweating and did not look up from the floor, but he heard Mario still moaning with his eyes closed, and went to him. He took his face in both his hands and tried to calm him. Mario did not answer. He put his cheek next to his and whispered to him. Mario was crying now. And suddenly, a frantic dash was heard below as of horses galloping, and the sound of sabers and shouts and voices barking orders, and of concentrated fire, again and again, and then the clatter of the machine guns.

They began to fire from the floor towards the stairs. But from the streets came another volley and the window next to Mario shattered, and the bullets were criss-crossing now, making the ceiling plaster fly, drilling holes in the walls, and smashing the lamps to pieces. Below, the firing grew in intensity and the machine guns were heard closer and closer.

Mario was firing mechanically, without aiming any more. The butt of his carbine punished his cheek and shoulder, but he felt no pain, only a vast burn that extended from his throat to his chest and left a void there. On the other side of the barricade there was something undefined, a danger that was not of men, but of shadows impossible to name or understand, that grew by deploying, and stopped for an instant to exchange obscene remarks, curses directed not at him, not personally, but in a vague and sinister way, shadows that came from his childhood, from a bronze bed where his mother slept alone and in which, at times she screamed or cried, or from a night table whose shadow, projected by the indirect light of an oil lamp, grew on the wall and ceiling. Mario fired blindly, feeling his eyes grow red from the smoke of his carbine.

He felt that nothing was going to happen to him. At most, a

beating at interrogation. That is . . . if they were defeated and taken prisoner. The possibility of the beating chilled his stomach. Maybe they wouldn't even beat them. Hold them for a week, two, perhaps a month and, afterwards, exile them. That's at the very worst. Exiled to the south, near the ranch of a former political crony of his father.

But Lucho. His death was like an accident. It had nothing to do with the putsch. Who told him to stick his head out the window anyway? You have to be real stupid. He looked at his wristwatch. After one. Just. The cops were firing from the sixth floor. Some trick! They had left them a way out. They'd never think of defending the entire building.

"Listen . . . the radio's not working."

"Find another channel. We mustn't lose contact."

The voice was drowned out by a new volley of shots that resounded in the corridor.

"Dammit! They are getting too close. Iginio! Listen!"

Iginio looked up again from the floor behind the door, a smile on his sad face, his much too white teeth showing.

"Get as close as you can to the corridor; be careful; see if they're already on the stairs. Watch out!"

Iginio smiled again and without a word crawled off using his elbows and knees, as his father had taught him. He stopped on the threshold of the door and his head seemed to flatten out and blend with the floor, like a lizard's. A bullet whistled over him and sank into the rear wall. He retreated.

"They're not on the stairs," he said.

"They're firing from below. They don't dare come up. They're chicken . . . ."

There was absolute silence.

"The important thing is to hold out for a couple of hours longer, and then go out when the army . . . ."

"Or not go out."

"It's all the same. We've done our part. Now it's the Führer's turn."

"It's enough for a regiment to follow him . . . . Join him: that's enough."

He didn't quite get these words out when a cannon resounded in the distance. It seemed to come from the center of town, perhaps from the other side of the palace. They exchanged a look of surprise and then someone shouted jubilantly.

A second cannon shot followed. Then silence.

"That cannon sounds near . . . very near."

In the Alameda the second cannon shot sent the gates of the university flying. The police, hugging the wall, entered at a run and took the building. They formed the students in two files and marched them off, arms on high, through the Alameda. There, a command sent them towards the north side of the palace. At the side door, General Arriagada, armed with a carbine—leaning backwards, belly sticking out—shouted in his frog voice as they went by:

"Have them all taken up and let no one come down!"

Later, he gave another order to a messenger: "Tell Commander González that I say crap on him and to step up the action . . . . Tell him not to embarrass me and that at five o'clock I'm going to have the artillery open fire and they'll all be killed."

The group of those who had surrendered continued to march along the middle of the street. People watching from behind the police cordons looked at them in wonder as if they had stepped out of the pages of a history book into the streets of a different era. The students didn't respond to the taunts, but they trembled as they approached the Social Security Building.

At three in the afternoon a voice rang out from below, quite near:

"It's me, Yuric; hold your fire."

"Peer out, Iginio . . . . Be careful, see if it's true."

Iginio stretched out like a lizard again and slid off on his belly.

"It's Yuric," he said.

"Let him come up."

"Don't let him come up, it's a trick!"

But Yuric was already up and made his way through the furniture of the barricade.

"I believe we've won," said Iginio.

"It's a trick. Don't let him come up!"

Yuric entered the room; tall and blond-headed, he looked about desperately; his coat was open and his shirt collar unbuttoned.

"We're screwed . . . " he said. "Pérez . . . we're screwed, there's no way out of it."

Pérez was in front of him, gazing at him with his ironic expression, spanning him with his broad shoulders.

"Believe me. We're lost. The cops took over the university with their artillery.... We had six casualties, Pérez, they're down below ... the dead ... There's no military revolt. They have all backed down. Ibáñez surrendered. They are holding him ... I tell you we've lost. Where are the rest?"

"Upstairs. We have enough ammunition to hold out all afternoon."

"All afternoon? Then what?"

"Someone's coming."

They all hit the floor. Up the stairs, shoving tables and chairs, came a dark, pop-eyed youth; his mouth was open and he seemed to be choking.

"It's Cuello."

"What's the matter?"

"They give us five more minutes ... they're going to flush us out with bombs ...."

"Get in here. Cut the horseshit. Wake up!"

Cuello shook all over and hung on to Peréz' chest.

"They're going to kill us ... " he said.

"What'll we do, Parada?"

"What'll we do? Surrender. These bastards have already given up. It's all over."

"And the Führer?"

No one answered.

"Try to get through on the radio again."

Pérez stood there looking out the window. Above the Carrera Hotel the sky stretched out cloudless, like a distant blue flag. Fancy flower pots were beginning to appear on the hotel terrace in anticipation of the season. The city was quiet. Some stores were closed, the employees watching, hiding behind the doors of restaurants. But the city would continue to seem strange to them. People would see them go by like the other prisoners, rifle barrels at their backs, and no one would say anything. They'd talk about it later at dinner, and belch. A bunch of punks trying to take over. Who'd want to get involved? Who wants to get involved when the country is reeling? Who speaks out? Would someone speak out as they went by, arms on high, along the streets?

"What guarantees?"

"We could slip in among the employees."

For the first time that afternoon, Mario felt the strange certainty that he'd get out of it alive and return home to closet himself with his football magazines, and that he'd seek out Elisa and Juan Luis to tell them about the jewel robbery and that they'd help him, saying Lucho was to blame. What would he care now? And he'd return what he hadn't sold yet, and turn in his Nazi uniform, and convince Iginio that his father was an s.o.b., and then they'd go back to the Forestal gang, back to the same girls with the light dresses and shining eyes, back to the beaches, back to the summer. He was safe, thank God.

"We must surrender."

"Go, Iginio, and tell those upstairs to come down, all of them, and no firing. We'll take Lucho with us. Four of us can carry him."

They went down to the sixth floor where the shapeless mass, like a dark snake, writhing in the corners, invisible, had been lying in wait for them. Mario walked next to Iginio, behind Pérez and Parada. He looked down the bend of the stairs between floors, saw the officers, submachine guns in hand. They had removed their belts and unbuttoned their coats. A fat man in civilian clothes, hat over his eyes, also had his revolver trained on them.

"Halt!" shouted an officer. "Herd them in there! Tighter."

Mario felt the warmth of Iginio's body pressing against him, looked at him, saw the smile on his face, showing his great white teeth; saw how Pérez gained stature and how he did not lose his disdainful manner. He felt himself shoved from behind by his companions, felt a tremor of panic coming from the bottom of the stairs. An overwhelming anguish convulsed his chest and rose in a wave to his throat. He tried to say something, call someone, look for help; he looked in confusion around him, saw only cheekbones, eyebrows, pistols, cartridge belts. He prayed hurriedly. "Most holy Virgin, help me . . . do not forsake me . . . ." The first volley rang out. He felt a blow. He felt a blow as from a rock in his belly, let out a scream, and his mouth filled with blood, and another blow and another scream, and he sank suddenly into a red wave and fell on his back beating the air.

A new gust of bullets shook the entire group. And they fell on top of one another. A few moans were heard.

"Come boys, let's put an end to this!"

An officer bent down over the bodies and began to shoot them methodically in the head.

The second group of prisoners was making its way down the stairs. Another officer stepped in front of them.

"Come on down! Step over them, dammit . . . " he shouted when he saw them hesitate before the pile of bodies on the floor.

"Come down, you bastards! Aren't you s.o.b.s fond of revolutions?"

They finished them off where they fell. Then, from the rear came the shapeless mass of cops, searching among the bodies, striking the dying with their gun butts, lifting watches, rings, and wallets, moving around like green rats, let loose in a bloody Indian raid.

"*Blut und Boden.*" The signal reached us a bit faintly because, on the way, the wires got covered with blood, and instead of a martial voice, we heard a scream, and the steps we were waiting for suddenly turned out to be the click of a policeman's heel on the bloody tile of the morgue, and later, the slow and muffled brushing of sandals pushing sawdust to erase the traces of viscera on the floor.

And who is to blame? September is a patriotic month for us, and families go out to Cousiño Park looking for the shade of the tired eucalyptus, lay out their tablecloths on the grass, take out their guitars, eat and drink. A down-and-outer, seated on the criminal's bench, with the cold of the cell in his creaky joints, passes his hand over his eyes and thinks that there is a certain contradiction between the galloping of the lancers, the roar of planes, the vibration of the tanks, and the jug of fresh chicha that the president will start drinking late that afternoon. The country demands sacrifices: there is a hierarchy that must be respected—a sad fact, at times, but inevitable—and for the country to be liberated, a student or a worker must fall, and a soldier will have to raise a saber over history,

However, the Führer has stood up to contradict him. The Führer has put on his brown shirt, newly pressed, has put away his speeches in his briefcase and has gone to say good-bye to his mistress, has drunk a glass of aguardiente with a steady hand and a determined gesture: 'To the hero's death!' 'To the hero's triumph!' Then, he has dashed off frantically to hide in the farms of Quilicura. There, resting against the trunk of a willow, earphones on his ears, he has turned toward the West and has enunciated his order of the day: 'To save a people from wretchedness, blood.' And the sky of the tiny country, not accustomed to human bonfires, answered him at once. Entirely too soon. Through the groves of Quilicura a flock of ducks let him have a volley of dung and the Führer, standing, arrogant, illuminated, received the white paste, soft, still warm and steaming, on his head. What to do? A bullet, a bullet in the temple. But times have changed. Climb a stage to die? Such stages no longer exist. Now people die in the savings and loan associations, in classrooms, in tenements, and we can't die one at a time, we have to die many at a time. Don't you see that it is necessary to affix a label to the vest of each of those massacred? Why, do you think? Well, because the world has grown a great deal and our dead, consequently, need their identification tag. So we make a mistake? Everyone has the right to make a mistake. I don't say this irreverently. Understand me. But it's all over.

Night has fallen in the Social Security Building. No one lies dying in the corridors, and the elevators are stopped. From time to time, a chair or a piece of glass still falls somewhere and the echo resounds through the passageways, seeks out the empty voices and goes out into the cold air. Time has welled up slowly in the bends of the stairs and a growing bloodstain drips and drips from one step to another, interminably. There is no order among the dead. In spite of the silence. They have gone to lie everywhere, in grotesque postures, between the second and seventh floors: some astride others as if they wanted to flee in a desperate gallop. But there is also a soft walking of bare feet over thick blood. Through the empty floors, along the corridors in darkness, through the cold offices, wander lieutenants and second lieutenants, their coats stained, their hands trembling, without daring to call out to one another, looking for a machine gun that has opened fire by itself and that will never stop, a machine gun that fires up and down, and from side to side, that fires through the open windows towards the starry night, from one end of the country to the other. Cammas, Angellini, Rojas, Ochoa, Quezada, stopping the bullets with their hands, refusing to leave the building, neither at midnight nor at dawn, caught forever in a certain trap for young dead.

In Forestal Park, next to a tower of a gothic castle, where there was nothing but garden tools, we used to lean our bicycles against the trees, look for the darkness of a grotto and, behind the lagoon, the boats, and the ice-cream vendors with their wheels of fortune, we used to kiss without knowing each other. A smell of high school boys and girls prevailed, a good smell that at times came from gymnasiums, from pools, or from classrooms, books, chalk, pencils, and at times from churches, from confessionals, or candy and, at times from intimate things that we all used to hug, a bit feverish, somewhat drunk, adolescents with many strange things in our faces and big circles under our eyes. We used go out to the sunset and hurl ourselves like a flock of angels on bicycles, our faces to the wind, laughing, and shouting. And, so, like a lightning flash, the dead from the Social Security Building keep going by on bicycles, their coats flying. And that is the image that keeps circling around the park. Not that of Alessandri, standing next to the Mapocho River, cane in hand, his gigantic dog at his side, surrounded by secret police, in front of the truckload of Nazis that shout insults at him and flee, afterwards, in terror. No; the other one.

It is true they lay on their backs on the morgue floor, bleeding, shot up. Nevertheless, the trees I know have not changed greatly, they are the same, and I know that the siren of the Purisima barracks is also the same, and the hill and the statue of the Virgin are the same, and the smoke from the factories of Bella Vista has not ceased to climb up and cannot be anything but the same one. Things, then, will endure. And the bicycles that descend by themselves, at great speed, toward General Baquedano, are exactly the same and we know the wheel of fortune of the ice-cream vendors that goes round, and round, and round, and also the bodiless hand that turns it and waits, turns it and waits.

XIII

How eloquent everybody was at the time! Pradenas talked here, Schnake talked there. In congress, radical González Videla hurled inkwells, and the conservatives hurled them back. The government closed *La Opinión* and *Topaze*, went on kicking congressmen, students, and workers in the behind. Along the downtown streets, paddy wagons came and went spitting bullets, letting loose their shock troops that clubbed and sabered the streets clean. Groups of desperate people gathered at corners, raised a flag, listened to a speech, threw leaflets in the air, broke a few windows, and fled pursued by the mounted police. Important politicians, labor and student leaders disappeared, and reappeared drowned in northern beaches, imprisoned in some village of Aysen, or dumped into some alley near General Mackenna Street, with Palma's brand on their behinds.

Verdoux accompanied Juan Luis and Pepe to identify Mario's body at the Morgue. Dressed in black—black suit and overcoat that looked as if they had been rescued from some magician's trunk—he insulted the government in front of the doctors and the curious onlookers. He had a photographer come in and take pictures of certain wounds suspiciously like bayonet thrusts and atrocities. Afterwards, he left flanked by the two young men who had remained silent.

"The revolt of these children," said Verdoux, "has not been a people's revolt. For the people, it had the earmarks of everything that happens downtown, that is, in a world apart, foreign, incomprehensible. People only go downtown for Easter and New Year's, and maybe for some parade or procession; and they always feel like fish out of water. I don't mean that they can't shout and even fight downtown. They do it, but they return to their neighborhood. For many people, the Nazi putsch was a caper by 'dudes'," Verdoux was smiling. "Not the consequences, naturally," he added, becoming serious once more. "After all is said and done, a revolution such as this is a bloody event, food for the yellow press, and we all know how a crime unites the population, be it the murder of a taxi driver, of an old widow, or of a group of students. Our people pass from the terrified but avid, considerations of the murder, to a superstitious devotion and the decision to do what the victim did not do, and to do him justice by lighting candles for him. And that, my children, that impulse is what brings about true revolutions. They start with a body, some candles at Morandé and Moneda Streets, then some paper flowers, a picture, and another picture, and many more; then will come some crutches, wooden feet, rubber hands, glass eyes; then, money, and since there will be no room for a grotto, they will continue across the street."

Juan Luis was a bit ashamed of his friend's histrionics. How could Verdoux talk like that about everything, turning the tragedy into another folkloric chapter for his monographs? Had the revolt been "an affair for dudes?" Among the sixty-one Nazis murdered there were three mechanics, a stonemason, a barber, an electrician, a plumber, a draftsman, two chauffeurs, a machinist, a bread delivery man, several workmen without a trade, twenty-seven government employees, a newspaperman, sixteen students, and a lawyer. People were not asking for vengeance for those deaths, and would go their way without a second look, in search of something that would take up more room in the country than those bodies.

But he was not going to argue now. Sometime, perhaps, but

not now.

"Do you want us to go up with you?" asked Verdoux.

Juan Luis imagined what the interview between Verdoux and Doña Raquel would be like. Good heavens, no! Under no circumstances.

"Thanks, Verdoux. I prefer to go up alone. I'd like to talk with Elisa alone."

"Did Elisa return?" asked Pepe.

"She returned Monday, the same day of . . ."he did not know what to say: the revolt? Mario's death? of Mario's and Lucho's deaths?

"Oh! That's all right."

"Look, Pepe, wait for me at Elias' tonight; if she feels up to it, I'll go with her."

They left and he went up.

Señora Raquel, in black, had installed herself in the reception room, and was weeping there, surrounded by friends and relatives. In that diurnal darkness, the curtains drawn, she created a sort of frenzy in which sobs mingled with prayers, prophesies, oaths, and swearing. And since the others also were in black and carried rosaries, and were of like ages, and heads were similarly gray, and since they gesticulated, and comforted one another at the same time, it could have been said that, in that room, death wandered through mirrors without finding the exit.

Juan Luis stood in front of Señora Raquel and she interrogated him in a hard voice without removing her handkerchief from her eyes:

"Did you see him?"

"Yes. M'am."

She let out a howl and seemed to go into convulsions. "He looked very well," said Juan Luis, and the others looked at him with murderous eyes, "he looked as if. . ." he was about to say as if asleep, and he felt like screaming, too, "as if. . ."

"What did you say, young man?" asked a gentleman wearing a pince-nez, in a very teary voice.

"He is the young man who went to identify Mario's body," explained an old lady. "Aren't you the son of Hortensia and Manuel Acuña?"

"I think," said Juan Luis, and Señora Raquel came out of her convulsions and fixed tear-red eyes upon him, "that he died instantly. It must have been a single bullet in the heart, because there are no other wounds. Nothing."

"God in his mysterious ways must have allowed him to die without suffering."

"He probably knew nothing. He says that it was instantaneous, that it was a single . . . ."

"God wanted it that way."

"He has taken him in his wisdom, he has died a good Christian death."

"He must not have realized it, Raquelita; those things happen so rapidly."

Juan Luis withdrew, walking backwards; he felt for the door knob and disappeared. Tiptoeing along the glassed-in hall to the room of Elisa and the grandmother, he felt he had already lived that moment, it did not matter when—months, years, days before—or whether it had been some winter dawn or spring morning, and that in that bedroom Don Carlos still floated in his short nightshirt, emaciated, bearded, throat slit, surrounded by large pillows, and that he was going to peer into the other bedroom and Elisa was going to wink at him from the bed, while the grandmother slept, and that he would enter seeking a certain explanation for his wandering through the house of the dead. But as he opened the door, the vision changed. Elisa, in black, her hair tied in a bow at the nape of her neck, awaited him at the window, the pale September sun in her face, and the grandmother, all dressed up, was reading in a wicker sofa, swinging her feet.

He entered, passed near the grandmother, who didn't notice him, and approached Elisa. He took her hands, and said:

"They riddled them with bullets and knifed him. They had him on the floor, head way back, mouth open, eyes to the ceiling. Lucho's face was ripped by an explosion. They put a card with his name on Mario's coat to identify him. They will bring him in a box tonight for the wake. Everything is arranged." And then he could not stand her gaze and bowed his head, let go of her hands, and began to cry in a tired way, with the hoarse sobs of a man, not those of a boy any longer. Elisa embraced him, kissed his tears, and led him to the bed where they sat down.

The grandmother seemed to be reading the same page eternally. She slept with her eyes open, swinging her feet, perhaps she listened.

"Juan Luis," said Elisa, "don't cry. What you saw has nothing to do with him. Don't cry."

Juan Luis dried his tears and looked attentively at the light coming in the window. He played for a bit with her bracelet, doing and undoing the clasp, and in the bit of blue that he saw through the window, he made out clearly the vision that he could not or would not be able to explain to Elisa, ever. He had lived with a bleeding face before him, a face that appeared out of unexpected places and that at times, was his father's, or Don Carlos', or Mario's, or Elisa's, or his very own, and it was time to blot it out. Erase the blood, stop the bayonet, stop the murderous scoop, and begin to rebuild.

"In the summer, at the end of summer," answered Elisa. "I shall have my child here, so that everyone will know."

"Everybody knows. Your mother asked me point blank when we would get married, and my Uncle Ramón has sent for me. Only father has not said a thing, yet."

"We will live here."

"Or over there."

Juan Luis wanted to fix an image of themselves that would not become confused with the shadows and dolls that walked along the corridor. He could pick up a certain agitation in the glassed-in corridor, some indescribable movement, as if Mario went by on the way to the bathroom, feetless, pushing the air with his bullet-ridden body, or as if Don Carlos barred his way by spreading the wings of his nightshirt. In the living room, the old folks fingered their rosaries and jostled one another delicately, without saying a word. There, the ashes were coming to rest, floating for an instant, then settling to the floor.

"Oh!" said Uncle Ramón, removing the napkin from around his neck and wiping his mouth, "We are in agreement, then, that things have changed."

No one gave a sign of agreement. Perhaps they had eaten too

much, perhaps the wine plus the darkness of that badly-lit corridor, and the severe routine that Aunt Esther imposed on the table, were beginning to have their effect. Juan Luis toyed with his demitasse spoon, without looking up. At the other end of the table, Elisa watched him with apprehension. Juan Luis' father was wrapping himself in a thick cloud of smoke, and Señora Esther crushed her handkerchief in her right hand, as if announcing that, at any given moment, she was going to cry. Only Uncle Ramón appreciated in its meanest details the scene and the tension he had gradually produced.

"Yes, then, things have changed!"

"What things?" asked Señora Esther, raising her head and looking hard at him. "What things have changed? Or are you referring to people, to the fact that people have changed . . ."

"This young man has changed . . . has changed a great deal. And this girl is not alien to that change. Isn't it true, Elisa? What do you think?"

In reality, during the meal there had been no talk about them, the pregnancy, the wedding, or Juan Luis' allowance. They had talked—Don Ramón had talked—about politics. Only after dessert, when the coffee was served, had Don Ramón brutally asked Juan Luis when he intended to get married and what he was going to work at. All those at table sank into their chairs, and either looked at the floor or played with the silver; or smoked in desperation.

"I don't know, uncle," said Elisa without taking her eyes off Juan Luis.

Why do you abuse yourself, father? Why do you have to go on lowering yourself? Have you had to pay such a price for your silly sense of family duty? Have the petty touches you exist on humiliate you? Just who fleeced whom? Who hid behind your sister's money, used her as a shield to hide his failures and, by pretending to be a wise guy, wants to be taken for tough and unbeatable?

"You have learned a lesson, my boy," Don Ramón told Juan Luis, aiming the tip of his cigarette at him.

And you'll learn yours, old fox. In fact, we've all learned a lesson. That's right. Some more, others less, some first, others later. Some'll learn entirely too late. It won't be of much use.

"Because you'll be a gentleman, a professional man, you'll be a family man, a credit to your parents and relatives."

... a bank or ministry clerk, right, assemblyman of some youth organization, an enterprising young mason, a solid lodge-brother, a future Grand Master ... new car, house on the beach, mistress, apartment downtown ... Bim Bam Bum ... dignified buffoon. No, godfather ... you are wrong. Never! Your world has already crumbled. The house was flooded from all sides, its bottom fell out, rats had invaded its vital parts.

"Yes, uncle, everything has changed."

Not quite. You haven't changed much, young man, I know you, apprentice of a man; nor your father, my poor brother, from whom you learned the art to worm your way in; nor my husband, who'll go on being a hypocrite. Superficially, perhaps. An odd-mannered bunch of hipsters appear to have taken your place. Puritanical in their ignorance of civilized things. Who can deny it? But, they'll fashion their own snare: banks, proprietorships, embassies, inheritances, weddings, tricks, their own sewers. You want to be taken for one of them? ... To drag this girl in the avalanche and pretend you are sailing full steam ahead with the democracy of talent? Mmmm! I know you, you'll recover from your philanthropy as from the measles. I can see the gold chain awaiting you when you get paunchy.

"You see? We are in agreement, then, things have changed. For the better. Everything can be fixed up, and you can adjust the load along the way," said Don Ramón, "let's drink to the family, to these young people, to the good old times, Manuel ... the good old times. But not here, in the library, little Esther, with some good cognac ... how do things look to you, Manuel?" he asked, getting up and putting an arm around his brother-in-law's shoulders.

Spring finally came, like a sudden light, barely touching the snow-capped mountains, and quickly becoming a golden dust, floating high above the trees of Santiago valley. Chile was gradually waking up as best it could. In some places: a beam of light, in others, a sudden setting of the sea. Valparaíso emerged from the winter shaking off the algae. The forests and beaches in the remote south ventured forth to dry out in the sun and sweep away the mud.

This is exactly what the spring of '38 was: the battle for October. The country split into two enemy factions. Everybody went out into the streets. One group to defend the established order, the other to establish a new order. The old oligarchy paraded through the streets clinking dollars. In the barrios, seated on straw-bottom chairs, men listened to radio bulletins and compiled figures beneath the protecting gaze of the pigs' heads.

The ultra-conservative Gustavo Ross was winning in the farming regions of the central valley where the conservative bosses brought silent peons to polling places, stuck a ballot in their pockets, guided their hands or signed for them, and then counted the votes. Aguirre Cerda, the Popular Front candidate, was holding his own in the copper, nitrate, and coal regions. The large cities were up for grabs.

Leftist forces decided, then, to attack Ross in his own redoubt in order to prevent him from buying votes. Throughout the country people from the slums invaded Ross' headquarters, meting out blows, overturning chairs and tables, tearing up posters and pictures of the candidate, placing stink bombs in strategic offices.

Fighting continued throughout the day.

The government radio favored Ross, pushing him a little. Liked a baked rock, Ross, however, refused to budge.

Rumors spread through the cities. Remember Spain? The Popular Front is already invading convents, sacking churches, killing priests. A few faint hearts got ready to abandon everything. They left in disguise, without knowing why or where they would go.

Around five in the afternoon the reports by radio stations began to change their headlines: "Aguirre wins in the northern provinces," they said, and: "Aguirre wins big in Valparaíso." The Ministry of the Interior continued to count the votes of the large haciendas, to count them over and over again, trying to budge Ross with them. It didn't work. At seven in the evening, the loudspeakers were blaring in Santiago, Valparaíso, Concepción, Antofagasta,

Iquique: "The Popular Front Victorious! Aguirre Cerda Wins!"

By nine o'clock the entire city of Santiago seemed to blaze. Thousands and thousands of people came out of the slums with lighted torches aloft, flooding the streets and avenues, converging upon the government palace.

Those faithful to Ross bolted their doors and remained, rifle in hand, whispering, praying. The mass of people passed by in a frenzied dash, descending upon Santiago like a huge tide. Coats and shirts flying, dazzled, an overwhelming victory cry in their throats, dragging children along, pursued by the image of the shanty-towns that bit at their heels like a dog.

Downtown! Downtown!

And downtown went Aguirre Cerda, smoking his cigarette butt, in the arms of the multitude. And downtown went Elías, the baker, the plumber, the teacher, the students. Juan Luis ran with Pepe, Elisa between them, protecting her from the shoves and blows.

Aguirre Cerda appeared in the balcony of *El Mercurio*'s radio station and, turning his brown face to the night ablaze with torches and flags, slowly pronounced the words that millions were waiting to hear. Below, in the streets, in the gardens of Congress, towards the Plaza de Armas and Alameda, the multitude swelled, swaying in the night. Aguirre had won; could anyone snatch the victory from him?

"Look out, look out!" said a smiling Juan Luis to Elisa. "We've already lost Pepe...."

She smiled too, nodding and reassuring him. Juan Luis saw her flushed face, beads of perspiration on her forehead, her bloodshot eyes. The multitude kept growing and, at the words of the leader, increased its pressure, swelled in powerful waves and began to shift like a high sea. People were laughing and singing, holding hands to form a human chain. Juan Luis held Elisa by the arms. Soon he could see nothing but the red sky above the people's heads, as well as the tiny balcony where Aguirre gestured trying to calm the crowd.

Then he lost Elisa. A sudden current coming from the neighboring streets shook that sea and separated them. Choking, Juan Luis tried to fight his way through, fearing that she could be crushed against the wall, fall, and be trampled by the mob. He struck some blows, but was unable to move. People continued to sing and shout around him, and now held him in a tight embrace. He saw Elisa's face a few yards away. Pale, eyes half-closed, she was still smiling at him, encouraging him. Then he also tried to smile.

"At Elias'!" he shouted. "We'll meet at Elias'!"

She nodded, moving farther and farther away, dragged off by the mob, moving on the dark waves that pounded the city. He could hear her no longer. In a new swaying of the multitude, among bobbing heads and upraised fists, Elisa disappeared.

A year has neither a beginning nor an end. It is like a turning, revolving, forgotten record that will continue to play throughout life. Are its words any less real because we are no longer there to listen to them? On the other hand, its grooves that will always surround us are real, as the two warriors that dance in them, and the diamond needle that lights their way and guides them. Who could stop all this?

Nothing succeeded in defining itself in the line of fire, because the year was ever changing, the multitude always moving, the wave forever embracing, the hand eternally ready to grasp. Other years stirred the surface of that image—like the wind does the water in a pool—breaking its lines, until those same years and others, together, deposited their load and reestablished the dizzying vision forever.

Tomorrow, those warriors will pass through this same city without weapons, and instead of helmets, shields, and emblems, they will bear the fruits of the red summer. They will go forth to walk through the wide cities where the dead were left on their backs, covered with ferns, cast in lime and moss, and they'll greet us once again, and we'll answer that greeting and their questions in the voice that life, re-making itself, has given us.

The spring of the young warriors was, therefore, a cruel one, because they slowly fashioned it out of blood. But, their shadows have kept growing. Like the tangled ribbons, you might say, of a Maypole in the evening sun.